Bolan considered exploding the grenades remotely

He dismissed the thought immediately. Too risky to civilians. Risking the lives of noncombatants was not acceptable.

Mack Bolan was in the business of conserving life, and killed only when necessitated by factors of duty or self-defense. He didn't believe the ends always justified the means, and he refused to do anything to put more blood on his hands.

When it came to the rules of engagement, Bolan had never believed it was right to salve his conscience with some "greater good" theory that civilian casualties were the natural collateral damage of warfare. Bolan valued human life much more than that.

Bolan fought for those who were unable to fight for themselves.

Don Pendleton's Mack Bolan

Hard Passage

A GOLD EAGLE BOOK FROM

WORLDWIDE®

TORONTO • NEW YORK • LONDON
AMSTERDAM • PARIS • SYDNEY • HAMBURG
STOCKHOLM • ATHENS • TOKYO • MILAN
MADRID • WARSAW • BUDAPEST • AUCKLAND

Recycling programs
for this product may
not exist in your area.

First edition March 2009

ISBN-13: 978-0-373-61528-5
ISBN-10: 0-373-61528-0

Special thanks and acknowledgment to
Jon Guenther for his contribution to this work.

HARD PASSAGE

Printed in U.S.A.

Courage and perseverance have a magical talisman, before which difficulties disappear and obstacles vanish into thin air.

—John Quincy Adams
(1767–1848)

There are those who say what I do takes courage. The thing is, fighting alone takes skill. Courage is a willingness to persevere—to never give up fighting for what's right even when the odds are stacked against you.

—Mack Bolan

To the men and women in the American armed forces

PROLOGUE

"I'm freezing, Leo!" Sergei Cherenko said.

Leonid Rostov looked at his friend with dismay and tried not to let Cherenko see him shiver. A biting, icy wind—usual for February in St. Petersburg—cut straight through the meager lining of his coat and chilled him to the bone. Rostov watched the snow swirl around them, his hands tucked inside his coat, his fingers numb. They had been standing in place for more than two hours, eyes glued to the nondescript building where men and women were meeting to decide the fates of Rostov and Cherenko.

"Why can't we just go in there?" Cherenko demanded.

Rostov removed his hands from inside his coat long enough to blow into them, and said, "Because it would be the fastest way to getting our throats cut."

Cherenko's cheeks reddened more. "But they could not possibly know we are here!"

"Shush!" Rostov scolded him. "Keep your voice down, Sergei. Do you want to die where you stand?"

What Cherenko took for paranoia, Rostov knew to be prudence. Recent violence had increased against those who betrayed the Sevooborot Molodjozhny—also known as the SMJ—and Rostov didn't feel like becoming another of their statistics. Many had attributed the violent outbreaks against foreign immigrants—particularly those of Arabic heritage—to the works of the Sevooborot. In truth, the youthful revolutionaries couldn't have cared less about the immigration problems in Russia. The fascists and social purists were responsible for most of that carnage, and their activities were confined to cities where large populations of foreign exchange students attended college, Moscow being one example.

Rostov and Cherenko had been members in good standing with the Sevooborot until two weeks earlier. Rostov had no trouble with the violence perpetrated by his comrades, even that against locals, but he didn't believe it was wise to involve outsiders in the great undertaking Sevooborot was about to embark on. When he made his opinion known to other members they betrayed him to the leadership, and before long he received an ultimatum to immediately and unequivocally renounce his claims or suffer penalties. Rostov refused and they forced him out, along with Cherenko. Cherenko, who had never done any wrong, became a sacrificial lamb solely because of his friendship and history with Rostov. The warning had come unbidden from a few men inside the group sympathetic to Rostov and Cherenko. The pair had been awakened in the dead of night, then rushed sleepy-eyed through the cold and crunching snow to a waiting automobile.

Two weeks passed and the safehouse where Rostov and Cherenko had been staying was compromised. With the help of his girlfriend's connections in her job with a local government office in St. Petersburg, Rostov and Cherenko managed to contact the American government with a plea for asylum and immunity in trade for information about a plot against the United States.

Now they stood directly across the street from the small hotel where Peace Corps volunteers met. Among the group was a pair of undercover agents with forged documents that would get Rostov and Cherenko out of Russia and into the United States. Neither man really had a plan for what he would do after that, but for the moment the most important thing was to make contact without detection by their former colleagues. The Sevooborot had eyes and ears everywhere.

Rostov settled on the best course of action and with a self-assuring nod took two steps in the snow before he felt Cherenko's hand fall on his shoulder. Rostov turned to look at his friend and saw Cherenko's eyes weren't focused on him but rather on something up the road. Through the grayish light of dusk and the white tendrils of snow he made out the gloomy whitewash of fast approaching headlights.

Rostov stepped into the shadows of the building and grabbed his friend's hand, pulling the man down with him as he crouched. For at least an hour the street had been relatively deserted, people staying off the roads due to the inclement weather. Most citizens knew when to stay indoors, which left one of two possibilities: one, the occupants were outsiders; two, they were counting on the fact most people had the good sense to stay off the streets. Something in Rostov's psyche told him the latter scenario seemed more likely. A minute later his suspicions were confirmed when the vehicle stopped at the curb in front of the hotel and four men in black leather jackets with machine pistols spilled from it.

The men looked in all directions, a bit wildly, and Rostov caught himself holding his breath. Fortunately, the gunners didn't see the two men crouched in the shadows of the tobacco shop across from the hotel. Rostov and Cherenko watched with a mixture of fascination and horror as the men turned, barged through the revolving door of the hotel and faded from view. For a time, they heard nothing but the sounds of the violent storm and the muffled idle of the waiting car's engine.

And then an idea crept into Rostov's mind.

AGENT LYLE CARRON OF THE Central Intelligence Agency's counterespionage unit watched the Peace Corps volunteers with feigned interest. He had only marginal curiosity in the activities of the people arrayed along the rows of tables in the hotel conference room, and he cared even less about their itinerary over the next few days. The thing that concerned Carron most as he checked his watch were the two young men who had missed their deadline.

Carron gazed at his counterpart across the room. The Company had just given the young, fresh-faced accountant from Langley his first assignment here for no other reason than his fluency in Russian. Big deal. Carron was fluent in Russian, too, seeing as how he'd operated with fair regularity in this country ever since the dissolution of the Soviet Union. And while he admired the youthful exuberance of his fair-haired companion, what he really wished was that they had sent another veteran with him on this mission. Now he had to babysit three kids instead of just Rostov and Cherenko.

George Balford didn't meet Carron's gaze—he didn't even notice Carron had looked in his direction—because he had his nose in the pamphlets and materials passed out by the chair of this workshop session. Carron thought about yanking the kid for a little sidebar in the restroom, but he didn't want to risk the rendezvous with their two contacts. Carron had found it difficult to fit into the role of a Peace Corps volunteer. Obviously, he was older than the rest of them and a couple had remarked on that oddity. One young woman sitting next to him on the bus ride from the airport to the hotel had asked a lot of questions, so Carron had to make small talk and still keep his answers general enough that she wouldn't spot him for the fraud he was.

Carron mused at her potential reaction had he broken down and said, "Listen, lady, I'm not part of the Peace Corps! I'm a covert agent for the CIA here in Russia to meet members of the Sevooborot who plan to break a terrorist plot against the U.S. wide open! Okay? You happy now?"

The thought of her stunned silence brought a smile to Carron's face, but he shook himself back to reality and looked at his watch again. Balls. Where the crap were those two Russians? If Carron had to sit through another mundane workshop he might have to shoot himself with the pistol he'd found stashed securely inside his hotel room. This entire mission stunk anyway to Carron. What would a couple of young hoods inside the SMJ know about a plot by the Jemaah al-Islamiyah to supply arms and fuel the Youths Revolution in Russia? Why any of that would have an impact on the United States remained a mystery to Carron. Not that he cared all that much. His job was simply to see the pair safely out of the country, and that's exactly what he planned to do.

The sound of people clapping thundered abruptly in Carron's ears, and he realized they had drawn the session to a close. Good, he could hit the head and relieve himself before the next one started in ten minutes. Carron got to his feet, indicated his destination with a gesture to Balford—the young guy simply nodded an acknowledgment—and then hurried for the restrooms down the hall just outside the conference room.

Most of the volunteers rushed the podium to get some face time with the presenter, so Carron pretty much had the bathroom to himself. It wasn't all that great, but it was clean and functional with a guy waiting inside to do everything from shine shoes and buff fingernails to spray him with the most horrendous smelling colognes on the market. Carron did his business, washed his hands and made for a quick exit. As he stepped from the restroom, he noticed four men in leather jackets enter the front door and rush the conference room. At the same moment, he spotted the wicked glint of light on the gunmetal of the weapons they held.

Carron reached beneath his coat and withdrew his .45-caliber pistol, but he traveled only three steps before screams and shouts from the conference room echoed into the hallway. The CIA agent picked up the pace, weapon held directly in front of him in a two-handed grip, but he was still some distance from the closed door of the conference room when he heard shouts followed by gunfire. First came the single report of a pistol immediately followed by short bursts from several submachine guns. Carron didn't have to think about what it meant. Balford had probably died in that short-lived cacophony of violence.

He reached the door and crouched to consider his options. Not that Carron really had any. This wasn't happening as he had planned. At least now he had some explanation for why Rostov and Cherenko were late. They were either dead—fallen at the hands of the SMJ—or they had expected this and were hiding in fear of their lives. In any case, Carron had bigger problems. There was no doubt in his mind that these aggressors were part of the SMJ, but he wondered how they'd known about the rendezvous. Was there a leak inside the Company or had it come from those connections made by Leonid Rostov's girlfriend? Maybe the whole thing had been a hoax from the beginning, a way to get moles inside America. That didn't make sense, either, that the SMJ would go to that kind of trouble for such a transparent charade.

No, this had to be something else. Something bigger. And as Carron waited in the hallway, his heart thudding against his chest, he couldn't help but wonder just how deep, and how far up, it actually went.

LEONID ROSTOV CRAWLED agonizingly through eight inches of snow and slush toward the idling sedan. He realized how futile his plan would be if another car decided to come down the street. They wouldn't be able to see him through the thickening snowfall, and in all likelihood would run over him. Rostov tried to ignore such morose thoughts and focused on the task at hand. He could almost feel Cherenko's eyes on him as he crawled across the street.

When he reached the sedan, Rostov rose to one knee and tried the passenger door handle. It gave under his hand. Smiling with satisfaction, Rostov reached beneath his coat and drew the 9 mm Makarov pistol that was holstered beneath his arm. He then jerked the handle upward and yanked back on the door. He jumped in and stuck his pistol's muzzle within an inch of the face of the surprised driver. In the heartbeat before the brief flash of the shot, Rostov recognized the young man as Josef Brish, a low-ranking member of the Sevooborot. Brish's head exploded under the impact of the 9 mm slug that punched through the side of his forehead and blew his brains out.

Rostov turned and waved for Cherenko to join him, then opened the driver's door and shoved Brish's corpse from the cab. By the time his friend joined him, Rostov was nearly out of breath from the exertion.

"Are you okay?" Cherenko asked with mild concern.

Rostov nodded, although he continued fighting to catch his breath. He'd been experiencing shortness of breath and dizziness for the past few weeks. Rostov had smoked for a number of years as a teenager but had since given it up. Their recent exile had prevented Rostov from seeing a doctor. Well, he could get the care he needed once they were safely in America. *If* they ever got to America.

"Shut the door," Rostov finally managed to say as his wheezing abated. "We must go now."

He put the sedan into low gear and pulled from the curb slowly to avoid skidding. They couldn't afford to dig themselves into a rut and end up going nowhere fast. Once they had traveled a few blocks, the two men began to feel better although they didn't speak. They were watching every side road, every mirror, for any and every potential threat.

After a time Cherenko said, "I think we have gotten away with it."

Rostov looked in his rearview mirror and replied, "You may be right. But we cannot assume anything."

"How did they know, Leo?"

"I don't know, I don't know." Rostov's thick eyebrows pinched together in concentration. "The fingers of the Revolution run deep, though. You should know this by now. We are not safe as long as we remain in Russia."

"Should we call Kisa?"

"No!" Rostov barked at the mention of his lover's name. When he saw Cherenko wince, he patted his arm and said more quietly, "That would put her in too much danger. They are probably monitoring her calls, in which case she may already be in trouble."

"Do you think that's how they knew?" Cherenko ventured.

"It's possible."

"So what do we do now?"

"All that we can do, my friend. We wait."

CHAPTER ONE

St. Petersburg, Russia

Mack Bolan gazed out his hotel-room window and saw four armed men exit a sedan in front of the building. He immediately moved from the window to the nearby table, where he shrugged into the nylon shoulder holster that bore his Beretta 93-R. Then he donned a cream-colored sports jacket to hide the weapon.

As Bolan left the room and headed for a set of back stairs that provided the fastest unobstructed route to the first floor, he thought back on Hal Brognola's briefing.

"HER NAME IS Kisa Naryshkin," said Hal Brognola, director of the Sensitive Operations group, America's ultracovert antiterrorist organization based at Stony Man Farm in Virginia. "And according to our intelligence, she's the only link we have to Leonid Rostov and Sergei Cherenko.

"While this one falls totally under the jurisdiction of

the CIA, we would feel a whole lot better with you there to act as backup, Striker," Brognola had told him.

"You're worried this might go hard," Bolan replied.

Brognola nodded. "Yeah. The guy they have there to oversee the transfer is Lyle Carron, and he's got a lot of years with the Company. He's one of their top agents on the Russian desk, as I understand it. George Balford's another story, though. The guy's only three months out of Langley, background in accounting."

Bolan frowned. "When is the CIA going to learn that bean counters aren't exactly the best choice for these types of operations? A sensitive case like this requires a certain expertise."

"That was our assessment, as well," said Barbara Price, Stony Man's mission controller. "That's why we felt it was best to call you in on this one. Rostov and Cherenko claim to have information critical to uncovering some type of terrorist attack against the United States by the Jemaah al-Islamiyah. Apparently the Sevooborot Molodjozhny, also known as both the Youth Revolution and the SMJ, has made some type of handshake agreement with them, where the JI will provide the SMJ arms and training."

"For what?" Bolan asked.

"That's what we don't know," Brognola replied. "All Rostov and Cherenko can tell us right now is that this has something to do with a plot against America."

"Sounds thin," Bolan said. "If the JI's planning a terrorist attack against us, I don't see any logical connection to a militant youth organization inside Russia."

"Maybe not, but the President thinks it's vital we keep our thumb on this one until the transfer's complete. That's where you come in."

Under other circumstances Mack Bolan might have passed, but something in his gut told him this went deep enough that he needed to get closer. And as he had no love for either militant Russian youths or Islamic terrorists—especially since both groups were quite outspoken of their hatred for America and her people—the Executioner decided to accept the mission and see what came of it.

THE EXECUTIONER PUSHED through the door at the first-floor landing that opened onto a hallway running along the east-side front of the hotel. He got his first view of the scene unfolding ahead. The doors were closed, shooting and screams had ensued, and a lone armed man had crouched at the door leading into the conference room, apparently unsure of what to do next. Bolan catfooted up the hall and entered through the double doors of an adjoining conference room. In the early hours of that morning, he'd paced the empty halls and accessed each conference room—mapping the approximate square footage and other important details of this wing—and then returned to his room where he sketched the layout. From his recon, Bolan had made some tactical decisions and picked the lock of the door leading to the room adjoining the one where the CIA agents would be waiting to rendezvous with Rostov and Cherenko. It was at that point Bolan had detached the divider separating the two conference rooms and left it slightly ajar to facilitate an alternate entrance and access if it became necessary.

Unfortunately it had.

Bolan let the door close behind him with a barely audible click. He waited long enough for his eyes to adjust to the light that emanated from the adjoining conference room, then made his way to the divider. Sidling up to the break in the divider, he took in the site with a practiced eye. The four men had moved the hostages to the back wall and lined them up single file on their knees with their hands on top of their heads. Good. That would keep the innocents out of his line of fire.

He then noticed the bloodied body of a young, fresh-faced man, a pistol lying just out of reach. It was George Balford. He recognized the face from the dossier provided by Stony Man. The poor kid hadn't even known what hit him, probably, and if he had, he certainly hadn't expected such a short career. So that meant Carron was out of the room when the gunmen had entered.

Bolan moved the divider slightly as the gunmen paced up and down the line, shouting at their hostages in a mix of Russian and English. He sighted on the closest gunman first, took a deep breath, let out half and then squeezed the trigger. The Beretta coughed discreetly as the 9 mm subsonic bullet crossed the expanse in a millisecond and punched through the target's throat. The SMG clattered on the floor as the gunner raised his hands to his throat, then staggered.

The Executioner already had the second man in his sights before the body of the first hit the ground, and he squeezed off another shot. The round punched into the gunner's breastbone and continued into his lung. The impact drove the man backward into his partner, who was apparently reacting to the falling body of the first man. While the third man tried to disentangle himself from his falling partner, the fourth gunman realized something was wrong and reacted, furiously scanning the area, fanning his weapon left and right.

The sound of a door flying open briefly drew everyone's attention from the carnage. Bolan's eyes flicked toward the front in time to see Carron burst through the doorway. The fourth man at the far end now had a visible target and swung his SMG into target acquisition, but he was too late. The .45-caliber pistol in Carron's grip boomed twice. Both rounds landed on target, punching through the man's stomach. Bolan gritted his teeth against the possibility one of them might continue through and strike a hostage, but his fears were never realized.

Bolan reacquired a sight picture on the remaining gunner as the man triggered a burst in Carron's direction that sent the CIA agent diving for cover. The weapon skewed upward and delivered a flurry of rounds harmlessly into the corkboard ceiling as the Executioner pumped two slugs through the man's skull. The bullets split his head clean open and dumped him to the floor.

In a snap decision, Bolan backed from the divider and raced across the room. He opened the door, peered into the hallway and then made for the steps when he verified it was empty. As the Executioner pushed through the door and climbed the stairwell he considered the situation at hand. The St. Petersburg police would undoubtedly swarm the building in the next ten minutes, which didn't give him much time. He couldn't remain in his room—they would conduct a door-to-door search, to be sure, and that meant a lot of uncomfortable questions. He would have to exit by the first-floor window of the rear stairwell. He could stow the pistol in a locker of one of the nearby train stations, so if they cordoned the area he wouldn't get caught with a weapon.

Bolan went quickly through his room, left the clothes hanging in the closet and the bag of toiletries on the sink, and removed only his forged identification and passport and heavy overcoat. He made his exit through the rear stairwell window unobserved, donned the overcoat once outside, then headed to a nearby payphone. He dialed the hotel, asked if he had any messages, then hung up immediately. That would probably provide a fairly decent alibi if he was questioned by police at any later point. Bolan then headed for the train station where he could dump his armament.

Then it would become a waiting game. He would need to touch base with Stony Man at some point to see if he could get a line on Carron. There was no point in keeping his cover. He would need some backup in his search for the two missing contacts, and Carron seemed the most sensible one to provide that given he was out to accomplish the same end as Bolan. Things were shaping up just as they always seemed to for the Executioner.

Yeah. Business as usual.

EVEN WITH THEIR ADVANCED computer systems, it took Stony Man more than four hours to track down Lyle Carron. By the time Bolan found him in a small coffee shop on the outskirts of St. Petersburg, the massive clock on a nearby church had nearly struck 10:00 p.m. and another three inches of snow had fallen. Bolan shook the snow from his overcoat as he came through the door. He nodded at the barista, ordered a coffee in Russian and then moved over to Carron's table.

"Mind if I sit down?" Bolan asked quietly.

Carron's eyes focused on Bolan's with surprise, then

the company guy gestured to a seat in front of him. Bolan sat but the two men said nothing until the barista arrived with a carafe of hot coffee and then departed. Wisps of steam danced off the coffee as Bolan poured a cup for himself and then refilled Carron's. The Company man looked bothered, his face gaunt and drawn, and Bolan had been in the business long enough to know what was eating at him.

"It wasn't your fault," Bolan said. "Balford, I mean."

Carron looked Bolan in the eyes, something few men seemed able to do without looking away just as quickly. While the CIA agent didn't say anything, Bolan could tell Carron was sizing him up. Many other men had looked into those same twin points of ice blue and shrunk under the stare. Carron seemed to take little more than a passing interest, obviously trying to decide whether he could trust Bolan.

"How did you find me?" When Bolan frowned, Carron waved it away and added quickly, "Never mind. Dumb question." He took a sip of coffee and said, "You're not Company."

It wasn't a question and Bolan shook his head. He extended his hand and said, "Name's Cooper. Or Matt, if you prefer."

"NSA?"

"Let's just say I'm not on any page in the book," Bolan said with a wan smile.

"The other shooter at the hotel. You?"

Bolan nodded. "Sorry I didn't stick around, but I had to beat feet for the same reasons you did."

"I'd like to know who sent you," Carron said matter-of-factly. "And why."

"And I'll be happy to tell you," Bolan said. "But

first I have a question for you. What do you think may have happened Rostov and Cherenko?"

Carron shrugged and let out a sigh. "I figure they made someone who was onto them, maybe they had a tail. They would have known it was too risky to make the rendezvous or lead their friends from the SMJ to the hotel. Probably took them on a wild-goose chase. Either that or the SMJ caught up to them *before* they could meet us, tortured them for the time and place, then sent some boys to take care of me and George."

"What about the car? You didn't try to follow it?"

"What car?"

"The one that deposited the four hardcases outside the front door."

Carron shook his head and frowned. "There wasn't any car there. I used the front for my own exit, and only thing I saw was a corpse. Figured that was your handiwork, too."

"No dice," Bolan replied.

The Executioner felt a knot settle in his stomach. Somebody had obviously ambushed the driver, left his carcass on the sidewalk and taken the car. All of that had probably happened during Bolan's trip to the first floor and the subsequent gun battle. He hadn't even thought about that; he figured the driver would either get spooked after a certain amount of time elapsed and split, or the cops would pen him in and nab him when they arrived.

"The fact someone smoked the driver and got away means they were waiting for them," Bolan finally said. "Either that or they saw an opportunity and decided to exploit it."

"Yeah," Carron replied. "And I don't think it takes a genius to figure out who did it."

"I sat watch on that street for more than an hour," Bolan said. "And I never saw Rostov or Cherenko. Never saw anybody."

"Not your fault. The weather was shit and you couldn't have figured the SMJ would try making a play with me and Balford covering all bets. Besides, you weren't there as the primary."

Bolan reacted to that.

The CIA man smiled. "Don't look so surprised. The Company has some sources, too."

"So you knew they sent me?"

"Well, not you specifically, but I figured they'd send someone," Carron replied. "Let's face it. It would've been stupid for the upper echelon in Wonderland to put all of their eggs in one basket. I think that's what got me incensed more than anything. They put out George and me as sacrificial lambs, almost like they were expecting us to blow it. Okay, I'm thick-skinned and I can take it, but George was barely out of college. Just a kid, Cooper."

Carron lit a cigarette and poured them more coffee, then said, "I get it, though. And I understand them sending you as backup. The information Rostov and Cherenko have is obviously too important to trust without some type of failsafe operation in place. For what it's worth, pal, I'm still glad you were there to cover my six."

"Fact of the matter is, we *both* lost this one," Bolan said.

"Maybe just the battle," Carron replied with a wink. "War's not over yet. Just what do these two know that's so important? Any idea?"

Bolan weighed his one of two possible responses. He liked Carron, genuinely trusted him, but he couldn't be sure how much he should let on he knew. Of course, Carron would have had a general idea anyway, although maybe not privy to all the details Stony Man had given Bolan. Still, the Executioner would need all the allies he could get if he were to find Rostov and Cherenko and get them out of the country. Carron had all of their documents, and he also knew the Russian sector pretty well if the information contained in his dossier was any indication. Besides, he'd lost his partner to this mission already and Bolan doubted he'd be able to keep that guy at any distance. Bolan had succeeded on missions like this partly because he knew when it was appropriate to take a lone-wolf stance versus when to accept an offer of help.

"I can give you a lot more details," Bolan said. "But before I do, you should know I expect we'll be working together from this point forward. And since we're now in backup plan mode, and I'm the backup, I call the shots. You read me?"

"I read you," Carron said, leaning forward on his elbows. "We follow your lead."

"So we agree. Now, Rostov and Cherenko's introduction to our people came by way of a woman named Kisa Naryshkin. Apparently she's Rostov's girlfriend or fiancée, something like that."

"You're thinking we should reach out to her."

Bolan shrugged. "That's a possibility if we don't turn up any solid leads on Rostov and Cherenko, but I worry about compromising her cover. In fact, what happened at the hotel may indicate she's already been compromised."

"So how do you propose we find them?"

"I'd say it's a pretty safe bet they're our mysterious

carjackers," Bolan replied. He gestured at the window and continued, "We can also assume they won't get far in this weather."

"Agreed." Carron took a last, deep drag from his cigarette, then stubbed it in the ashtray. "Where do you want to start looking?"

"Well, this is your neighborhood," Bolan said. "If you were a pair of ex-militant youths in a stolen vehicle, where would you hide?"

Carron scratched his chin and stared at the ceiling in thought for a time. Finally he replied, "It's not where they're hiding that's important. That could be like trying to find a needle in a haystack. I'd suggest we find the ones who are after them. And for that, I know *exactly* where to look."

CHAPTER TWO

A cool morning wind gusted across the veranda of Anatoly Satyev's retreat home in a private community outside Reno. Satyev's mansion was one of several secreted within the Sierra Vista on more than seven hundred acres sprawled around a central golf course and private resort. Only the richest and most influential people lived there.

Once a high-ranking military power broker inside the Soviet Union before its dissolution, the tide of change had forced Satyev to flee his country. He'd barely escaped with his life, and it had taken a number of years to secure his holdings and move his liquid assets safely out of the now-defunct commerce system. The cash from his investments had proved more than adequate to satiate his eclectic if not rather lavish tastes and within a few years he'd establish a sound reputation within the American business community.

With his personal and professional reputation now reestablished in a new land, Satyev set upon a course for reinstating the Communist Party in his homeland while profiting from the socialist fanaticism of those who considered themselves pure revolutionaries.

This morning, though, Satyev had awakened to a new sensation, one he'd not experienced for more than a decade: dread. And he was going to make sure that the man who arrived soon heard about it. That man was Jurg Kovlun, a former Spetsnaz commando and head of Satyev's personal security force during his tenure with the Party. Kovlun showed up shortly after Satyev finished his breakfast in front of an open-pit fire that his servants had lit to keep off the morning chill.

"Good morning, sir," Kovlun said.

Satyev waved him into a seat across from him at the table. He reached into the pocket of his robe and opened a silver case. "Cigarette?"

Kovlun nodded and gingerly removed one. Satyev took one for himself, which he affixed to a long cigarette holder, gestured for a light, and then once they were both comfortable and smoking he dismissed the house servant who had attended them.

"I'm not happy, Jurg," Satyev said. "What is going on with this operation?"

"I'm sorry, Comrade Colonel, but I'm afraid I do not understand."

Satyev pulled the long stem of the holder from his mouth, exhaling slowly through his nose as he repeated "You don't understand" several times. "I see. Well, let me ask it another way. Why the fuck are two members of the Sevooborot running around the Mother Country shooting off their mouths about our agreement with the Jemaah al-Islamiyah? Hmm? And more importantly, why the fuck are they breathing? Hmm? Can you explain that, Comrade?"

"Ah, yes I have just recently heard of this."

"Why have you just recently heard of it?" Satyev demanded.

"Well, I—"

"Never mind," Satyev cut in, raising a hand. "I'm sure I don't want to know why your men aren't keeping you properly informed. That is not my problem to work out. Rather, it is yours. And you will work it out, Jurg, or I'm going to become very angry with you, and I'm sure you do not want that."

"No, sir," Kovlun replied quickly and he took a few short, successive puffs from his cigarette.

"Take care of this, and I mean soon. Otherwise, I'll have to find someone else to handle this little problem. Understood?"

A few quicker, more nervous puffs. "Perfectly."

"Fine. Now, tell me about the rest of the operation and how it's proceeding."

"We've secured the weapons we were promised, and the training is almost complete. I expect the first operation to begin tomorrow night."

"Where will it begin?"

"It starts in Seattle. By the timeline you've given us, we'll then move operations slowly down the West Coast until we reach Los Angeles. Then we will begin to expand toward the east. We expect everything to be completed within the year, just as you originally planned it."

"Good, good," Satyev said with a nod. "I cannot be any more satisfied with this news. What of our personnel issues?"

"We're still having a bit of trouble getting some of the JI's men into the country. None of our personnel have had a problem, but with the crackdowns it's more difficult to get Muslim males through customs without them being subjected to some scrutiny."

"Maybe I can do something about that," Satyev replied. "Maybe we need to change the cover stories. Perhaps we can convince the American government they are mostly students, refugees of the recent violence against foreign immigration into Russia."

"That might speed things up considerably, sir," Kovlun agreed.

"I'll see what I can do." Satyev made a show of looking at his watch. "In the meantime, you have a plane to catch. I want you in place in Seattle well before the operations begin. You are to personally oversee every phase of it."

"Of course, Comrade Colonel." Kovlun jumped to his feet, nodded at Satyev in respect and then headed for the patio doors.

"And, Kovlun?"

"Yes, sir?"

"Don't forget to take care of that little problem we discussed. Rostov and Cherenko can never testify. Never. Do whatever you have to, but make sure those two are dead before the sun sets."

"Consider it done, sir," Kovlun replied.

WHEN KISA NARYSHKIN MET Leonid Rostov, she never expected he would be part of the Sevooborot; she definitely never expected to fall in love with him.

In some ways, their relationship had been doomed from the beginning. When she first discovered he was a member of one of the most violent youth gangs in all of Russia, she felt betrayed and incensed that he could deceive her about his business dealings. She remembered the encounter that night in her parents' home where she was house-sitting while they were away on vacation. She recalled how they argued, how she screamed "I hate you" over and over again, and demanded that he decide between her or his murderous cohorts. That was when he'd broken down and professed his love for her, and they sat in the middle of the living-room floor, crying and holding each other. That was the same night they made love for the first time, when she had fully and completely given herself to him.

And that was the night she agreed to help him get out.

"But only if you help Sergei, too."

Naryshkin's contacts in the Russian government had proved the saving grace for her love and his friend. It hadn't taken much to convince certain people that Rostov had information of considerable value to the United States. A whisper in the ears of a few select people working at the municipal records building. Someone had to have told the right people because less than a week passed before Naryshkin received a plain, unmarked envelope on her desk. Inside were instructions for the meeting.

She arrived two minutes early at the gift shop of a massive building, a new construction at the edge of Alexander Park, known as the Palace of the People. A work of the St. Petersburg Committee of Temperance, the building included an opera house and massive dining area, and the gift shop stuffed with souvenirs and trinkets of every kind acted as a type of guardian near the entrance. The back of that shop served as the meeting place.

The man who met with Kisa Naryshkin didn't offer his name or agency, and she decided it better not to ask about such things, but when the conversation got under way she had no doubts this man could help her beloved Leo.

"I've been led to understand," said the distinguished-looking man with gray eyes, salt-and-pepper hair and a British accent, "that you know a man who holds a high-ranking position inside the SMJ."

Naryshkin nodded, the stray dark hairs of her head dancing in the golden morning rays that shone through the skylight. "It is my boyfriend, actually, Leonid Rostov. He is a member of the Sevooborot. I do not know his ranking inside of it. And his friend," she added quickly as an afterthought. "The deal is for his friend, as well. Sergei Cherenko."

The man smiled not unpleasantly. "You must understand, Miss Naryshkin, that there isn't necessarily any deal on the table right now. My friends must be able to verify the validity of the information before the benefactors in question would be willing to make any arrangements."

"Leo said you might say that," she replied, just as she'd rehearsed with him two days earlier. She reached into her small handbag and removed a thick envelope, which she slid across the table at the man. "That contains the dates and details of certain crimes committed by the Sevooborot but never solved by local police or Interpol. These are details never released. There are also the names of the perpetrators, where they can be found and the location of evidence that should be sufficient to prosecute them."

The man didn't make a move for the envelope, something that surprised her. She had never practiced that part with Leo, and she wasn't sure how to respond if the conversation took a turn in a direction that wasn't part of the script.

For a long time, the man said nothing. He just looked at her and smiled. Finally he said, "I'm sure there's some validity to the contents of this envelope."

"There is, I can assure, sir. Check it out."

"Oh, you can be sure we'll validate the information. You have no need to worry about that. But to arrange for the safe passage of these two young men out of Russia without the SMJ finding out about it will be much more complex. You see, Miss Naryshkin, the SMJ has a growing number of connections and supporters within St. Petersburg. That support has extended to places like Moscow and Vladivostok."

"Why should good and influential people wish to support a gang of hoodlums like the Sevooborot?"

"It would take me too long to explain the politics of your question," the man replied. "And this is neither the time nor place for such a discussion."

"You think me too naive or meager of intellect to understand it," Naryshkin replied with a haughty raise of her chin.

"I did not say that."

"You didn't have to. I could see it in your expression and condescending manner." She tapped a long fingernail on the table and let a moment of silence lapse before asking, "Do you know who my father is, sir?"

"Of course."

"Then you know I am an educated woman," she replied. "And you must also know that I have quite a number of influences inside the Russian government."

"I never said I doubted *you,* madam," the man replied. He sat back in his chair, folded his arms and crossed his legs. "I'm simply trying to avoid any measure of antagonism by entertaining a conversation that can undoubtedly end in nothing but an argument, one that should serve no purpose as it pertains to Rostov and Cherenko."

"So there's something about all of this you don't wish to tell me," Naryshkin concluded.

The smile again. "That would be correct."

That's how it began and everything seemed to move at a blinding pace after that. Within a few days she received a second envelope, this one in her mail slot, with another envelope inside of it stamped with the letters "LR" in block letters. When Naryshkin delivered it to Leo and asked him about its contents, he declined to talk to her further about it. She could understand his concern, his desire to protect her, and at the time she'd had the meeting with a man she assumed to be some type of British agent, she hadn't even considered what would become of them if Leo left the country.

"I don't know yet," he told her. "But I promise you that I *will* find a way for us to be together. No matter how long it takes me. I promise you. I love you."

More than a month had passed since their last meeting and she had neither heard from nor seen him. For all she knew, he'd already left the country along with the Cherenko. One of her closest girlfriends, Sonya Vdovin, happened to be part of the Sevooborot scene, partying at a lot of the same clubs as its members. But Naryshkin had decided not to publicly condemn her friend, rather she kept her mouth shut and pumped the young woman for any information she could get.

"No, I haven't seen Leo around," Vdovin would say. "I haven't seen Sergei, either. Which is really too bad because he's quite…how do I say it, *adept* in bed." And then a mischievous smile would play at her lips. "Yes, that's a good word."

So Naryshkin lay alone in bed each night, wondering and worrying, finally drifting off to sleep in the wee hours of the morning after waiting for him to call. Eventually she started to give up and she hated herself for thinking that way. Leo had made her a promise and whatever else he might have done or not done, she loved him and she knew him well enough to know that he was a man of his word. And then one night, this night, the phone rang.

She answered it breathlessly. "Hello?"

"Hello, my sweet."

"Oh, Le—"

"Don't use names!" he snapped.

Naryshkin swallowed her voice along with a big chunk of disappointment. She yearned to see him, to talk to him, to touch him at that very moment but she didn't dare. Finally she asked, "How are you?"

"I am okay."

"Are you…" She hesitated, not sure how to ask the question, but then she didn't have to worry about it.

"No, I am not," he said. His voice cracked when he added, "Something went wrong, dearest. Something went horribly wrong. Good people are now likely dead."

Before she could conjure a reply he moved away from the phone, a fit of coughing and wheezing having overtaken him. That cough and shortness of breath had grown progressively worse. Naryshkin had feigned an allergy to get a doctor friend of her father's to prescribe an inhaler of powerful medicine. Medical care in Russia still wasn't adequate to meet the needs of many people. She had provided the last inhaler to him more than a month ago, so she knew he had to have exhausted his supply of medicine by now.

"You do not sound good," she said. "Hello?"

It was Sergei Cherenko's voice that came on the line. "Hello."

"Is he okay?"

"He's not doing well. I'm worried about him. I am also worried for myself."

"Where are you? Let me come get you."

"No," Sergei replied. "He would never forgive me if I put you in any sort of danger. In fact, I would never forgive myself."

"Don't be silly."

"It is not silliness, it's practicality! This has become a very dangerous game for us, and I'm not sure how much longer we are going to be able to play it. We need your help but the only way we'll accept it is if you immediately get in touch with your contacts. Let them know things didn't happen like they should have. Tell them 'The meet did not happen. We are going to the alternate plan.' Do you have that?"

"Yes, I have it. But—"

"I must go now."

"No, wait! Let me speak to him."

"He is still having trouble. He cannot speak right now."

"Okay," she said, doing her best to be brave and hide the disappointment in her voice. "You take care of him. And yourself."

But Naryshkin then realized she was talking to dead air—Sergei had hung up the phone. She slowly re-

placed the receiver in the latch hook of the phone ped-
estal and considered this news. What had happened? It
should have been so easy and yet here they were, calling her, still inside Russia—maybe still even in St. Petersburg—with the mother of all storms outside. She
knew what Sergei's comments had meant. The meeting hadn't taken place and they were now going to their
alternate plan, one that involved traveling to Murmansk
where they would seek passage aboard a trawler or
small cargo carrier.

The woman started to pick up the phone and then
thought better of it. Leo hadn't wanted her to use any
names, which meant he believed someone might be
tapping her phone. In fact, members of the Sevooborot
might even have her under surveillance, although she'd
been mindful to keep her eyes open for any observers
since her last night with Leo. Not that she hadn't worn
her emotions on her sleeve. Both of her parents had repeatedly inquired as to what was bothering her ever
since their return, but she simply laughed it off and
concocted excuses about how hard she'd been working,
how stressful her job was and so forth. Her father offered to intervene but she expressly forbade him, warning that she was an adult now and that he'd taught her
to stand upon her own two feet. That was usually
enough to end the conversation.

This time, though, she knew it would become dangerous to do this alone. After sitting on the edge of her
bed, chewing thoughtfully on her lower lip, Naryshkin
made a decision and rose to dress. It was time to face
this situation with all the courage and veracity she'd
been taught, and to reach out for help to the only two
people left in the world she trusted. There had never

been anything her father and mother couldn't overcome in the past. Yes. Her father had once been an influential man in the government. He had many connections. And he would help her, especially when she professed her undying love for Leo. After all, her father was a hopeless romantic who could refuse his family nothing.

Yes. She would go to them immediately, wake them from their beds if she had to.

But Naryshkin was so focused on her mission, she failed to notice the two men who observed her leave her two-story flat, get into her car and begin the long, arduous drive to her father's house.

CHAPTER THREE

"I have to hand it to you, Carron," Mack Bolan said. "I might never have thought of this."

Carron chuckled and replied, "Yeah. I figure if you want to catch the mouse but don't know where he's hiding, then your next best option's to sit on the cat."

In this case, they were sitting on an entire den of cats. One of the things Carron had learned during the past few years working the Russian sector were the hangouts of every SMJ cell in St. Petersburg. This wouldn't have necessarily been difficult information to come by given Stony Man's significant reach into the intelligence community, but it certainly would have taken time. It was this fact that made Bolan glad he decided to enlist Carron's help.

The snow stopped falling while they were in the café and the pair managed to get a taxi ride to the train station where Bolan had stored his weaponry. Another stop at a CIA safehouse allowed Carron time to check with his superiors and gave Bolan the opportunity to bring Stony Man up to date on the mission status. A second cab ride had brought them to a club, one that served alcohol and catered to the underage crowd.

It disgusted Bolan that such establishments were permitted to exist, although he knew the problem wasn't isolated to St. Petersburg.

"We can't save them all," Carron had responded when Bolan voiced his concern.

"We can if we do it a few kids at a time," had been Bolan's reply.

The two men watched the entrance for about twenty minutes before Bolan checked his watch. "Almost 2330."

"Sounds like it's about time to crash the party."

"My thought exactly," Bolan said. "You're fluent in Russian. How about I back your play this time around?"

"No problem."

The two men stepped from the shelter of the awning and hurried carefully across the slippery street. Vehicles had been arriving infrequently to deposit their occupants outside the front door of the club. At the moment, the sidewalk was empty and they didn't see anyone hanging around nearby. The weather and the weeknight hour seemed to have kept the majority of people indoors, leaving only the more young and daring crowd to venture into the nightlife. Carron had told Bolan that in the summer this part of town was typically packed with pedestrians and all the shops were open.

The pair reached the door and Bolan opened it to admit Carron first. They crossed a very dark and narrow vestibule, and beyond that was another entryway, this one a dark, heavy curtain, through which the briefest flash of lights and the steady thump of electronic dance music encompassed them. Carron pushed the curtain aside and was immediately detained by a huge, bald man. Bolan didn't understand the full exchange but he caught the gist of the conversation.

"Hold it," the bouncer said. "This is a private party."

"I was invited," Carron replied.

"I don't think you were," the door guy said, and he jabbed a finger into Carron's shoulder.

In the blink of an eye the man's finger disappeared from sight, enfolded by Carron's left hand. The bouncer's knees bent some in a show of submission as Carron bent the finger backward to the breaking point. A second man, a bit smaller than the door guy, stepped forward to intervene, but Bolan intercepted him with the barrel of his Beretta 93-R in the guy's ribs. He held the weapon in such a way nobody inside the club could see it.

Bolan favored the man with a cold smile. "We're not here for trouble, so don't start any."

"What do you want?" the man asked in English.

"We're looking for two guys, names of Rostov and Cherenko," Bolan replied. "We have it on good advice they may hang out here."

The man's face paled. "They are not here."

Carron then said something to the bouncer in Russian. The man winced with the increased pressure applied to his finger and then jerked his thumb toward the back of the club. Through the smoky haze and the flashing lights Carron and Bolan could make out an older man surrounded by at least half a dozen beautiful women. Carron fired off a couple more questions, then released his hold on the bouncer. The bouncer's eyes were filled with hatred but he made no attempt to detain them from entering the club.

Carron leaned close to Bolan's ear to be heard over the incessant beat of the music. "He says we should talk to the blond woman over there. Her name's Sonya Vdovin. She's like part of the SMJ's entourage, or something."

"I didn't know militant youth gangs had groupies," the Executioner remarked.

Carron shrugged. "I guess."

Bolan took point now with Carron watching his back. They advanced on the raised booth adjacent to the dance floor, approaching it from two directions. The man seated at the center of the booth wore a silk jacket in L.A. Lakers purple, and sunglasses. As many glittering, gaudy rings adorned his fingers as the number of women strewed sensuously across the massive booth surrounding his table. Bolan searched his mental files for a name to put to that smug face but came up empty. Apparently this one liked to keep a low profile. Bolan could only assume he was part of SMJ's top echelon, and young as he might be, that still made him one of the enemy.

Among the man's little harem were mostly dark browns and auburns, with one blond seated two spots to the man's left. Sonya Vdovin.

A brief conversation took place in Russian between Carron and the pimp look-alike before total chaos erupted in the club. Bolan spotted the flash of strobes on metal in his peripheral vision and turned in time to see a pair of young men on approach, machine pistols held too close to their bodies to be effective in that space. Bolan reacted automatically, whipping the Beretta 93-R from shoulder leather. He drew a split-second bead on the first gunner and squeezed the trigger.

The Beretta's report couldn't even be heard above the music but that made the shot no less effective. The 9 mm Parabellum round pounded into the man's breastbone and pitched him into a table occupied by a man and woman a couple of booths down. The second gunman skidded to a halt and brought his SMG to bear, but Bolan already had him tagged. The Executioner fired a double-tap this time that drilled the first slug into his opponent's chest and the second through his upper lip. The proximity of the shot flipped the guy off his feet and dumped him over the railing lining the walkway. His body smacked the dance floor and the people below began to scream and shrink away from the corpse.

Bolan stepped back and nearly lost his footing on some steps as the man in the Lakers jacket suddenly up-ended the table and produced a machine pistol. The soldier managed to keep his feet but in that brief moment he could only shout a warning at Carron. The Company man had drawn his pistol in the moment during Bolan's initial encounter, but his focus had been on the battle and he forgot to cover his flank from the table man. Even as Bolan raised the Beretta and sighted on the hood, the rattle of the Uzi submachine gun resounded above the shouting and scrambling of the club's patrons. A flurry of red splotches peppered the front of Carron's shirt as he triggered his own weapon reflexively and sent a .45-caliber bullet into the kneecap of a woman seated next to the SMJ gunner. The force of the blasts from the SMJ gunner then drove him into an empty table. Carron crashed to the floor amid splinters of wood, torn polyester and glass from a broken candle holder.

The Executioner triggered four successive shots, but he knew he was too late. He drove the distraction from his mind as the SMJ gang member's body slammed into the wall and tumbled off the seat, coming to a rest on the floor amid booze, food and blood.

The women had already made themselves scarce in the melee, and Bolan had to search long and hard before he spotted the flash of blond hair that signaled Sonya Vdovin. Bolan went after her as she disappeared through a back exit of the club. He nearly reached the doorway when the hulking bouncer blocked his way. Bolan never lost momentum as he left his feet and closed the gap with a perfectly executed flying kick to the bouncer's stomach. The kick drove the man back with enough force to break down the door of the rear exit. Bolan landed catlike on his feet and jumped over the bouncer's body now sprawled unconscious across the splintered door.

The Executioner pushed through a metal door that opened onto a back alley and looked both ways but saw nothing. He was about to turn back but then looked down and noticed a pair of tracks in the snow that could only have been made by high heels. He followed them with his eyes as they crossed the alley and then stopped at a garbage container. Bolan glanced upward just as he heard a clang from above and saw Vdovin making her way up a fire escape. Bolan thought about following, then realized she couldn't go anywhere from there except back down the stairs of the building—assuming she could access the roof door—or down the fire escape on the opposite side.

Bolan could easily cover either one without a whole lot of effort.

The Executioner raced to the front of the building next to the club, then headed into the alleyway on the far side where he stepped into the shadows of the structure beyond it. His position allowed him to watch both the alley and the front of the building. Several minutes elapsed before Bolan heard the first wail of police sirens. If Vdovin didn't make her play soon, he would have to leave to avoid the cops and that would put him back to square one—he couldn't afford to give up his only lead.

As predicted, the faint clang of high heels on metal reverberated in the cold, thin air and Bolan followed Sonya Vdovin's shadowy progress as she descended the fire escape. He moved deeper into the alley, finding concealment behind a large cardboard box, and considered drawing his Beretta. He thought better of it. If he wanted information, he needed Vdovin on his side and he figured sticking a gun her face wouldn't be a good start to their relationship. Then again, he couldn't be entirely sure where her loyalties lay—she did hang out with one of the worst criminal elements in the city, after all, and he doubted she behaved like an angel while in their company.

Bolan made his move as soon as Vdovin's feet touched the ground. He stepped from the shadows as she walked past him and drew up on her left flank. He wrapped a hand tightly around her elbow and steered her onto the sidewalk. Her eyes grew big and she started to open her mouth to scream when Bolan clamped his left hand over it.

"Quiet," he commanded. "I'm not going to hurt you. I need your help."

She tried to kick at him with her spiked heels, but Bolan moved out of the line of attack. He swung her body into the wall, not hard enough to hurt her but with adequate force to get the message across he wasn't fooling around. Hand still over her mouth, Bolan leaned close.

"I already said I wasn't going to hurt you, so there's no more reason to fight me."

Tears glistened as they pooled in her lower eyelids. Bolan felt her body shudder against his own and realized she wasn't wearing a jacket. He slowly let his hand off her mouth, released his hold and quickly shrugged out of his coat. He held it out and she stepped off the wall to allow him enough room to drape it around her shoulders. He still wore the sport jacket beneath the overcoat so the Beretta remained concealed in shoulder leather.

"Come on," he said more quietly. "Let's go someplace we can talk."

THE SOMEPLACE TURNED OUT to be a cozy bistro-style restaurant a mile from the club.

The waiter took their orders for coffee, bread and a soup appetizer. Vdovin had kept the overcoat draped across her shoulders when they entered the place so as not to call much attention to the skimpy blouse and short skirt she wore beneath it. She looked older than her twenty years, so her appearance on Bolan's arm didn't seem out of place with the other patrons, most of whom looked to be from high society. The place was also crowded, which surprised Bolan until Vdovin explained, according to the waiter, that a late opera had just ended.

"Your English is good," Bolan said. "With barely any trace of an accent."

Vdovin smiled briefly. "I was born in Russia but spent a number of years in Australia."

"That explains the strange inflections."

"My parents were not popular people. I was too young to remember, but they were forced from the country during the revolution. I only returned a few years ago."

"And got in with the best crowd right off," Bolan quipped.

"You've no right to judge me for that," she countered.

"You're right. Sorry. But I'm sure you know by now I'm not out to hurt you. All I want to know is where I can find Rostov and Cherenko."

She snorted. "Of course. You and half of the people I know in the Sevooborot. But I don't know where they are. And even if I did, I would not betray my friends."

"I thought Rostov and Cherenko were your friends."

Vdovin signaled for the cigarette girl who came over and extended a tray arrayed with a variety of smokes. Vdovin selected one, waited for the cigarette to be lit and then looked expectantly at Bolan. The Executioner shook his head at the cigarette girl as he handed her a generous tip and she sashayed from the table. Bolan looked around them but nobody seemed to notice them.

"You were saying?" he prompted.

"I have nothing to do with Leo and Sergei, either for or against. I only knew them for a short time, and I broke all contact with them once I had learned they betrayed the Sevooborot. My only connection with them is my friendship with Kisa."

"Kisa… Kisa Naryshkin?"

Vdovin seemed to let her guard down some. "You know Kisa?"

"Not personally," Bolan said with a shake of his head. "But I know she's Rostov's girlfriend, and I know she could be in serious danger from people inside the SMJ."

"She is in no danger from the Sevooborot."

"Want to bet?" Bolan countered. "I think there's something you don't understand here. Those people you like to hang out with aren't in this just for the sake of Mother Russia. Don't get that in your head for a second. They're driven by two things, power and money, and they're willing to steal or kill or whatever else they have to do to accomplish their ends."

"I do not believe you," she said. "I *know* these people. They are my friends."

"Time to find some new friends, Sonya." Bolan leaned over the table and lowered his voice. "You act like this is some kind of country club you belong to. I have intelligence that these supposed friends of yours are in bed with members of the Jemaah al-Islamiyah. Are you familiar with that group?"

Vdovin shook her head.

"Well, let me give you a clue. The JI is one of the most influential terrorist organizations in Southeast Asia. They're responsible for the murder of thousands of innocent people."

Vdovin took a long drag off her cigarette, sat back and folded one arm across her body defensively, holding the cigarette high in her opposing hand. "I do not believe you."

"Whether you believe me or not isn't important," Bolan said. "And it doesn't change the fact the JI is active in places like Afghanistan, the Philippines and Indonesia, to make no mention of the campaigns they sponsor in a half dozen other countries."

"My friends fight against those people. They stop them from coming into our country and stealing jobs and murdering our people."

Bolan's smile was frosty, at best. "I think you're confused, Sonya. The SMJ has made some kind of deal with the JI. Now I don't know what it's for, but Rostov and Cherenko know. That's why your friends in the SMJ want them dead."

"Leo betrayed the code of silence," Vdovin insisted. "Anything that was done to him or *is* done to him is because of that. And in the course of betraying the Sevooborot, he brought down Sergei, as well."

"I'm not part of these people. Why did they try to kill me?"

"Because you came to kill them."

Bolan shook his head. "No dice. We came looking for you, not them. The man you were with tonight. Who was he?"

"I have told you before, I will not betray my friends."

"What about Kisa?" Bolan said. "You said she was your friend."

"And so she is."

"Who do you think arranged to get Rostov and Cherenko out of the country?" Bolan replied. "You don't think your precious revolutionaries won't try to kill her once they find out?"

"They will probably do nothing," she said. "She is not even part of the Sevooborot."

"Really," Bolan said. "Then I guess it would surprise you to know they've had her under surveillance for some time now."

"How do you know this?"

The Executioner decided to go for broke and play his only trump card. "The same way I knew how to find you. Listen, Sonya, you don't have to believe anything I say. But two good men have already died at the hands of your friends, and I'm here to make sure nobody else falls. Now I can do that with or without your help, but in any case you need to wise up and see what's going on around you."

"I have already told you that I don't know where to find Leo and Sergei."

"But Kisa confided in you," he said.

"Yes."

"If she were in trouble, where would she go for help? Would she come to you?"

At first, Vdovin didn't answer—she just sat and stared—and Bolan wondered if she had finally decided to shut down and not answer any questions. Slowly, he realized that she was thinking about what he'd said. Something had dawned on her, some small bit of their discussion had taken hold, and she was now beginning to see Bolan had told her the truth.

Finally, Vdovin shook her head. "No. There is only one person she would go to for help. Her father."

Bolan nodded grimly and replied, "Tell me where to find him."

CHAPTER FOUR

Kisa Naryshkin's parents greeted her warmly but tir-
edly when she arrived at their home.

After summoning a house servant to put on a pot of
tea, they adjourned to the parlor where Kisa's father lit
a fire. She watched him work with the same fascination
she always held for him, and her mother watched her
with same amusement she always had when Kisa
watched her father. Tolenka Valdimirovich Naryshkin
had served with the GRU, the main intelligence arm of
the General Staff, Armed Forces of the Russian Federa-
tion. Tolenka's distinguished career began in 1962
where he served as adjutant to a low-level officer in the
supply distribution logistics arena. The GRU promoted
him quickly through the ranks and he worked with both
Soviet signal intelligence and field reconnaissance before being transferred to the Division of Human Intelligence. On several occasions during the eighties and
nineties, a number of foreign intelligence services had
approached Tolenka Naryshkin with offers to perform
counterespionage activities against his own country,

but according to Kisa's mother he refused every offer and reported it immediately to his superiors. This was something Kisa had learned very early in her life about her father: no matter how much it might benefit him, monetarily or otherwise, he would not betray his friends or his country.

Another thing that separated Tolenka from other men in his position was his sense of justice. Kisa had grown up—an only child as complications during her birth had left her mother sterile—hearing her father say regularly that he believed in the general goodness of most people. While many considered this naïveté, an odd trait for a military intelligence officer, Tolenka preferred to call it "natural humanistic optimism" and refused to offer any explanation or defense for his beliefs. What many failed to understand, although his daughter knew this simply by watching her father's interactions with others, was that Tolenka Naryshkin had a way of bringing out the very best in people. This had made him both a successful intelligence gatherer and administrator in the GRU.

The traits of steadfastness, truth and fairness that Kisa had come to know about her father made it all the more difficult to tell him what she was about to tell him. Certainly he would view her actions as unethical, maybe even as betrayal. All she could do was to hope he would understand. That didn't make it any easier when he sat next to her on the sofa and watched her intently with his gray eyes.

Tolenka smiled. "I wondered when you would come to us with whatever's been troubling you these past two months. I have to admit I didn't expect a visit at such a late hour."

Kisa smiled and shrugged, lowering her eyes and looking briefly at her mother for support.

"What I have to say is difficult, Father," she began.

"You know you can tell me anything."

"I do," she said, and quickly added, "and I know you love me."

"What's troubling you, Kisa?" her mother prompted.

"Please, don't interrupt me again or this will become too difficult," she said. "I have done something of which I am ashamed. But it has gone very wrong, Father, and I don't know what to do. So I am coming to you to admit of my indiscretions and ask you to help me."

Tolenka's eyes narrowed slightly for only a moment, then he nodded.

"About five weeks ago, I used contacts inside my office to arrange defection of two men to the United States." Kisa's mother took a sharp, inward breath and looked at Tolenka, who didn't react. "One of these men was Leonid Rostov, the man I'd been dating. You met him once. You remember?"

Tolenka nodded.

Kisa took a deep breath and plodded on. "He had a friend, Sergei Cherenko, who I also helped get out of the country because both of their lives were endangered by the same people."

"Who, dear?" her mother asked.

Kisa fixed her mother with a level gaze. "Leo and Sergei were members of the Sevooborot."

Now it was Tolenka Naryshkin's turn to react. He stood and shoved his hands in the pockets of his smoking jacket, marched to the fire and stared with a steely expression at the growing flames. Kisa could tell he'd become angered by her mention of the revolutionary organization. Her father considered them traitors to the country, murderers and dissenters who refused to let the revolution die. Things had improved vastly in Russia over the past nine years, particularly in their part of the country. People no longer had to fear being yanked out of their bed by the secret police in the dead of morning for their political affiliations, or fret over the possible repercussions when a volume of family members suddenly went missing. While things weren't perfect, not by far, they were much improved.

Tolenka said quietly, "Go on, Kisa. Tell me everything."

And that's exactly what Kisa Naryshkin did. She laid it out for her parents, every last detail, stealing regular glances at her father to see how he reacted to certain parts of her tale. She felt horrible having betrayed him like she did, but she could not have stood by and done nothing—risked the possibility of her true love being murdered—as long as she had the connections and resources to give Leo and Sergei a fighting chance.

When she completed her story, she began to cry softly and her mother moved over to the sofa and wrapped comforting arms around her. "You poor child. You've taken all this grown-up responsibility upon yourself."

Tolenka Naryshkin said nothing for a very long time; he just stared into the fire while his daughter cried. Finally he turned and sat in his wingback chair and fixed his daughter with a sympathetic expression.

"When you told us of this, my first thought was to my career and how this might have affected me. But since I retired last year, this is of null effect. What hurts my heart more than anything is that you did not come to me with this in the beginning. However, you are my daughter and there is very little I would not do for you or your mother. In fact, there is almost nothing I wouldn't do."

Kisa's eyes rested on him.

Tolenka sighed. "You really love this man, do you?"

She nodded.

"And what about him? He feels the same way?"

Kisa nodded again. "He was going to send for me once he was safely out of the country and he'd told the Americans about the terrorist plot. And I will go to him."

Tolenka smiled and reached out a hand to her. "Then tell me how Father can help."

Kisa emitted a soppy giggle and then rushed to her father's arms. He hugged her and they held the embrace for nearly a minute. When Kisa had regained some control of her emotional outburst she sat on the table and told her mother and father of the phone call and the alternate plan for Leo and Sergei to catch a boat from Murmansk. Her father considered this information carefully, sat a minute in thoughtful contemplation then rose and crossed to the telephone.

"I will reach out to my contacts in Murmansk," he said. "I'm sure I can get them safely aboard a—"

The window of the parlor suddenly erupted and a gust of cold air whished at the flames of the fire, causing them to flicker and rise with the additional air flow. Kisa screamed as a man clad in black boots and camouflage pants entered. A black ski mask covered his face but all three of the Naryshkin family members understood the intent from the automatic weapon slung over his shoulder. Another dressed just like him followed afterward.

Tolenka Naryshkin looked quickly around, rushed to the fireplace and grabbed the wrought-iron poker from the tool stand. He rushed the first man and swung the poker, catching the intruder with a glancing blow that bounced off his shoulder and subsequently grazed the masked man's head. The guy recoiled from the attack, a bit surprised at the resistance. Tolenka's mother hauled her daughter to her feet by an arm and ordered her to run before pushing her in the direction of the door. Kisa got as far as the door before stopping to look back. Her father was now embroiled in a vicious, hand-to-hand struggle with the second combatant while the first tried to scramble to his feet and help his comrade. The man never made it that far as Kisa's mother leaped onto the man's back and began to beat her fists on his shoulders. At one point, she clawed at his face and ripped part of the mask away, taking blood and flesh along with it. The man howled in pain and in one vicious show of strength he threw Kisa's mother off his back.

Kisa watched in horror as her mother landed hard on the ground and smacked her head against a wall-mounted radiator. Blood gushed from the wound and a sickening crack resounded through the air. Kisa started screaming at the man and he started to raise the machine pistol but her father—who had somehow gotten into the precarious position of having one arm pinned behind his back and the other wrapped around his own throat—kicked furiously at the weapon. The muzzle tracked upward just as the gunner squeezed the trigger and plaster rained down from where a volley of bullets chewed into the wall and ceiling above her head.

"Kisa...run!"

She hesitated another moment and then burst out of the parlor and raced for the exit. She was halfway down the hallway when the front door shot inward, swinging violently against the back wall. The entryway framed a tall, muscular man dressed in skintight black from head to toe. He held a pistol in his right fist and various implements of war dangled from the harness he wore. A pair of icy blue eyes inset on hard, chiseled features locked on Kisa and brought her to a skidding halt.

"You okay?" he asked.

Kisa didn't say anything for a moment, struck dumb by the awesome sight of the grim specter who entered her house and approached with a confident stride that could only have been forged out of a lifetime of hardships and violence. She seemed unable to form words, but she did manage to point toward the back room and mouth a cry for help.

The man nodded and rushed past her.

THE LAST THING Mack Bolan had expected to see on his arrival at the house of Kisa's father was a band of SMJ thugs ring the property before two of them made a forced entry through a window.

The Executioner elected to penetrate the house via the front door, the one place his enemies had not thought of, which would permit him quick and ready access to most of the first floor yet facilitate a hit-and-get scenario if the situation called for it. As soon as the SMJ hoods crashed through the window, Bolan went EVA and approached the front door, drawing his Beretta 93-R on the move and adjusting the selector switch to 3-round bursts. One kick with his two-hundred-plus pounds behind it proved sufficient to the task. The door rocketed aside and Bolan's eyes locked on those belonging to the frightened face of a young woman: Kisa Naryshkin.

"You okay?"

She seemed unable to find her voice, but the pointing and whimpering was enough information for Bolan to act on. The warrior moved swiftly past her and toward the room where the pair of SMJ hoods had made entry. He had nearly reached the doorway when one of the militant youths emerged with a machine pistol in his hands. Bolan raised the Beretta and squeezed the trigger, the triburst vaporizing the man's skull. The almost headless corpse shot backward and exited through the massive floor-to ceiling window of the back hallway.

Bolan turned into the room in time to see the second SMJ terrorist whipping an older man with his SMG. The young hoodlum stopped and looked at Bolan in shock. The Executioner wiped the man's surprised expression from his face with a 3-round burst to the chest. The impact flipped the man off his victim; his body slid across the polished, wooden floor and smacked to a halt against the back wall of the parlor. Bolan crossed to the victim. Blood seeped from a deep laceration across his cheek but otherwise he was breathing and thrashing about in semiconsciousness. He'd live. Bolan then noticed the woman and crouched next to her to check for a pulse at the neck: also alive. He rose as Kisa entered the room.

"You speak English?" he asked. When she nodded he said, "Call for help and stay locked in here until I return."

Bolan closed the door behind him, then headed up the

hallway. He reached a front room on the opposite side of the house in time to catch two more SMJ gunners, each coming through one of the two windows. The men appeared surprised to see Bolan waiting there, pistol drawn. They foolishly tried to bring their SMGs to bear, but the Executioner easily had the drop on them. His first burst sent one of the men back out the window with a trio of bullet holes to the chest. The second toppled inward, triggering a fusillade of rounds that gouged through a rug and into the wooden floor beneath it as Bolan's second burst caught him at belly, sternum and chin.

Bolan switched out magazines as he wheeled and left the study. He entered a room on the other side of the hallway and crouched in a corner where he could cover the entire dining area. He heard a window break and watched a moment later as a small, elderly woman in a housecoat burst through the swing door of the kitchen and ran screaming toward an exit door at the far end of the dining room. Two SMJ youths followed through that door, machine pistols held at the ready.

Bolan steadied the Beretta 93-R in a two-handed grip and squeezed the trigger. The 9 mm Parabellum slugs struck the first unsuspecting gunman in the chest and slammed him against a china cabinet. The other gunner reacted with incredible speed and swept the entire area with a furious stream of sizzlers from his AKSU assault rifle, but he was well high of Bolan's position in the shadows. Undaunted by the rounds buzzing over his head and slapping into the plaster walls, the Executioner took time to sight on the gun-toting hoodlum. He squeezed off a double-tap that drilled six rounds through the man's chest, several puncturing a lung and his aorta.

The AKSU flew from the enemy's fingers and he staggered to his knees before toppling onto his side. His body twitched several times as he bled out.

And with that, Bolan accounted for the six men he'd observed surrounding the residence.

Satisfied he'd neutralized all aggressors, Bolan rose and returned to the parlor. He rapped his knuckles softly against the door and called Kisa by name. She opened it a moment later and admitted him. Her father now sat on the edge of the sofa at the head of the woman who they had placed there. The man held a bloody handkerchief to his face while keeping vigil on the woman, who Bolan had to assume was his wife.

"You're out of danger now," Bolan said.

The man nodded and then extended his free hand. "I don't know who you are, sir, but we owe you our lives."

Bolan shook the man's hand and replied, "You're welcome. But it's best you forget it now."

Kisa stepped forward and laid a hand on Bolan's forearm. "Are you from America? Were you the one they sent to help my Leo?"

Bolan shook his head. "No, I was the backup plan. These men who attacked you are with the SMJ. They've already killed two American intelligence officers, and you might have been next if your friend, Sonya, hadn't decided to tell me where you were."

"I see," Kisa replied.

"I don't think you do. With the two men who were supposed to get Rostov and Cherenko out of the country dead, it's now up to me to find them and finish the job. I'm on your side, but I'll need your full cooperation."

"And you shall have it," the man replied.

"Father—" Kisa began, but the old man shook his head.

"No, Kisa, this man has saved my family."

He looked at Bolan and said, "My name is Tolenka Naryshkin. I am Kisa's father. I am recently retired from military intelligence."

"The GRU," Bolan said.

Tolenka nodded and continued, "I will not bother to ask your name, as I'm sure you would not be able to give me your real one. Under any other circumstance, I would report you immediately to the police. And while I am a soldier and statesman, I am also a family man and a patriot. And I recognize when another soldier is doing something for a greater cause."

Tolenka held out his hand and, after staring at the man a moment, Bolan removed the Beretta from his holster and dropped it into Tolenka's palm. "Now you should take Kisa and go. She will be able to tell you where to find these men."

Bolan nodded and turned toward Kisa. "Will you help me?"

Kisa looked at her father who smiled at her, and then nodded at Bolan. As they departed, Tolenka said, "I trust that once you have found them, you will release my daughter back to me safely."

Bolan stopped and turned to look at Tolenka. Although the guy had just had the hell beaten out of him and now stood guard over the brutalized body of his wife, he still seemed to hold his air of poise and dignity. A proud man, indeed; a man devoted to duty and honor; a man Mack Bolan understood.

With a short nod, Bolan replied, "You have my word."

And with that, the Executioner sealed the understanding between them. Yeah, he would keep his promise.

Even if it cost him his life.

CHAPTER FIVE

It took them more than an hour meandering along some unkempt back streets to avoid roadblocks before they reached the airport in St. Petersburg. Under normal circumstances it wouldn't have been difficult, but the recent outbreak of violence had the local cops scrambling to choke roadways with random inspection teams. Bolan elected to ride shotgun and let Kisa Naryshkin take the wheel. He might have considered driving in other circumstances, but this was her territory and she knew it much better than he did.

He could also keep his eyes open for tails.

For most of the drive they didn't speak to each other, and then when they did it was small-talk. Bolan couldn't say he minded all that much. This was the first combat stretch he'd allowed himself since his encounter with the SMJ at the hotel more than nine hours before. That was okay, though, since the trip to Murmansk would take a few hours by plane—there would be plenty of time for chitchat.

Bolan had thought about using his cell phone to contact Stony Man but decided against it. He'd already phoned Jack Grimaldi and advised they would be leaving for Murmansk. The Stony Man pilot promised flight readiness by the time they arrived, and it wouldn't be difficult to get flight clearance since they were flying within the country. All he'd have to do would be to file an amended flight plan. Business travel between the two cities by private jet wasn't all that much out of the ordinary, although the time of morning might have set a few of the more curious types wondering. Still, Grimaldi had indicated to Bolan it wouldn't be a problem.

When they arrived at the airport, they left Naryshkin's car in a long-term parking garage and took a shuttle to the main terminal. They then passed through a checkpoint where neither of their documents got more than a cursory inspection. Bolan's cover story as an American businessmen and Naryshkin posing as his interpreter seemed legitimate enough. Especially when the young woman showed her government credentials, which allowed her to travel unhindered through most of the country with considerable immunity from detainment. Bolan couldn't help but wonder if the relatively few questions and disinterested scrutiny they experienced might not have been the result of a phone call or two being made by a certain former member of the GRU.

Whatever the case, they were airborne in no time and they settled in for their flight over coffee and a sandwich for Bolan, while Naryshkin consumed a hot cocoa and a pair of cheese Danishes with the voracity of someone who hadn't eaten in a week. Bolan let her food settle some before turning their conversation to the topic at hand.

"You're sure that Leo and Sergei will take a train to Murmansk?" he began.

Naryshkin nodded as she licked the remnants of her food from her fingers. "It is the plan we had discussed. And if you're correct about the estimated time they left, it would make perfect sense. There was a train that left the Ladoga Station in St. Petersburg for Murmansk at 5:50 p.m."

"What time does it arrive?"

"I cannot recall exactly, but we will be plenty ahead of them. About 10:00 p.m. tomorrow, I believe."

Bolan whistled. "Yeah, that's a long haul."

"There is one stop in between," she said, looking at her watch, "but I believe we are too late for that."

"Where's the stop?"

"A passenger station in Petrozavodsk."

Bolan nodded as he looked at his own watch. It was just going on 0200 hours. "Didn't they worry the SMJ would be covering the train stations?"

"The passenger trains, yes. But this is an express cargo carrier. I was able to arrange for those seats just for times like these. Those in the Sevooborot would not have ever thought to look at a cargo train, because there is very little room for other than crews to travel on them. We figured it was the safest way to go since the chances were pretty good they knew nothing of my involvement."

"I have to admit I'm impressed."

Naryshkin smiled and lowered her head, her cheeks flushing with embarrassment. "I wish I could say that I had not learned a trick or two from Father growing up, but then I would be lying."

"You don't have to be ashamed," Bolan replied. "We're all a product of our upbringing in one way or another. It's what we choose to do with it that counts."

"When we reach Murmansk, if we find them, you will let me see Leo?"

"I promise to do my best. But understand my first duty is to make sure you come through this alive. I gave my word to your father and I intend to keep it."

The Russian expressed her disappointment. "I understand. No guarantees."

"You should try to get some sleep," Bolan counseled her. "You're going to need it."

She nodded and immediately inclined her seat and closed her eyes. Within ten minutes she was out like a light.

Unable to sleep, Bolan took the time to further study the files of Rostov and Cherenko. He'd already reviewed them twice in his hotel and knew they contained scant information. He had to admit that predicting their next move hadn't been easy once the meet had gone to hell at the hotel. The other consideration was how the SMJ had beaten him at nearly every turn. There could have been a mole inside the Company, although Bolan figured it would have to be someone pretty high in the food chain, not to mention he doubted the SMJ had enough money to make it worth the risk.

That left Bolan considering the strong possibility that Rostov and Cherenko had been on the level when they cited a partnership between the SMJ and JI. Maybe a group of young revolutionaries didn't have the resources to get inside the American intelligence community, but the JI certainly did, and they had proved it on more than one occasion. Bolan recalled the alliance the JI had formed with Japanese terrorists resulting in the theft of an entire U.S. aircraft with a top-secret, unmanned combat airplane aboard. Had it not been for the combined efforts of Able Team and Phoenix Force, they might have gotten away with it.

What Bolan still couldn't piece together centered on how an alliance with the SMJ could benefit the Islamic terrorist group. That mystery probably couldn't be solved until Rostov and Cherenko were safely in custody and on their way to the States. And until he found them, Bolan could do little more than run interference and hope this time around the information from Kisa Naryshkin would put him one step ahead of the competition.

The Executioner sensed his mission had barely begun.

JURG KOVLUN WALKED along the back lane of the underground shooting range and watched with satisfaction as the trainees grouped their shots on the paper targets with admirable precision. His training, coupled with the weapons provided by their contacts in the Jemaah al-Islamiyah, had produced the most excellent results. These were the results that the colonel should have been congratulating him for instead of criticizing him for the handling of two Russian punks who weren't under his control to begin with.

Why couldn't the SMJ police their own screw-ups? What did he look like, anyway? He was a professional soldier, a Spetsnaz veteran, not a nanny! There were moments when Kovlun wondered if it had ever been worth his time to join this crazy plan of the colonel's. While he believed in Anatoly Satyev's genius as a businessman, he'd never much trusted the man's military tactics or strategic abilities. Fighting a war like this one took more than simple money-changing and cheap disinformation campaigns. Such a cause as theirs required sound battle plans and the ability to position men appropriately. For example, why conduct business with the JI in Russia on their terms? Why not do the business dealings on neutral ground? And why, especially, had they chosen to involve young revolutionaries? Weren't seasoned professionals more appropriate for the tasks at hand?

Well, Kovlun couldn't deny that the results had been greater than he expected. Of course, Satyev had permitted him a free hand in the training of these gang members, and it hadn't taken much effort to bring the impressionable trainers in the Sevooborot around to his way of doing things. Through sheer discipline and the transfer of knowledge, Kovlun had turned more than forty SMJ recruits posing as American gang-bangers into a fighting force ready to do the colonel's bidding.

They had also chosen this particular location for a very good reason. Portland, Oregon, would serve as a proving ground, of sorts, since the police department here sponsored a local FBI office that specialized in gang activity. These officers and special agents were better trained and equipped to combat gang violence than those in just about any other city in America, Los Angeles included; Kovlun knew that was saying a lot. If these young men could put down the police resistance here, they would be unstoppable anywhere else. The other thing they had going for this plan was a general denial by Americans that gang violence wasn't a serious problem except in the largest cities. The flaw in that theory, aside from its mass acceptance, was that America had one of the worst gang problems in the world and, per capita, more gang-related murders, robberies and rapes than any other country. This wasn't exactly a statistic the nation would accept easily, and by that fact alone Kovlun figured the colonel's plan had a marginal chance at succeeding.

Kovlun finished his inspection and then ordered the range master to wrap it up before heading upstairs to the club. It lay dark and relatively empty, being only ten o'clock in the morning, but in twelve more hours it would be filled to capacity with teenagers and young adults, the perfect cover from which to launch their first major strike.

Kovlun nodded in greeting at his two lieutenants, Mikhail Pilkin and Aleksander Briansky. Pilkin had been in the Sevooborot since a very young man, actually a second-generation revolutionary of his father—one of the co-founding members of the organization and now a statistic in the files of the Moscow special police unit appointed to combat youth gangs. Briansky, a former native of the Ukraine, had fled his country and come to St. Petersburg for work, only to discover there was a lot more money to be made with his special affinity for guns. Briansky remained the chief armorer for the group, as well as a unit leader, and Pilkin oversaw most of the tactical operations based on Kovlun's orders.

The two were hunkered over a map of Portland spread across the stage at the front of the club.

"What say you?" Briansky greeted Kovlun in traditional fashion.

Kovlun nodded and replied, "Their shooting. It is much improved."

Pilkin was smoking a cigarette and in a cloud of exhaled smoke he replied, "Aleks performed a few modifications on the guns we received from the Arabs. They're much tighter now."

"We also took out the rattle in some of them," Briansky added. "It wouldn't do to have them making noise during the operation, Comrade."

Kovlun furrowed his brown at hearing about the defect. "I agree. That was good thinking. I will have to speak with our supplier."

"Would it not be better if we were to just shoot him between the eyes the next time he gives us crap weapons?" Pilkin asked.

"Save the hard-on for your many girlfriends, Mikhail," Kovlun warned.

"Sorry, Comrade, but I don't much trust the Arabs."

"I don't trust them, either, but for now we're forced to work with them. I have assurances from my people that once we've accomplished this mission we will no longer have to deal with them."

Briansky's eyebrows rose. "Does that mean we will also be able to start choosing our own targets?"

"I choose our targets," Kovlun countered. "Now and in the future. Not you, not anybody else. Got it?"

Briansky nodded.

Kovlun didn't like having to slap them down—they had actually turned out to be fairly competent operatives despite their youth—but he'd learned as a leader that young men full of piss and iron who were anxious for a fight occasionally needed to have their reins jerked so they didn't go off half-cocked and do something stupid.

"Have you heard the status on the little problem I brought to you earlier, Mikhail?"

Pilkin shook his head. "We're still working on it. Which reminds me that we may have another problem with that."

"I don't want to hear of any more problems. I've already had my ass torn apart one time for this and I don't want to bear any further criticism. Cherenko and Rostov are part of the Sevooborot, not part of this unit, and that means they shouldn't be *my* problem. I thought I'd made that clear the first time."

"You did, but this is a new development, and I have to tell you about it, especially when there's a chance it could compromise our operations here."

Kovlun's hair stood on the back of his neck. "And what is that?"

"An American agent," Pilkin replied. "Not the two men from the CIA. We managed to take care of them easily enough. This is another man, one we do not recognize and who doesn't show up on file with any of our contacts inside the intelligence networks. Even the Brit who made the initial contact with Kisa Naryshkin can't tell us who this man is."

"So what?" Kovlun said. "I don't see the problem. He's one man."

"Yes," Briansky interjected. "But this 'one man' has already taken out more than two dozen of our best operatives. So he may be one man but he fights like an army! Unless, of course, the reports we've received are exaggerated."

Pilkin continued, "Not to mention that he somehow found out about the idea you had to grab Kisa Naryshkin and hold her out as bait until Leo Rostov came calling for her. Now the American's disappeared with her and we have no idea where they've gone."

"What about her old man?" Kovlun demanded.

"He's onto us, too. He's got so many guns watching him now there's no way we could get to him even if we wanted to. *And* he's chosen to protect this American by claiming it was *him* who took out all of the men at the house."

"Yeah, as if anyone would actually believe that," Briansky added with a disgusted wheeze.

Kovlun had lit a cigarette and begun to pace the floor. "Oh, they'll believe whatever General Tolenka Naryshkin tells them to believe, you can be sure of that. I'm not even confident *my* people can get their hooks into him. And if he's covering for the American, your resources will never be able to track a man who doesn't allegedly exist."

"The cops are too busy cleaning up the mess of bodies this man has already left behind," Briansky pointed out.

Not to mention that most of them are Sevooborot, Kovlun thought. Which meant they wouldn't be looking too hard for the perpetrator, especially not when they heard stories about some lone, shadowy American who committed all these heinous acts. The St. Petersburg police didn't have much cause to feel empathetic when a young revolutionary fell under violent means. They had certainly committed enough acts of violence against others, many of them low-ranking members of the Russian government. The Sevooborot couldn't very well expect the full weight of justice to rush to their aid when the tables were turned. Kovlun understood that, and he'd never really been a fan of civilian revolutionaries trying to overthrow the government by force of arms. That was better left to those trained for that kind of activity.

Finally, Kovlun said, "I would agree this does present a bit of a problem. Very well. I'll make some phone calls and see what I can find out about your mysterious American. In the meantime, the shooting drills are wrapping up and I want inspections on equipment and weapons to start immediately after lunch. Your units will depart for their respective targets at 2000 hours sharp. The men are free to engage in recreation on site once inspections are completed, but nobody leaves and no alcohol from now until we've returned. Any man caught sneaking a drink will be shot on sight. The same goes for drugs."

"Yes, Comrade," the men declared in unison.

Kovlun wheeled and headed for the club exit. He needed to head downtown, find a decent place to have a late breakfast. On his way, he would make those phone calls. Yes, he would find this American, if he even existed.

And then he would destroy him.

CHAPTER SIX

"Coffee?" Barbara Price inquired, the carafe poised over Hal Brognola's cup.

The big Fed pulled the unlit cigar from his mouth and held up a hand. "No thanks, and especially no thanks if Bear made it. His coffee's strong enough to straighten the prehensile toes on a chimp."

Aaron "the Bear" Kurtzman, head of the Farm's cyberteam, looked up from where he'd busied himself at the computer terminal and frowned. "I'm hurt, Hal. I thought everybody liked my coffee."

"Everybody does like your coffee, Aaron," Price said, arching one eyebrow and fixing Brognola with an amused gaze. "But not everyone has Ironman's constitution."

Brognola shrugged and chuckled, then felt the rise of heartburn in his chest and tugged a roll of antacids from his vest pocket. He popped three, studied the package for a moment, then sampled one more for good measure before returning the half roll to his pocket. The burn started to subside almost instantaneously, as it always did, and Brognola sighed with relief. At least now he could focus on the briefing.

"Okay, let's get started," Price said after topping off Kurtzman's cup. Price was Stony Man's mission controller and often held the lives of the Farm's action teams in her capable hands.

Kurtzman tapped a key on the terminal and the lights dimmed as the face of a young man in the uniform of a Soviet army officer materialized on the massive screen on the far wall.

"Bear has compiled every scrap of intelligence we have on the SMJ, aka the Youth Revolution," Price began, "and cross-referenced that with potential suspects who might have some reason to profit from their activities. We pulled quite a number of names out of the hat, but this man is our prime candidate."

"Anatoly Satyev," Brognola interjected.

"You know him," Price said.

"You bet. He would have been one of my first choices, too. High-ranking officer, colonel as I recall, in the KGB and a first-rate pain in this country's butt. Current location?"

Price shook her head. "We're not sure. Satyev dropped off the radar for quite some time after the fall of the Soviet Union. About seven years, actually. He resurfaced in 1998 with an entirely new agenda, new credentials, the works. Even with our extensive resources we haven't been able to pinpoint him or his source of operations. We know he maintains several businesses, some paper corporations and a few legit, under a variety of pseudonyms. He's appointed CEOs for every company he ever started, though."

"Pardon the interruption," Kurtzman chimed in, "but there are a lot of suspicions from agencies like the NSA and FBI that he may be here in the United States. We just haven't been able to find him."

"What about photo recognition?" Brognola asked. "Surely the guy has to have a driver's license or passport…something to identify him."

"Well, if he does, he hasn't gone through official channels of any kind to obtain those identities."

"A guy like Satyev would go through the best paper guys in world, anyway," Price continued, "the vast majority of whom we have under surveillance. In all that time we've seen nothing, which leads us to conclude either he has others do all his work and monitor his business interests for him or he's altered his appearance."

Brognola grunted. "Keep working on it, Bear. I want to know where this guy is as soon as possible. What else?"

Price nodded to Kurtzman and he displayed the photograph of a second man, this one much younger and wearing the uniform of a Spetsnaz commando.

"This man we have identified as Jurg Kovlun, although he's using the alias Georg Mirovich here in the U.S., according to the California DMV," Price said.

"What's his connection?" Brognola inquired.

"There is none that we can ascertain, at least not to the SMJ, although he did work for a special detail that operated under none other than Colonel Satyev."

"Too much to be a coincidence."

"Right." Price pulled a manila folder from the stack on the table in front of her and passed it to Brognola. "This contains a complete dossier on Kovlun's activities. To no great surprise, he's been under observation by the FBI off and on for the past couple of years, and then one day they just dropped it and nobody's been on to him since."

Brognola furrowed his brow. "Why?"

"I wish we could tell you. Call it bureaucratic red tape or just plain apathy, but none of our sources inside the FBI can give us the first clue why their agents stopped following him. In fact, nobody could even tell me why they'd initiated a surveillance order to begin with. There's no originating paperwork on it, and no follow-up orders from the offices by any of their agents in charge."

"What about any agents assigned to the case?" Brognola asked.

"There were two and they're both dead," Kurtzman replied grimly. "One was killed during an operation a few years ago. The other died mysteriously just three weeks ago by what a medical examiner ruled as, and I quote, 'a coronary event of indeterminate origin,' end quote."

"Heart attack?" Brognola said. "A thirty-six-year-old FBI agent? Why do I not buy that?"

"We don't, either," Price said. "But it would be very difficult to get an order to exhume his body for a second opinion without very strong, incontrovertible evidence, especially when we don't think such activities will tell us much more than we know now."

"Damn," Brognola grumbled. "I wish Striker were here right now. I'd bet he'd have some insight."

"He hasn't checked in lately?"

Brognola shook his head. "No, and frankly I'm growing concerned. Oh, I'm not worried about him personally, mind you." Brognola dismissed the thought with a wave. "Striker's proved he can take care of himself without any help from us. What bothers me is that I think something's about to break wide open, and it doesn't appear we're any closer to this thing than we were forty-eight hours ago."

Price frowned. "Well, if you have any suggestions on how we might proceed, I'd be glad to hear them."

Brognola shook his head. "I'm sure you've hit every avenue you know. Tell me more about the plausibility of this theory the SMJ might be working with the JI."

"We did encounter some rumblings from British intelligence done by MI-6 agents currently inside Russia that there might be a connection, although none of our own intelligence assets inside Moscow can confirm it one way or the other," Price stated.

"Didn't Kisa Naryshkin originally make contact with us through a British agent?"

Price nodded and leaned forward in her seat to flip through the folders until she came upon the one she wanted and slid it neatly from the stack. She opened it and thumbed through a couple of pages before finding the details she sought. "Yes, it's here. The agent's name is Carson Barbour, former Russian translator for three years with MI-5 before he was transferred to counterespionage in MI-6. And by order of the Crown, no less. Seems he had a few friends in the highest circles of Parliament."

"Sounds like," Brognola agreed.

"We learned of Kisa Naryshkin's offer when Barbour first debriefed her about two months ago. He passed the information to our own case officers, who then took it to their superiors at the Company for evaluation," Kurtzman added helpfully.

"And then they told their two friends who told their two friends…" Brognola sighed deeply. "I get it. Still, Striker's last report indicated a leak in the information chain somewhere. I want you two to work up everybody involved with this operation, from the director of the CIA on down. And let's start with Barbour. Put a tail on him, if you have to, but I want that guy watched. He's closer to Striker than anyone, and if we can't be there to help him we can at least cover his backside. What frustrates me most is this thing might have cracked open anywhere."

"And isn't it funny how right after we make the transfer arrangements, the only man who could give us some idea of Kovlun's activities winds up on an ME's table in Washington, D.C.?"

"He's got a point there, Hal," Price said, "and it's too much to be mere coincidence, which is why we started looking at Kovlun."

Brognola had begun to skim the reports. "I noticed here that Kovlun went incommunicado about the same time as Satyev, by the way."

Price nodded. "There's no question these men are up to something. We think they're both in the U.S. right now, and we believe if they're working together they just might have had a hand in masterminding this deal between the SMJ and the JI."

"Okay, let's assume we're right about this," Brognola said. "The only thing I see the JI could offer the SMJ is support for their cause in Russia. Arms and intelligence, primarily, and maybe even some manpower. They might also create a sanctuary network for them in Islamic nations near Russia. But how the SMJ could make a return on the JI's investment is the biggest mystery, and yet Rostov and Cherenko swore this alliance is based on some terrorist plot against America. None of it makes sense."

"Maybe we're trying too hard," Kurtzman said.

Price looked askance. "What do you mean?"

"Sometimes in a situation like this we just don't have enough intelligence to form a cogent theory. Maybe what we're going to have to do is wait it out and see what happens."

"I think Bear has a good point," Brognola agreed. "In his last report, Striker said he felt like he was real close to scooping up Rostov and Cherenko. Since they're the only ones who can really tell us anything useful, we're probably wasting good time discussing this. I think we ought to proceed on what we have. Let's get something in the National Crime Information Center for both Satyev and Kovlun. Make it a minor infraction, failure to appear on a traffic citation, something like that. That should be enough to filter it to all the local agencies but not send up major flags."

"I agree," Price said. "We don't want any eager beavers spooking them."

"Is that wise?" Kurtzman asked. "Kovlun and Satyev are well-trained, former military. Things could get ugly if some unsuspecting state trooper pulls one of them over and tries to apprehend him."

"Put it out as a report-only," Brognola said. "That should minimize the risks to local police agencies."

Kurtzman nodded and headed to the Computer Room where he could work on drafting the bogus warrant. Price brought him up to speed on other minor items and then set about her own business, leaving the Stony Man chief alone with his thoughts. Brognola couldn't help feeling frustrated; they would have put together a more solid theory by now on most missions. This one had been handed to them pretty quick, though, with not a lot of time for planning. All they could do now was to put out the national alert net and see what happened. It was like sitting on their hands, hedging a long-odds bet, but he knew they had no other choice.

Brognola could only hope Mack Bolan was having better luck.

CARSON BARBOUR HAD NEVER expected a call like the one he received while at his residence, packing for a one-way trip.

His part of this entire deal should have been closed, but instead he was now embroiled in a search for a lone American and the daughter of a powerful former Russian officer in the GRU. And the American was potentially a ghost. Wasn't that the word his unnamed Russian contact had used? Yes, by jove, he had called this mysterious American a ghost. Barbour should have been getting ready to get on the private flight he'd chartered under an assumed identity and get out of this accursed, frozen country. Instead this new development had forced a change of plans and now he was bound for Murmansk.

In one respect, it surprised Barbour that Kisa Naryshkin had actually used a real identity card with inspectors at the airport. This, coupled with the two calls her father had made over his home phone wiretapped by MI-6, spelled out their plan in no uncertain terms. Barbour hadn't figured Tolenka Naryshkin would let his daughter travel alone—plus there was no way he bought the man's story about taking on six armed gunmen when he made his call to St. Petersburg police headquarters—which meant the girl was probably accompanied by either some of Naryshkin's men or this American.

Barbour also had to wonder who it was behind the recent outbreak of violence in the city against the SMJ. He didn't buy all of that chaos as the handiwork of the CIA man, Carron. There had to be another explanation, and they were now expecting Barbour to figure it out. The only problem was that Carson Barbour couldn't even be sure who he was working for. That was strictly against his policy most of the time, although he'd made an exception in this case because the money was so good. While the SMJ had considerable resources throughout Russia, he didn't believe they had the kind of intelligence and bank account he'd sampled. Barbour had never met any of his contacts face-to-face, but things were always in the drop locations he was given and always accompanied by a generous amount of untraceable euros in small notes.

Well, at least his command of the language and its culture would get him around the country with relative ease; this, and his excellent forged credentials as a Russian citizen provided by MI-6 had served him well. And whoever he'd been working for this past two years provided him with enough money to make up for his requirements to live modestly as a citizen in a middle-class neighborhood. It had taken Barbour many months, years really, to settle into the community—enough that people didn't pay him much mind but not so much that if he turned up missing somebody would immediately call the police.

Barbour had made sure to pay his rent a year in advance, so with several months remaining it wasn't likely his landlady would come calling. The housekeeping service would come in once a week, as usual, to tidy up. They probably wouldn't even notice he was gone for a while, since he kept his place immaculate. He'd just embarked on a two-week vacation as far as it concerned the local employer he'd engaged since first moving to this area of St. Petersburg more than three years ago. So he had accounted for all of this, planned it to the last detail. Even if they notified the St. Petersburg police he was missing, it wouldn't necessarily raise any concerns, and he'd planned to leave enough false trails that they could spend years searching for him and still come up empty-handed.

So Barbour left before dawn that morning with a single bag, hardly large enough to attract attention really, locked his apartment door behind him, an act he deemed profound in that it was as if he'd closed the door on this chapter of his life. He went downstairs and caught a waiting taxi to the airport where a jet waited to take him to Murmansk. If he didn't miss his guess, he was only an hour or two behind Kisa Naryshkin and her escort. He'd already put out feelers with confidential informants to be alert to their arrival. The CIs didn't come cheap, but they were effective.

Barbour had also placed a phone call to the local cell leader of the SMJ, instructing him to put his people in Murmansk on watch. He didn't give a bloody nickel for the fates of the two squeals, Rostov and Cherenko, but he couldn't afford to risk Kisa Naryshkin flapping her gums about him to anyone. He would have to deal with her and this alleged American co-conspirator, yet somehow make it look like they might have had something to do with his own disappearance. He'd originally thought he could make his people in MI-6 think he'd fallen victim to the FSB, perhaps even the SVR—the modern equivalent of the KGB—but now that scenario wouldn't hold together under close scrutiny. Since he'd been forced into this last-minute change of plans, he would have to concoct a new strategy.

Quite all right, though, Carson Barbour thought.

It would only make his disappearance look that much more convincing.

CHAPTER SEVEN

A light dusting of snow covered the tarmac of Murmansk Airport, but despite the gloomy weather Grimaldi received permission to land immediately.

Bolan gently shook Kisa Naryshkin awake. After the woman excused herself to the lavatory, Bolan stripped from his blacksuit and donned a pair of wool, charcoal slacks and a silvery turtleneck sweater. He then slid back into his shoulder holster and procured a Beretta 93-R from a hidden armory aboard the modified Learjet 36A. Bolan checked the action, loaded a clip, put the weapon in battery, made sure a round was in the pipe, then added two more clips to the carrier on the opposite side. He was shrugging into a heavy, suede coat when Naryshkin emerged from the lavatory a minute later, dabbing her face with a hand towel. She smiled at the big American, who returned it briefly.

"We've completed the tow into our hangar," Grimaldi told Bolan as he exited the cockpit. "There's a sedan waiting just outside. You should be able to leave the airport without trouble."

"That'd be a nice change," Bolan quipped.

"There are only about eight flights a day from this particular location," Grimaldi explained. "It's not overly busy, so they don't consider this a hot target for hijackings or other strange goings-on."

"I wonder if anyone's told them that's what makes this place a perfect haven for terrorists?" Bolan said. "But then most Russian airport cops make next to nothing. Easier to bribe them to look the other way."

The Stony Man pilot nodded. "Wish I could act surprised."

"Well, at least it will work to our advantage," Bolan said. "Hang tight, Jack. I'll be back in no time."

Bolan looked in Naryshkin's direction. "Ready?"

She nodded, and the two deplaned and headed to an adjoining office where Bolan found keys to the waiting rental. Along with the Beretta 93-R, Stony Man's contacts provided some additional hardware in the trunk of the luxury sedan adorned with diplomatic plates, along with a satchel containing spare sets of warm clothing in Bolan and Naryshkin's respective sizes, along with a fully equipped carbine version of the FNC assault rifle. A feat of firearm engineering by Fabrique Nationale Herstal SA, the 5.56 mm FNC had become a personal favorite of Bolan's for its reliability and versatility. He appreciated the weapon because it provided him a high-power, high-velocity resolution in a tough, carbine-style package that had proved itself time and again in his operations. A bag marked as "Diplomatic Satchel" in both English and Russian contained several 30-round box magazines for the weapon along with a half dozen RGN hand grenades.

Naryshkin furrowed her brow, worry evident in her voice. "What happens if we're caught with this?"

"Nothing," Bolan said, gesturing toward the diplomatic sign and then tapping the license plate of the car. "These were provided by contacts inside the American Bureau of Diplomatic Security. They give us full diplomatic immunity. The local authorities can't even detain our vehicle except in the case they declare martial law, and I don't see that anywhere in Murmansk's future. Do you?"

Naryshkin smiled. "You thought of everything. Much like my father, I think. I believe my Leo will be safe with you."

"I'll try to measure up."

When they were in the car and clear of the airport, Bolan said, "Okay, a few ground rules. First, you do what I tell you and when I tell you. I say jump, you ask how high and I say run, you ask how far and how fast. Understood?"

The woman nodded but kept her eyes on the road ahead.

"Second," Bolan continued, "I promised I'd try to give you another chance to see your boyfriend, but that doesn't negate my word to your father. Returning you in one piece to him supersedes a possible reunion. Third, no outside contact with anyone for any reason unless you go through me, because we have a leak in security and that could sign both our death warrants. Last, you follow my rules to the letter. Nothing will buy you a faster ticket out of here than if you break one of them. Are we clear?"

"I agree. We play by your rules."

She looked him in the eye when she said it, so Bolan felt he could rely on her to keep her word. He had to admire Kisa Naryshkin: tough, resourceful and honorable.

"What do we do now?" she asked.

"I'm going to find a place to stow you for a while so you can eat and catch a decent few hours of sleep. Then I'm going to do some reconnaissance of the train station and the docks."

"If you can get to Leo and Sergei at the train, why would you need to look over the docks?"

Bolan glanced at her out of the corner of his eye and said, "In my line of work, you learn to cover all your bases. Don't assume anything will go as planned, don't fail to learn the terrain you might operate in intimately and never, ever underestimate the resourcefulness or resolve of your enemy."

"This does not sound like a very happy life."

"It's not meant to be," Bolan replied.

She made no reply and they rode the remainder of the trip in silence. By the time Bolan rolled up to a hotel in the heart of Murmansk, the sun had risen and the purple-golden haze of dawn's first rays brought warmth to the bitterly chilly air. Bolan elected to skip the valet in favor of parking the vehicle himself. He didn't trust the sedan to the curiosity of a young man when he spotted the diplomatic plates, not to mention he was on unfamiliar turf with no decent intelligence on the SMJ's foothold in Murmansk. They checked into the hotel without incident.

Bolan waited while his companion showered and changed clothes, then sat her down on the love seat and took a place across from her on the coffee table. "Don't order any room service and don't answer the door. I put the privacy sign on the door, so housekeeping shouldn't disturb you, but keep the dead bolt in place all the same."

"Do you think I'm safe here?"

Bolan extended a hand and rubbed her shoulder in a sign of comfort. "You're much safer here than tagging along with me. I doubt anyone's looking for us, but there's no point in taking any chances."

Naryshkin nodded slowly, then, after locking eyes with him, she leaned forward and threw her arms around his neck. The move surprised Bolan, but not nearly as much as the kiss she planted on each side of his face where it met his neck. In other circumstances it might have meant something more, but Bolan knew in her culture this was a sign of affection and respect, like a sister might demonstrate toward an overly protective brother. Bolan cupped her chin, smiled with a wink and got to his feet. She followed him to the door so she could lock it behind him.

"Remember," he said as he opened the door. "Don't open this for anyone but me. Someone tries to break in, you call security and lock yourself in the bathroom. Got it?"

She nodded and he left her, stopping and waiting until he heard the click of the dead bolt before heading to the car. Once out of the hotel lot Bolan headed straight for the docks. According to Naryshkin, Rostov and Cherenko planned to hook up with a trawler or other similar vessel where they could gain passage out of the country. In one respect, Bolan saw a spark of brilliance in their plan. While they remained in Russia they were fugitives—both from the SMJ and the law—but once they were in international waters the only agency that had jurisdiction over them was Interpol. And since Interpol didn't have any reason to look for them, the two men would be relatively safe until they could arrange some alternate transportation into the United States.

And with any luck, the Executioner would find them before the enemy did.

THE CALL CAME VERY EARLY in the morning from the one Bratus called simply "the Brit."

Of course, Olaf Stroski knew all about the man whose real name was Carson Barbour; knew he was a British agent for MI-6; knew how he was assigned to lead the life of an upstanding Russian citizen while he spied on the Russkies for Her Majesty, the queen; knew how he'd succumbed to disillusionment like so many other British agents before him. He knew all of these things because he'd paid a good amount of money to know them—just the same way he'd paid a good amount of money to Barbour on behalf of his partners in the Jemaah al-Islamiyah.

The beauty of this whole deal, which was quite pretty as a picture, was that Barbour believed Stroski worked for him instead of the other way around. This wasn't the only time that Stroski had decided to play the role of the hired goon, a bootlicker who would do anything to make an easy buck. So it came as no surprise when Stroski's cell phone—the one that Barbour paid for—rang and roused him from a deep sleep, induced by imbibing a bit too much fine Russia vodka.

"I have a mission for you," Barbour had told him in flawless Russian.

Of course, he always had a mission for Stroski. It further amused the man when Barbour would play his pathetic spy games, but Stroski let the man have his fun. What did it hurt, after all? Stroski was well compensated for his efforts. Barbour could be generous to a fault.

In his other life, the one he lived when not kowtowing to every hustler and cheap hood in Murmansk and surrounding areas, Stroski headed the largest recruiting agency for the Sevooborot in the country. Personally, he didn't give a damn for the organization, as he considered himself neither a revolutionary nor a pioneer of the youth movement. In fact, Stroski's childhood in Murmansk had been quite unremarkable. He'd been an orphan by ten, an accomplished thief by twelve and wanted by Moscow police on a murder rap by the time he reached eighteen.

Stroski realized he wouldn't survive in prison. He would either commit suicide or someone inside would do him for sure, so he convinced a high-ranking member of the Sevooborot that he'd be ideal for recruiting top talent for the youth revolution movement. Before he knew it, he'd bought himself a one-way ticket to the greatest hell on Earth, where half a million people suffered nearly twenty-four hours of darkness six weeks a year and citizens would actually leave glass bottles on the sidewalks for the poor. Still, it didn't take long for Stroski to fit right into his environment. Part of the deal had included a stipend, a decent sum of money that a resourceful guy like him had no trouble tripling. By the time he reached twenty-two, Stroski had amassed what made up a small fortune in contrast to the income of most of Murmansk's citizens, and he'd learned long ago as an orphan that sharing did nothing but make one poor very quickly.

With his money and a new life in place, Stroski set about creating what amounted to a virtual empire. His recruitment tactics were crude, at first: lure young, impressionable types with women and sex and then suddenly cut them off. When they came begging and pleading on their knees, he promised them their life back if they agreed to pledge their allegiance to the Sevooborot. Most of them would promise just about anything. The only tactic Stroski steered clear of was drugs. Not only were they illegal and expensive, they put Stroski too close to police scrutiny, and he couldn't afford that. Second, it wouldn't do much good to recruit a bunch of hopheads so strung out they couldn't perform adequately.

Nowadays, Stroski resided in a high-rise apartment, had all the women and vodka he wished and ran a premiere business that selected the finest recruits for their revolution. He had earned himself quite a name, enough that their Arab contacts had selected him to be their liaison with Stroski's partners in Moscow. Yes, he smiled when he thought of the term. Somewhere along the line his relationship had changed from that of employee to business relation. Stroski wielded enough power in Murmansk that he could call his own shots—name his own price, even, although he kept it reasonable to stifle the competition—which included oversight of a private army of the best the Sevooborot had to offer. He called them "operational security," although his benefactors in Moscow chose to refer to them by other names.

Either way, Stroski had built a reputation for being cheap and fast but delivering quality results, regardless of the role he played. He predicated this success on his ability to call the game while making whoever he dealt with on the other end think it was their game. What did he care who took the credit as long as he could continue to live the lifestyle to which he'd become accustomed?

So after he got the call, Stroski disentangled his arm from beneath the head of the woman he'd met at the club the previous evening and took a shower. He put on a pot of coffee, scrambled some eggs of which he only ate half and fed the remainder to his Doberman guard dog, and then bundled himself into a leather overcoat and made for the street. He could still smell his own drunkenness, so he called a taxi to take him rather than risk being caught by Murmansk officials driving under the influence. He could not allow a positive identification by the police. Although he'd grown a couple inches in height since he left Moscow, died his blond hair dark brown and obtained an alternate identity, Stroski knew his fingerprints were on file from his juvenile records and any detainment might result in an unmasking of his previous life.

When he reached the airport, Stroski paid the cabbie and ordered him to wait. If he spotted the people Barbour had told him to watch for, he didn't want to risk losing them. He knew his chances of returning to find the cab still there were about fifty-fifty, but a quick check of his watch told him he might get lucky. Barbour had just been leaving and he estimated his quarry would be approximately two hours ahead of him.

Stroski made his way along the slick sidewalk and entered the terminal, then walked three doors down and exited out of sight of the cabbie. He rounded the corner of the building and made his way through the predawn darkness to the fence that bordered the perimeter of the private airfield. He arrived in time to see a small jet, unmarked except for its American registration number, which he noted on a small pad of paper he kept with him at all times. There was no guarantee the number was legitimate, and even if it were he felt sure it would come back to some bogus person or organization.

The Russian waited for a time, standing stock-still as he shivered in the cold. He wished he'd dressed warmer, but there wasn't anything he could do about it now. Eventually, as always, his diligence paid off and he watched as a tall man and young, short woman emerged from the hangar and opened the trunk of a waiting vehicle. Stroski reached into his coat and withdrew the second item he carried virtually everywhere: a small pair of collapsible, 30-power field glasses. He put the binoculars to his eyes and checked the contents of the trunk and the vehicle's license plate. It was difficult to make out the license, but he finally determined they were diplomatic plates, the kind the government issued to high-ranking officials. Of course, they would want this so that the local police couldn't detain them.

Stroski smiled as he turned after watching the sedan depart and headed toward his cab. As he did, he removed his cell phone from his pocket and dialed a specific number. The Brit would want to know everything, especially that license number. While Stroski didn't have the connections to get information on the sedan or who might be using it, or even where it was going, the Brit had the connections who could easily find out. Most of all, though, the young man thought about the extra money he would make. Yes, the Brit would probably pay a bonus when Stroski confirmed the rumors about a mysterious American accompanying a young woman, and a trunk filled with what looked to be weapons.

Stroski had to admit that even this new development had piqued his curiosity.

CHAPTER EIGHT

Mack Bolan walked along the tracks of the empty station and studied his surroundings. He identified about a half dozen ambush points the enemy might be able to utilize to take out Rostov and Cherenko. What troubled him most was the fact that he couldn't possibly cover all of them alone. He'd either have to involve Grimaldi, something he didn't want to do unless it became necessary, or figure out a way to get the pair off the train without being spotted by anyone waiting for them.

As the Executioner left the station and headed for his car, he considered the possibility of rigging the grenades to explode remotely, then dismissed the thought. Too risky to civilians. Bolan had always tried to factor in the innocent population in his operations. Risking the lives of noncombatants wasn't acceptable, and he'd built a reputation on keeping the bloodshed to the enemy at all times—even it meant compromising an operational objective. Bolan was in the business of conserving life and always had been, killing only when necessitated by factors of duty or self-defense. He didn't believe the ends always justified the means, and he refused to do anything to put more blood on his hands. When it came to the rules of engagement, Bolan had never believed it was right to salve his conscience with some "greater good" theory that civilian casualties were the natural, collateral damage of warfare. Bolan valued human life much more than that.

Bolan drove from the station and headed toward the docks. He looked at his watch: roughly ten hours remained before Rostov and Cherenko's train was scheduled to arrive. There was plenty of time to scour the docks to see if he could determine the most likely exit scenarios in the event things fell apart at the station. Bolan had some faith that the throng of people crowding the station that night would make it difficult for the enemy to target Rostov and Cherenko. And Bolan had no doubt it was murder the SMJ had on its mind.

The Executioner also had to consider his other mission—the one that would get him information on the JI's plot to launch a terrorist attack back in the States. While Hal Brognola hadn't said anything to Bolan during their last conversation, he could sense the frustration just by the tone of the man's voice. He knew the guy too well not to pick up on the nuances of Brognola's tone. Yeah, Brognola probably felt like he was sitting on his hands, helpless because he couldn't contribute one iota of useful intelligence to the mission.

Bolan didn't see it that way. What Brognola failed to remember was that Bolan's experience had taught him to be resourceful and to learn not to rely on help from anyone to accomplish his mission. In fact, Bolan often preferred it that way, because then he didn't have other concerns to distract him. He could remain focused and more alert to potential trouble.

Like the kind he'd spotted in his rearview mirror, a nondescript Citroën. Bolan hadn't noticed any tails from the hotel, although that didn't mean a thing. The enemy had either used spotter cars or they'd picked him off here based on intelligence from someone inside their organization. So he hadn't been able to keep his movements a secret very long after all, not to mention they might have observed his activities at the train station. Bolan cursed himself. It wouldn't take the SMJ long to put two and two together; that meant he had to make sure his tail never got back to anyone with a report on his movements.

Time to go on the offensive.

Bolan got on the highway that took him north out of Murmansk and headed for the seaport at Kola Bay. According to the thermometer inside the sedan, the temperature was still well below freezing, near -17° Celsius, but the roads were clear and dry. He needed a bit of running room to give himself time to formulate a plan. Besides, traffic had thickened with people traveling to and from work in Murmansk, and the motorists didn't need to contend with a highway gun battle during their morning commute.

Bolan could wait.

THE EXECUTIONER TOOK THE EXIT, a long and lonely stretch of road that would take him through a large rural tract and eventually terminate at Kola Bay. He downshifted as he made the curving exit ramp and looked over his shoulder at the tailing vehicle. From that vantage point he could make out four occupants inside the Citroën—they had sent a full crew. Bolan knew that many bodies could only mean one thing: hit squad.

Bolan poured on the speed until the sedan swung onto the straightaway, then slowed. He wanted the tail to believe he wasn't interested in them, or at least that he hadn't taken any notice of the pursuit vehicle. If he kept far enough ahead, they wouldn't be able to gauge any of his reactions. Bolan was able to make his move a few minutes later, when he spotted a bend in the road surrounded by a patch of mature woodlands on the blind side of the curve.

"Perfect," Bolan murmured.

He rounded the corner, then put the vehicle into a skid that took him off the roadway and into a ditch. He then double-clutched as the vehicle slowed, powering it gracefully out of its slide and putting it into Reverse. The engine whined in protest and the transmission slammed a bit, but Bolan made sure to decrease his speed enough he didn't drop the transmission from the undercarriage. His vehicle now in Reverse, Bolan aimed for a spot between two trees, stopped and put the gearshift in Neutral. He turned and slapped the center button on the rear dash that disengaged the backseat and folded it, then reached beyond it to retrieve the FNC assault rifle.

Bolan checked the action of the weapon and rolled down his window. He waited nearly a half minute before the sound of the Citroën's engine reached his ears. The vehicle swung into the curve a minute later and shot straight past his position without even slowing. Bolan dropped the gearshift into Low and released the clutch, jerking the wheel back and forth to maintain his tread on the spongy woodland floor. The sedan came away from its hiding spot and he quickly made the road and accelerated to catch up. He'd hidden at the first sharp turn in the arc that skirted the wood line, which meant his tail wouldn't notice him until he'd gained speed and reached the straightaway.

By that time, it would be a bit too late for the enemy to do anything about it.

Bolan's plan came off perfectly. When he reached the straightaway, it took him only a few seconds to close the distance between the two vehicles. He maintained control of the wheel with his right hand as he reached across to snatch the assault rifle from its place on the passenger seat. Just as the soldier straight-armed the weapon out the window, he saw the two rear passengers scrambling for weapons. The Executioner waited another heartbeat, then triggered a sustained burst as he swept the muzzle across the back window. The window shattered and Bolan saw a violet and pink spray bathe the inside of the vehicle. Scratch one.

The driver began to swerve to the extreme sides of the road in an attempt to avoid more damage. Inside, the remaining occupant of the backseat had his own weapon clear and aimed out the window. He triggered off a wild burst from the SMG that went wide of Bolan's sedan. The Executioner tried to ride the shoulder so he might get off a shot on the vehicle's now unprotected right flank, but the driver's erratic steering prevented him from gaining an advantage. The rear fender of the Citroën struck the front driver's panel of Bolan's car and nearly sent him spinning out of control.

Bolan clenched his teeth and had to reposition his grip on the wheel to avoid a fishtail. He tapped the brake and steered onto the pavement, but the extra few seconds it took him to get his sedan under control tendered an advantage to his quarry, and they managed to gain some distance. Bolan knew the engine inside the Citroën was more powerful than his own, so if he wanted to make sure the gunners didn't get a chance to report back to their superiors, he needed to act.

With a new resolve, Bolan extended the FNC out the window once more, but this time he aimed low, triggering several short bursts, each a little closer to his intended target. He hit pay-dirt with his fourth volley, which drilled through the right rear tire and effectively shredded it. The enemy driver continued onward, bringing the rear end of the vehicle under control quickly. Eventually the flaps of tire flew clear; sparks began to fly from the wheel well and smoke rushed up where the metal bit into the roadway. The destroyed wheel wasn't enough to stop the vehicle, but it provided all the advantage Bolan needed to catch up.

The Executioner started to swing onto the right flank once more, but the driver again attempted to block him by moving to the right, as well. Unfortunately, the driver didn't account for the fact that with his right rear wheel dragging the vehicle down, he couldn't correct his steering as quickly. Bolan did. The soldier swung suddenly back onto the lane, crossed to the extreme shoulder and gained on the left flank. Before his quarry could respond, Bolan tapped the nose of his vehicle against the Citroën's rear fender and sent the car into a tail skid for which even the most experienced driver couldn't compensate. The Citroën continued its wild spin until it slid off the road and bounced to a halt in the ditch.

Bolan stood on his brakes and stopped his car with a power slide. He popped the trunk and went EVA before the occupants inside the Citroën recovered enough to react. The soldier palmed one of the RGN grenades, yanked the pin, then sprinted for the ditched vehicle. As he got close, the front seat passenger tried to open his door and get clear but the incline of the ditch prevented an exit. He saw Bolan approach and, realizing his dilemma, stuck his pistol out the window and fired wildly. The shots went considerably high over Bolan's head. By that time, the Executioner was in range and released the RGN. It bounced off the ditch and made a neat path through the open passenger window.

The big American went prone a heartbeat before the grenade blew. The explosion whooshed a fiery cloud of gas close enough to singe the hairs on the backs of Bolan's hands where he'd covered his head and neck. The entire interior of the car combusted, and when the Executioner next looked he saw nothing but reddish orange flames as they flickered through the charred holes in the windshield and roof.

He stood and looked around briefly before he returned to his car, stowed the weapons and got away from the combat site as quickly as possible. With any luck, when the police did finally arrive, the initial physical evidence would lead them to conclude the Citroën had a blowout, the driver lost control and the explosion was secondary to the crash. A closer look that might reveal subsequent evidence to the contrary would take a long time.

But by that time, the Executioner planned to be long gone.

"So it turns out this American isn't such a phantom after all," Carson Barbour said to Olaf Stroski who arrived in his personal vehicle with one of his men at the wheel to chauffeur them. "You're sure he left alone?"

"Positive."

"And what about the girl?"

"Still inside the hotel somewhere," Stroski replied. "It has been difficult to get information on the residents there. It is one of the largest hotels in Murmansk, very popular among the elite, typically reserved for prominent businessmen or diplomats. Or simply the filthy rich. The American's contacts did well in choosing such a place. Lots of security."

Barbour raised a hand and said, "I only wish facts in your answers to my questions. I'm not interested in excuses."

Barbour could see the anger in Stroski's expression—the young man truly desired to lash him with a biting reply. But Stroski knew his place and wisely decided to keep his peace. Good discretion in that boy, Barbour thought. The information Stroski provided Carson Barbour turned out to be spot-on, which made it less difficult for Barbour to reach out to his other connections in Murmansk and order them to put the hotel under observation.

"I have some friends," Stroski said quickly. "I told them to keep an eye on the American and to tail him if he left the hotel, whether or not the girl was with him."

Barbour snapped a hard look at Stroski. "Why did you do this?"

"You weren't here," Stroski said, shrugging. "What was I supposed to do?"

"You were supposed to back off."

"Well, you wouldn't even know about him leaving the hotel if I hadn't assigned a few of my friends to keep an eye on him."

Barbour thought a moment about a snarling reply of his own, but then reconsidered. He didn't think it in his best interests to tell Stroski anything about his other connections in Murmansk. Stroski wasn't all that big a fish in the pond anyway, and Barbour figured if he told Stroski he had other irons in the fire, the man might try to seize the advantage in some way. No, better to keep the bloody punk in his place with the rest of the dregs of society. He couldn't afford to have the kid in his business.

"All right," Barbour replied with a feigned smile, "so I can see you're just bucking for a little bonus." He reached into his coat and withdrew two bundles of one thousand ruble notes he'd promised Stroski for the work plus a bit something extra. All told, it equated to the sum of approximately five thousand pounds sterling. "You've earned it. Now what about these men you ordered to follow the American. How reliable are they?"

"They'll do their job," Stroski said, pocketing the money without even bothering to count it.

"And you ordered them not to make contact, I assume."

Stroski blinked.

Barbour took a deep breath. "You *did* tell them not to make contact. Right?"

"I, well, I didn't—"

"Oh, bloody hell!" Barbour slapped his foot on the floorboard of the luxury sedan and pounded on his knee. "You understand that we're dealing with a professional here, correct? This American, he's not just some lackey of the U.S. government. According to my intelligence this man is extremely dangerous and should only be handled with the utmost discretion!"

"My people can handle one man," Stroski said with a snort, although the tone in his voice told Barbour he had some doubts.

"No, they cannot, you dumb Russian pig! Some of the top soldiers in the Sevooborot couldn't handle this one man. That's why I told you to observe him and keep your eyes open. I never authorized you to engage him!"

"I did not say we ever engaged him," Stroski replied. "I simply ordered my people to follow him."

Barbour snorted in derision. "*Your* people. Listen to you! You view yourself as some hoity-toity of high society here in Murmansk. Who do you think you are, the next Russian emperor or something? You're a nothing, a nobody on the bottom-most rung of the social ladder. Why, I even doubt if—"

Barbour was looking out the window as he scolded away, not considering Stroski worthy to even deign him with his countenance. He wished now that he hadn't done that because even above his tirade he heard the unmistakable click of the hammer being cocked on a pistol. Barbour turned with surprise to find Stroski in the seat opposite him, a stainless-steel semiautomatic pistol in his fist and pointed directly at Barbour's face.

"I've heard enough, *Comrade,*" Stroski said. "And I've taken about all I plan from you. I was content to this point to let you think you were the superior in our little arrangement and that I worked for you, but now I'm simply full to the point of sickness with your personal attacks. You see, I can take many things from many people, but to call me a Russian pig is to insult me beyond my capacity. I will agree that maybe putting my men on this American's trail wasn't the brightest decision I've ever made, but to listen to you, *you* of all people, to speak to me in this fashion is another case entirely. So, I would pose this challenge to you. Open your fucking mouth in such a fashion again and I make a solemn promise to put a bullet right into it, which I'm confident would bring a tidy end to our relationship. Do you understand me?"

Barbour nodded slowly, horrified that he'd let this commoner, this peasant, get the drop on him like that. Of course, Barbour could only blame himself because he'd broken one of the most basic rules in his business—he'd grossly underestimated the enemy.

"My mistake," he said. "I apologize."

Stroski immediately slipped his weapon back into place beneath his coat. "It is forgotten. Now, I would like to hear a little bit more about the situation here in Murmansk, because I have the sense there is a little more money here involved than perhaps you originally led me to believe. Am I warm?"

Barbour merely nodded in reply, still a bit shocked as to what had just transpired.

"Well, then," Stroski said, leaning back in his seat and folding his hands in his lap. "Tell me more of this American. Don't leave out any details. Especially where it concerns that *lovely* woman accompanying him."

CHAPTER NINE

Kisa Naryshkin sat in front of the television with a blank stare.

This was her favorite show, a comedy from the United Kingdom—one of the few openly telecast in Russia outside the mundane programming of news, world news and talk news—yet she found herself distracted. The chief distraction was the dark-haired, blue-eyed American out there risking his neck to help her friends, particularly her beloved Leo. What distracted her more, however, was the thought that she could actually be in physical danger.

Growing up the daughter of an army intelligence officer, Naryshkin knew quite well the ills of the world. There were a lot of sick and twisted people walking freely throughout the streets of every major country, and Russia was no exception. Russia had its problems, to be sure, but among its blustery winds and frost and blankets of heavy, wet snow were also a strong and emboldened people who could be quite warm and accommodating when it suited them.

That made it more difficult for the young woman to understand why people were so intent on killing Leo and Sergei. Why didn't they just leave them alone and let them live their lives? What had they done so terrible to the Sevooborot that they felt the need to terrorize them? Well, she could only hope that Cooper would be able to facilitate their escape from the country. Once they were in the U.S., she hoped the Sevooborot wouldn't be able to touch them.

The jangle of a phone shook her from her daydreaming. It rang again, and Naryshkin stared hard at it for a long time. Cooper's instructions had been very clear about what to do if a visitor knocked on the door. But he'd said nothing about what to do if someone called. She got off the settee and padded barefoot to the front door. She double-checked the locks and made sure the sign still hung from the outside of the door before returning to the TV and her seat, by which time the phone had stopped ringing.

About two minutes elapsed before the phone started to ring again, and this time it went on long enough that it had begun to drive her crazy. Five minutes passed and then it began incessant ringing a third time. After about ten rings she decided she'd had quite enough and picked up the phone. She wouldn't say anything until the caller identified himself first, because at least if it was an attempt by those in the SMJ to determine if she was there they couldn't be certain it was actually her.

"It's me," the familiar voice of Matt Cooper said. She could hear some relief in his tone. "Are you okay?"

"I'm fine. Was that you before? Calling, I mean?"

"Yeah, I just kept trying because I thought either you might be asleep or decided not to answer."

"Well, you didn't—"

"I know," Bolan cut in. "That's not important right now. Are you safe?"

"I'm fine," she said, alert to the fact he seemed a little short with her. "Why?"

"I want you to pack your stuff and go directly downstairs to the lobby," he said. "Wait in view of the desk clerk and make sure you sit close to any people who might be down there."

"Okay, but what's—"

"I don't have time to explain this right now," Bolan said. "Remember, I say jump…"

She nodded into the phone without any thought he couldn't see her. "Okay, I remember. Fine, I will do it."

Naryshkin hung up and turned on her heel. She was halfway to her bedroom when a sudden thumping began at the door of the suite. She froze in her tracks. She hadn't ordered anything. In fact, nobody should have even known she was there. It's not as if the privacy sign hanging on the door had her name written all over it. Cooper wouldn't have called her from outside the room. Would he? Was this a test? More beating at the door, louder and more insistent, but the young woman ignored it. Cooper had instructed her not to open the door for anyone, and she knew him to be a man who meant what he said.

She rushed into her bedroom, shed her robe and quickly donned the fresh clothes the American had purchased for her. She then stuffed the dirty clothes into the small overnight bag and quickly put her coat on before returning to the living room. The banging on the door had ceased. Naryshkin waited for a minute, then tiptoed to the door and pressed her ear against the cold, hard wood. It was a heavy door, really, probably made of walnut or red oak. She tried to slow her breathing, which had grown rapid from excitement mixed with fear, and looked through the peephole. Nothing. She heard a dull thump through the door and then a renewed pounding against the wood caused her to shriek and jump backward. She brought her hand to her mouth to stifle any further outcry, but it was too late. As if the soles of her shoes had been nailed to the floor, her feet froze in place and she couldn't feel any of her muscles move when the door rocketed inward.

The two young men who advanced on her with outstretched arms were enough to jolt her back to reality, but she lost her balance and fell backward. One of the men bent and that's when Naryshkin delivered a kick with all her might. She couldn't be sure, but it had to have connected because the guy let out a grunt just a moment before his eyes bugged from his head and he cried out in agony as he cupped his groin. The young woman scrambled backward, got to her feet and rushed for her overnight bag. She heard the approach of footfalls behind her so she turned and swung the bag. The thick leather caught the second attacker square in the side of the face, opening a large cut under his eye and sending him sprawling.

Naryshkin burst out of the room and raced down the posh carpet to the end of the hallway. What floor were they on again? Right, the twelfth floor. She had eleven stories to go and not a lot of time to get there. Kisa rocketed down the steps as fast her legs would carry her. She looked behind her a couple of times but didn't see anything, so she decided not to check again in favor of getting to the safety of the lobby. The echoes of her gasps and cries through the cavernous stairwell taunted Naryshkin as she continued down the steps. At one point she lost her footing and took about half a flight on her rear end, but she regained her footing and continued as if her life depended on it.

Mostly because it did.

A cry of half fear and half triumph escaped through her tightened lips as she finally burst through the door of the first floor and rushed down another large hall for the lobby. As she drew near to the desk she spotted three men standing at the entrance: all wore the uniforms of policeman, but Naryshkin knew better. If those were cops, they were the youngest in the history of the force.

Naryshkin came to a halt just as one of the officers looked in her direction. He said something to his comrades out of the corner of his mouth as he reached for his holstered pistol. The young woman looked for cover, but there wasn't any place she could hide. The Sevooborot would have closed off every exit, covered every alternate route from the hotel. She watched helplessly as the leader of the threesome unleathered his pistol and pointed it straight at her, closing one eye even as he settled his sights on her. She didn't see the muzzle-flash because she'd closed her eyes to whisper a final prayer, but she heard the shot. She thought that odd because she didn't feel the pain of a bullet going through her.

The young woman opened her eyes to see the look of shock in the man's eyes as blood poured from a nasty, jagged hole in his forehead. A moment later he toppled forward and landed face-first on the carpeted floor with a thud. His two companions whirled, and she now had an unobstructed view of Matt Cooper as he came through the entrance at a flat run, triggering an automatic weapon with the vengeful fury of a death angel.

No real cop, even in Russia, would draw his pistol on a defenseless young woman in a crowded lobby. It took Bolan only a moment to reach that decision as he raised his assault rifle, aimed and fired in one motion. Two rounds entered the back of the man's head and he toppled prone to the carpeted floor with a smack.

The dead man's companions clawed for hardware, but Bolan easily had the drop on them. He took the first of the two with a short burst of 5.56 mm slugs that cracked his breastbone and sent him airborne. The second gunner managed to get his pistol clear before Bolan cut him across the stomach with a volley. The weapon clattered from the man's fingers and his body executed an awkward spin, which ultimately landed him against a wire display of tourist media. The man toppled to floor and sent pamphlets and maps flying in all directions.

Bolan rushed to Naryshkin, who stood there, dumbfounded, and grabbed her hand, yanking her toward the front door. They were halfway across the lobby when the soldier heard shouts. He risked a backward glance to see a pair of security officers appear from a bend in the hallway. Their pistols were drawing a bead on the retreating fugitives, but neither man got off a shot. Two more players, dressed in civilian clothes, emerged from a stairwell door and into the hallway, interfering with the security's line of fire.

The Executioner and his companion made it through the revolving door and onto the flagstone entryway.

They reached the sedan and got the passenger door open before several gunners vaulted a nearby hedge and charged the couple with SMGs leveled in their direction. Bolan shoved Naryshkin into the front seat as he knelt behind the open door. He steadied the FNC in two hands and swept the new arrivals with a sustained burst. The muzzle flashed angrily as Bolan's corkscrew pattern blanketed the enemy with rounds at a cyclic rate of 700 per minute. The high-velocity slugs punched through arms, legs and torsos without prejudice, tearing flesh and leaving exit holes in some cases. Bolan had dispatched the enemy kill squad in under ten seconds, and the hotel staff and a few guests had chosen to give him a respectful amount of room to do it. Nobody interfered with Bolan when he rushed around his car, jumped into the driver's seat and rocketed away from the hotel with a squeal of rubber against pavement.

The Executioner smoothly shifted into higher gears and made several turns on streets he didn't even know until he was certain nobody had pursued them. He looked at Naryshkin. The young woman gripped the dash with both hands, her long fingernails biting into it, her face pale and her breath coming in gasps.

"You okay?" he asked with concern. "Have you been shot? Kisa!"

Her head whipped sideways to look him in the eye.

"Are you okay?" he repeated.

She nodded quickly but said nothing.

Bolan returned his attention to the road. She'd calm down over time and then he could find out what happened to her. In the meantime, there had to be a reasonable explanation. He couldn't believe the SMJ had found them so quickly. Bolan couldn't be sure where the leak was coming from, but he knew there was one. He'd deal with that soon enough, but he first needed to find a safe place to hole up. Staying at a high-profile hotel hadn't been the best idea; they needed something smaller, inconspicuous and out of the way.

Maybe a local place. Yeah, that was it. They might have better luck in a small guest house or a B and B, or whatever they called the Russian equivalent. Naryshkin would be able to help them with that. Bolan considered calling her father, taking that offer for help, but he decided it was too risky. He already figured they had probably gotten some unbidden help from the elder Naryshkin, and it was entirely possible they had the guy's phones tapped. The SMJ had proved itself pretty resourceful to this point.

Naryshkin finally found her voice, shaky and faint as it was. "Thank you for your help. It looks like once again I owe you my life."

"You don't owe me anything," Bolan said. "I almost got you killed."

She looked at him. "You're not responsible for my actions, Matt."

"No, but I'm responsible for mine. I shouldn't have let myself get so far away from you once I spotted that tail."

"How did you know they were coming for me?"

Bolan shrugged. "I didn't. But I figured if they tracked me from the hotel, then they'd know you were with me, too. It wasn't hard to put it together."

"And if they did not?"

"Then no loss." He grinned. "It looks like my hunch was right, though."

"Now what do we do?"

"Find someplace quiet to hide. And then I need to contact my people."

BOLAN FOUND JUST THE PLACE he was looking for, a little motel on Lenina Street in downtown Murmansk. It was out-of-the-way and nobody gave them a second glance thanks to Naryshkin's perfect Russian and an ID card that allowed her to sign under her mother's maiden name. Bolan decided to stay entirely out of the picture so that if any of the SMJ's people came inquiring the motel clerk would be able to say he had not seen any young women accompanied by an older man, or any older men at all for that matter. And especially not an American.

"You will call your people now?" the young woman inquired once they were in room. When Bolan nodded, she said, "I will leave. Go get us something to eat and let you have privacy."

"No," Bolan said with a curt shake of his head. "You'll stay right here. I'm going to the pay phone I saw across the street."

Bolan made her secure the door behind him and then went to the phone booth he'd spotted on his way in. He dropped the appropriate amount of change into the slot and dialed a very specific number, one of about ten he had memorized. All of them went to the same place through a series of cutouts that would route the call to Stony Man Farm.

"It's your nickel," Aaron Kurtzman answered.

Bolan shook his head and grinned. "Not really."

Kurtzman's tone went serious. "Striker, you okay?"

"I'm good."

"Wait one, Hal's here and he wants to talk to you ASAP."

Bolan didn't bother to protest, knowing it wouldn't have done much good. If Brognola wanted to talk to him, then he had a good reason for it.

When Brognola came on the line, he sounded excited. "Striker, we got a breakthrough."

"Sounds big."

"This is big, believe me. There's definitely a leak in the system. Its name is Carson Barbour. Ring any bells?"

Bolan searched his memory, then replied, "Isn't that the MI-6 guy who originally reached out to the Company people in Moscow?"

"One and the same."

"And he's our leak."

"No question," Brognola said. "I had some of our connections run him down. He was observed leaving St. Petersburg on a private jet I just learned a short time ago was headed for Murmansk. We tried to call you but no luck. I was having Aaron arrange a communications downlink to Jack when you called."

"He and I aren't together right now," Bolan said. "But what you've told me explains quite a bit. It's obvious Barbour's working with the SMJ, and recent events also point to the fact Barbour can call on a number of their local resources."

"I have no way to verify it, but your theory fits the facts."

"Maybe he's the one who brokered the deal between them and the JI, as well."

"Could be," Brognola said. "But I'd caution you that where it concerns Rostov and Cherenko, the mission remains compromised as long as Barbour's in the picture."

"I'll take care of that," Bolan said. He followed with a complete rundown of the events that morning.

"Huh," Brognola grunted. "That's all very interesting."

"Well, it only makes sense they won't try to take Rostov and Cherenko inside the station. Too many witnesses. We both know the SMJ's people aren't big on that."

"When do you think they'll make their move?"

"I'd guess at the docks along Kola Bay. I'll head that way later to run down the angles."

"What about your friend there?"

"She's okay for now," Bolan said. "I don't think they'll be able to find us so easily this time. Especially now that I know what to look for."

"What's your next step?"

"I think it's time to put an end to our little problem here before Rostov and Cherenko even arrive," Bolan replied. "And I'm going to start with Carson Barbour."

CHAPTER TEN

After ensuring Kisa Naryshkin was tucked safely away at the motel, Bolan drove to a highway overpass that provided a bird's-eye view of the Murmansk Airport, and studied it through a pair of binoculars he'd bought at a shop near the motel. Things weren't particularly busy, a few vehicles pulling up at the terminal, others proceeding directly to the long-term-parking garage. One plane had just taken off and another was taxiing into position.

None of that interested the Executioner, however. Bolan had his mind on a more obscure prospect, the possibility that one of Carson Barbour's lackeys might just be waiting for him at the airport. It was a slim possibility, Bolan knew, but he didn't have any other leads. Stony Man's contacts had lost the trail after Barbour's departure from St. Petersburg. Bolan had considered returning to the hotel and picking up a lead on the SMJ, but he figured it was too risky—someone might identify him. So this was his next best bet, and something in Bolan's gut told him it would pay off.

First Bolan checked the hangar where their plane was parked. All seemed quiet. Then he scanned the remaining private hangars, but he didn't see any movement. Bolan lowered the binoculars and looked at his watch. The hit against the hotel had gone down less than an hour ago. His encounter with the tail had been a half hour before that, and about two hours before that when they checked into the hotel. They had probably been under observation since touching down at Murmansk Airport. In every case, the SMJ might not have had a foolproof way of identifying him, but they would have an iron-clad description of his vehicle: gold Volkswagen Passat Sedan VR6 with diplomatic plates. Yeah, it wouldn't be hard to spot a car like that among the few luxury vehicles that crowded the snow-packed streets of the city. Barbour would have every available man on the lookout for their vehicle, which meant if he couldn't go to them, then the Executioner would find a way to draw enough attention the SMJ would come to him. After all, Bolan's experience had taught him, it was much easier to track down a large group of people and follow their trail to a single person than vice versa.

The other thing the Executioner had considered was Kisa's encounter. They had tried to take her alive in the hotel room, and yet the thugs dressed as cops were clearly intent on killing her. That didn't make any sense to Bolan, and he had to wonder if more than one group was involved in the chase, as it would seem the various players had different agendas when it came to Kisa. Really, this was the second time they'd made a play for her. Why? So they connected her with Rostov and Cherenko, fine. Bolan could see that. But wasn't the SMJ's *real* interest in shutting up Rostov and Cherenko for good? Their only interest in Kisa had to be they didn't know where the two young men were, and they figured Kisa did.

His mind settled on a plan, Bolan eased off the shoulder of the bridge and into traffic. The skies had become overcast, gray, totally obscuring the sun. The Executioner reached to his pocket and withdrew his cellular phone. He dialed Grimaldi's number aboard the plane. The pilot answered on the second ring.

"I'm about two minutes out, and I'm alone."

"What happened?" Grimaldi asked, the concern evident in his voice.

"Nothing to our package," Bolan replied in reference to Kisa Naryshkin. "She's safe."

Bolan could hear evident relief in his friend's voice. "What's up?"

"Hal found the leak, and friends of the source are close. I'm just giving them something to occupy their time."

"What's the forecast?"

Bolan smiled, knowing Grimaldi had caught the reference and would be ready for his arrival. "Warm… real warm."

Portland, Oregon

ONLY ABOUT HALF THE GUESTS had arrived and the party was already in full swing.

Ornate, cast-iron street lamps cast a yellowish glow on the heavy, red carpet that led from the curb of Southwest Broadway to the glass doors of the Portland Center for the Performing Arts. The night's gala started at 8:00 p.m. sharp, when the lights would dim within the

Dolores Winningstad Theatre and some of the biggest names in the business would gather together for the annual jazz festival. A multitude was in attendance for the event, more than two thousand in all, and ranged from mere jazz enthusiasts to some of the biggest names on the charts.

It was this fact that convinced Jurg Kovlun this first operation would be nothing less than spectacular, because among the attendees were some of the biggest names in the gang world of Portland. Kovlun's intelligence had it that top echelon of both 18th Street and the head of the Woodlawn Park Bloods, aka the Bloods, would be in attendance; the latter of those because his mother was a huge fan of jazz. The Bloods were also the largest black gang in Portland, or at least deemed so by members of a police task force as the most active, and they had money and resources to reach into places normally not accessible by gangs, which was the entire point of this operation. Kovlun had decided to recruit 18th Street members, of course, because he had much less disdain for Hispanics than the blacks, to make no mention of the fact they had grown in numbers to the point they nearly tripled in membership since 2002. In fact, the attempt by Portland police and the FBI to stem the tide of gang activity through their joint task force seemed to have had no effect on the city and surrounding suburbs. As it stood now, Kovlun had it on good authority that a large number of gang members lived in nicer houses and had a better annual income than two-thirds of the working, middle-class citizens.

This made recruitment easier, both for the gangs and Jurg Kovlun, who had now built a veritable army for this operation.

Kovlun stood atop a building down the block, on the opposite side of the theater, and studied the scene through binoculars. They would have to time this one perfectly; there wouldn't be a second chance. Their operation here would undoubtedly start a chain reaction, one that would unfold within a matter of hours, and their men would have to be ready. They were prepared. He'd overseen their training personally, and although the colonel might take a hard line with him on issues, he did recognize and appreciate Kovlun's efforts in this area. Of course Kovlun knew that one day, a day he hoped not in the far too distant future, he would no longer have to worry about what Satyev thought.

"Unit One, report," Kovlun said into his shortwave radio.

"All clear and awaiting target," Mikhail Pilkin replied.

Pilkin's team would be responsible for executing the hit when the time came. Their objective was the most critical, as this is what Kovlun planned to use as the spark that would ignite a flame of gangland war such as had never been seen before. A sudden, massive gang war would take the task force completely off guard; they would not have the resources with which to combat such a war, and federal laws prohibited the use of military units such as reserves or National Guard to repel the violence. Not to mention the bleeding-heart Americans would never condone the use of deadly force against the youth of this generation, no matter what the circumstances.

"Unit Two, report," Kovlun commanded.

"Unit two is secure," Aleksander Briansky stated.

Kovlun smiled with a self-congratulatory nod. They couldn't be more ready for the moment to arrive.

As he thought about this, the car they had been waiting for turned the corner and took up position in the line of vehicles. The gala had begun to look like one of the famous awards shows held in Hollywood every year. There were several Mercedes sedans and stretch limos and even a few BMW luxury cars making their way to the drop-off point, where the red carpet ran from Broadway to the theater. Some people would exit and the waiting crowds along the police barricades would clap and cheer at the sight of certain arrivals.

"All units," Kovlun said into his radio. "Target is in sight."

And indeed it was, for the vehicle belonging to Luther Medford—the leader supreme of the Bloods—was a deep purple stretch Hummer, covered from hood to tail in a variety of ornamental designs set in polished gold-leaf and chrome. Kovlun's people had done their best to get inside Medford's organization to figure out if the Hummer had any other special features, such as protection from bombs and bullets. It did. Of course it did: Kovlun wouldn't have expected anything less from a man in Medford's position. The guy conducted very dangerous business with very dangerous people. The lineage of inheritance in a gang empire wasn't quite the same as in other more disciplined organizations, like Spetsnaz. In gangs, Kovlun knew that a competitor had no qualms about breaking into the house of another gang member in the middle of the night and cutting that man's throat just to step up a rung on the ladder. It was a highly competitive system these days, controlled only by those who could afford the most security and were willing to spread the wealth around.

Luther Medford, however, had built a reputation as a family man, who took care of his mother and younger siblings, and who enjoyed a life of prosperity in one of the nicest, as well as most heavily guarded, homes in Woodlawn Park. Among Medford's closest associates were twin brothers who oversaw most of Medford's business interests in Portland, along with enforcing his every whim whenever and wherever they met resistance. But this night would prove to be another story entirely, because his brothers were on a plane to the Bahamas, each with a quarter-million dollars to not be anywhere near the place when it went down.

Without the pair to lead the Bloods in warfare, this would be a messy and disorganized lot once word got out of Luther Medford's demise.

One by one the vehicles deposited the guests at the curb, bringing Medford's Hummer one step closer to the mark. Kovlun checked his watch, cognizant of the time: 7:23 p.m. They were right on schedule. Kovlun raised the binoculars to his eyes once more and put the radio near his mouth when a limo in front of Medford's vehicle stopped at the curb. The crowd let out a cheer as a tall black woman in evening dress and a heavy fur wrap easily worth twice the limo from which she emerged waved to them, blew a few kisses and then proceeded along the red carpet. She didn't even bother to stop for photographs as the flashbulbs of press and a few aficionados flickered randomly in an impressive light display. Kovlun didn't recognize her, neither did he care.

"Unit One, hold off until you have confirmed the target with me. Unit Two, stay in place until I give the signal. Don't get ahead of us."

Pilkin and Briansky acknowledged in the affirmative. Kovlun kept the binoculars to his eyes, and he felt his heart rate increase a little as the Hummer stopped at the curb. A man with arms so massive he looked ill-fitted in his tuxedo leaped from the front and rushed to the door. He shoved aside the curb attendant who had stepped forward to open the door and then did the honors. A short, rotund woman exited. She wore her hair in a silvery bouffant-style hairdo and the long, black evening gown she wore hung on her portly form. A younger, dark-haired woman wearing a red dress that flowed to the ground and was slit up the side to reveal a long, shapely leg emerged next, and was finally followed by Medford.

Kovlun could hear a few people cheer, and Medford waved to them like he was a guest of honor. Kovlun ordered the units to stand by. Pilkin's sniper was in a very limited position and he would only get maybe two or three seconds to take the shot. Medford stepped to the right of the woman and extended his arm as an escort to his mother while the long-legged, cocoa-skinned beauty—Kovlun assumed she was Medford's longtime girlfriend—remained a step behind them.

Kovlun keyed the radio. "Unit One…execute!"

He never heard the shot of the rifle, not that he expected to, but Kovlun watched the action through the magnified view with utter satisfaction. Medford's head snapped sideways and his body jerked just a moment before an older, rusted vehicle painted bright yellow cut into the line of cars and jumped the curb before coming to a halt. The four men from Pilkin's ground team, dressed in blue jeans and plaid shirts, the colors and uniform of 18th Street guns, burst from the vehicle and delivered a spray of autofire in the direction of Medford's entourage that sent the entire area into a stomping panic.

The SMJ youth directed their fire with deadly accuracy, cutting Medford, his mother and girlfriend to ribbons with a merciless barrage of hot lead. They also neutralized the two bodyguards who had been a couple of steps behind the trio. Despite the fact they had been informed of the security measures of the Hummer, Pilkin had instructed his men to fire on the vehicle, as well, since this would make it look more convincing. It was highly unlikely low-level hit men for the 18th Street would know anything about that and they would go ahead and fire on the Hummer anyway to send a statement to the opposing gang. After nearly thirty seconds of endless chaos, the four men jumped into their vehicle and drove away in a cloud of smoke from where they left rubber on pavement.

Kovlun put the radio to his mouth once more. "Unit Two…execute."

Nearly eight blocks away, Briansky nodded to his men when he heard the order come over the radio for his unit to proceed.

A dozen or so of their recruits from the ranks of the 18th Street, believing that they were operating under orders from their true leaders, jumped from the panel van and dashed across the street to the club owned by Luther Medford. Briansky followed about fifteen seconds behind the last youth. Although he didn't really have to see what was happening inside to know the results, Briansky had to admit he was at least curious to know how their men would actually perform under the circumstances.

He watched with satisfaction as the two young black men in suits who guarded the door looked up in surprise at the approach of armed assailants from their greatest rivals. The 18th Street gangsters raised their assorted machine pistols and SMGs as supplied by the JI and triggered short bursts that cut the pair down with little fanfare. The few witnesses who had been standing outside and waiting for entry dashed from the scene, shouting in panic. His men ignored them, as ordered. They wanted witnesses, as many as possible to tell the police about the men they saw, how they were dressed, how they looked like Hispanics. Everything.

The gunners continued into the club and Briansky entered just in time to see four of the gangbangers open up on the crowded dance floor. Glass lights and bottles of alcohol along shelves shattered in a spray from two more muzzles directed at the bar. This was nothing less than blatant, wholesale slaughter of innocent people, not to mention how much it would cut into the business of Luther Medford and the Woodlawn Park Bloods. There was no question when word reached whoever was next to succeed Medford that an all-out war would be declared between the two most powerful gangs in Portland. In fact, this would probably result in calling in of brother units from neighboring cities, not to mention the kind of racial tensions this would generate.

The plan was perfect, of this Briansky had complete confidence.

As soon as they had delivered as much mayhem as they could expend from the two or three clips of ammunition per man, Briansky turned and left the club totally unobserved. In the panic he doubted anybody would even be able to identify him.

He climbed into the passenger seat of the paneled van and ordered the driver to leave. The men had been instructed to scatter, change clothes, then make their way back to the club that served as their front by whatever means they could. They didn't want anybody who was pouring out of the club to identify the van as the escape vehicle because they would need to use it at least once more before destroying it. It would get a paint job and new plates, of course, but that was hardly the point. Jurg Kovlun had strategized this mission down to the last detail and Briansky had learned to follow his orders to the letter. Kovlun was a tactical genius and expected unquestioning obedience.

Briansky keyed his radio and said, "Unit Two to leader. Operational objectives complete."

"Understood," Kovlun replied.

Briansky smiled. Let the Americans think on *that*, for this was only the beginning of their woes.

CHAPTER ELEVEN

Bolan and Grimaldi waited inside the hangar near the exit door. The Executioner had left his VW sedan parked just outside and now he watched through the small, plate-glass window of the door in anticipation the enemy would eventually show up for the party. Grimaldi leaned against the door of the hangar near Bolan, a Sig Sauer P-229 pistol in his fist.

"Okay, I'm ready for action," Grimaldi informed his friend. "What do you have in mind?"

"Well, we know Barbour's the leak now, but what I couldn't figure out was how they'd found us so easily in a city of this size. That's when I realized we've probably been under observation since we arrived in Murmansk."

Grimaldi nodded. "So you figure they got the hangar under surveillance."

Bolan shrugged. "Or my vehicle, which in either case would yield the same results. If anyone's watching, they surely know we're here by now. It's only a matter of time before they send someone calling."

"Except you'll be ready this time."

Bolan nodded, then returned to his vigil of watching through the small window. He didn't have to wait long. At first he thought it was more of a mirage from the solid wall of gray that stretched across the tarmac as far as the eye could see, but then he saw the approach of several shadowy forms through the thickening mist, human forms with the familiar outlines of automatic weapons in their hands.

"Show time," Bolan told Grimaldi, and the two men took their places.

The Executioner waited behind a fifty-five-gallon oil drum, Beretta 93-R and .44 Magnum Desert Eagle both up and ready, as Grimaldi grabbed his cover behind a couple of spare-parts crates toward the back. They had decided to make their stand as far from the aircraft as possible to protect its tender, aluminum skin from perforation by a stray bullet.

The door hinges squeaked as the hit team made its entry and Bolan crouched deeper into the shadows. He watched their movements from a small gap between the barrel and an interior hangar wall. The final count came in at four, two armed with pistols and the other pair with SMGs. The numbers ticked off in Bolan's head as the enemy crept straight toward him. When the moment came, they executed his plan perfectly.

Bolan stood and exposed himself, giving the closest pair time to see him and track with their weapons.

That's when Grimaldi made his move.

The pilot emerged from cover, leveled his pistol and snapped off two shots. The first caught the closest guy in the skull and split his head wide open. The man's SMG clattered to the floor, the noise of its path obscured by the acoustics of gunfire inside the cavernous hangar. Grimaldi's second shot also landed on target, this one taking the gunner in the sternum. A shocked expression crossed the man's face, almost as if he couldn't believe he'd been shot, then he dropped his weapon as both hands went to his chest. He looked down at the blood as it began to seep quickly around his fingers, fell to his knees and toppled onto his face.

Bolan had raised his own weapon during Grimaldi's opening salvo and took careful aim on one of the hardmen. He squeezed the trigger and the Beretta coughed, the single round plowing into the target's shoulder, the impact pushing him backward to the ground. Simultaneously, Bolan raised the Desert Eagle and took the last man with a single shot to the chest. The 300-grain .44 Magnum round cracked the breast bone and shattered ribs. The round continued through, puncturing a lung and blowing a chunk of the man's spine out his back, the impact slamming him against the hangar door. He slid to the floor, dead.

The Executioner hurried to the winged hardman and delivered a solid punch to the downed man's jaw, rendering him unconscious.

"Nice job, Sarge," Grimaldi said as he clapped Bolan on the back.

"Don't thank me," Bolan replied with a grin. "I couldn't have done it without that eagle-eyed shooting of yours."

"What's next?" the ace pilot asked.

"We get these bodies out of here," Bolan said. "We can't leave them lying around for an inspector to find."

"We can stow them under some old tarps I spotted out back."

By the time they had completed the grisly job of removing the bodies and cleaning house, their prisoner was starting to come around. Bolan and Grimaldi dragged the man aboard the plane and secured his hands and feet with plastic riot cuffs, then dressed his wound. When he finally came to, Bolan took a seat across from him.

"It's your lucky day today, friend," the big American said.

The man just looked at him with resolute hatred, and Bolan realized that this guy was a kid really. Yet there was no mistaking that bloodlust in his eyes. Bolan had seen that look too many times in an enemy, and he could never quite get past that kind of fanaticism. What made people believe in a cause so much they were willing to murder and terrorize innocent people for it had been a part of the psychology of terrorism Bolan never quite understood. Carnage for the pure sake of it, and no other good reason.

Bolan fixed the young militant with a frosty expression. "I'm going to ask questions, and you're going to give me answers," he said in Russian. "If you cooperate and don't make trouble, you walk away from this alive when my mission here is complete."

"And if I do not choose to answer your questions?"

"I shoot you between the eyes," Bolan said. "In which case, we're back to you joining the carcasses of your friends out back."

The young man studied Bolan a moment and then smiled. "You bluff. I have information you want. You won't kill me."

Bolan produced the Desert Eagle, making sure his prisoner got a good look at the hand cannon for sheer effect, then pressed the stainless-steel muzzle against the bridge of the youth's nose.

"I found you," Bolan replied icily. "I can find another just like you."

"I see your point."

The big American nodded and returned the Desert Eagle to its holster. "Now, let's call this a fresh start. I know Carson Barbour's the one who set your people onto me. I want to know where he is and what holes he's operating out of."

"I don't know this Barbour you speak of," the youth replied. "I answer only to Olaf Stroski."

"And who is he?"

"He is the leader of our team. And I can promise you that he will not stand for this. As soon as he hears what you have done to me and my friends, he will come for you. And in force."

Bolan shook his head. "Not if I find him first. So what about Stroski? Who does he work for?"

"I do not know. But I do know that he is well respected in the Sevooborot and he has many powerful friends. As I say, once he knows what you have done, he will find you and destroy you. I doubt you shall live through this night."

"Enough of the sales pitch," Bolan said. "You haven't scared me. What about Rostov and Cherenko? How did you find out they would be coming to Murmansk?"

"Again, I do not know of these people. My job was to get the girl."

"Why? What does she mean to you?"

"Nothing to me," the prisoner replied quickly. "To Master Stroski, however, she is an object of beauty. He enjoys such fineries."

So that was it. This man, Stroski, was only interested in Kisa as a sex object, nothing more, which meant he saw Bolan as just an obstacle in his way.

"I'd be more than happy to discuss this personally with Stroski."

"He's going to want to talk to you himself," the young man said, sneering.

"Great," Bolan replied. "Then you won't mind telling me where I can find him."

As soon as darkness settled on Murmansk, the Executioner took his position on the rooftop of a three-story commercial flat across from the Volga Club. The club was one of the most popular hangouts in Murmansk, and Olaf Stroski had financed both the purchase of the old building—a former play theater—and its subsequent conversion to a nightclub that catered to everyone from college students to the prominent of society. It was the perfect front for Stroski to recruit new members for the SMJ, which also made it an ideal target for a Bolan blitz.

Bolan was rigged for battle in his midnight blacksuit and combat boots with neoprene soles. Implements of war hung from the load-bearing suspenders: Ka-Bar fighting knife, a garrote, spare clips for the FNC and a pair of fragmentation grenades. Bolan had slung the assault rifle along his right shoulder so he could bring it into action quickly. The air temperature, which neared zero, had necessitated storage of the Beretta and Desert Eagle in canvas holsters to discourage sweating during rapid transition from outside to indoors. The attraction of moisture could result in misfires and jams, something Bolan knew he couldn't afford in the heat of a firefight.

Bolan put the night-vision device to his eyes and scanned the front of the club. A pair of men in heavy overcoats, gloves and fur hats stood guard at the front door, and the Executioner surmised several more probably had the interior covered, which meant a swift and silent penetration through the roof. Bolan scanned the front of the club once more, then returned the goggles to the hip satchel and withdrew a flat-black cylinder of metal about two inches in diameter and a foot long.

Bolan had never attempted to use the device at this temperature extreme, but he saw no reason for concern. The cylinder contained a collapsible three-tine grappler composed of titanium alloy and fifty meters of high-tensile core mountaineer's cord rated at 1000 pounds. The yank of a safety pin at its base and slap of the rubber grommet at the end detonated the propellant cap.

Bolan took aim and slapped the plunger. Special vents in the side of the tube permitted a slow, steady hiss of escaping gas barely above the sound of a whisper. The grappler arced gracefully over the street and connected with the roof on the other side. Bolan retracted the grappler gently, like a fisherman with a large catch on the line, until the tines bit into an object and locked the rope tight. He then tied off that end and stepped onto the parapet, shimmying across the taut line gloved hand over gloved hand, keeping one eye on the men below as he moved. Less than a half minute later he made it over the parapet of the club rooftop undetected.

Bolan dropped soundlessly onto the roof and advanced to an entrance to the upper floor. He made a quick inspection of the lock and started to withdraw a pick set, then thought better and tried the handle. It turned smoothly and the door popped open with a spring-loaded click.

Some security, Bolan thought.

The Executioner stepped inside, closed the door behind him and was engulfed in blackness. He crouched and waited, eyes closed and ears attuned to any noise or movement as his eyes adjusted to the dark. After several minutes, the Executioner rose and descended the steps, back to the wall and his Ka-Bar held at the ready. The fact the rooftop entrance had been unsecured surprised him, which meant either the enemy had been careless or there were other security measures in place.

He reached a small landing where he encountered a locked, secured door. He ran his fingers along the sides and top of the door frame until he encountered a small, rectangular object of metal about four inches wide and an inch or so thick. An alarm.

Bolan sheathed his combat knife and drew the Beretta before reaching for the handle. The door opened with the same click as the rooftop latch, and the Executioner figured he'd have less than a minute before Stroski's hardcases responded. He stepped into a dimly lit corridor. A midnight-blue shag carpet ran the length of the hall, whose walls were painted a dull maroon. Black-light fixtures lined either side of the half dozen closed doors, which were coated with thick, black enamel. For a moment Bolan thought maybe he'd stepped into the pad of a 1970s brothel for hippies. He crouched against the wall to wait.

Moments later a pair of heavies emerged through a stairwell door at the far end of the corridor. They were attired in black suits, white shirts and ties, which glowed brightly under the black lights. Bolan's blacksuit merged him with the wall and that bought him the advantage. The pair of security toughs didn't spot him until he stood and tracked them with the Beretta.

The men clawed for hardware but to no avail. The silenced Beretta coughed twice, the first round taking one of the men in the head and ripping away a better part of his lower jaw. The second round drove the remaining hardcase back and slammed him into the stairwell door, the impact driving him through it and depositing him on his back. His corpse acted as a wedge to keep the door open.

Bolan crossed the hallway to the door, stepped over the corpse and onto the stairwell landing. The sound of footfalls slapping the stairs reached his ears and Bolan crouched and whipped up the Beretta as two more suits rounded the corner of the midfloor landing below. The lead man looked up with total surprise a moment before Bolan squeezed the trigger and drilled a 9 mm Parabellum round between his eyes. Blood and brain matter exploded out the back and splattered his comrade as his body slammed into the wall. The second man tripped over his partner, and his hands were slippery with gore as he tried to gain hold of his weapon. Bolan showed no mercy, knowing if he let off the assault for even a moment, it might cost him the advantage of surprise. The Beretta chugged once more. The round caught the guy in the throat and ruptured the soft tissue of his esophagus. Both hands went to his throat and pink, frothy sputum bubbled from between his fingers a moment later. The guy dropped like a stone to the floor and lay still.

The Bolan effect had come to Club Volga.

CHAPTER TWELVE

Olaf Stroski hadn't expected this much trouble.

This entire operation should have been simpler, but Stroski had to admit that the Brit was right: this lone American was trouble. For his part, Stroski couldn't have cared less about any of that. The young woman interested him the most when he learned she was the daughter of a former GRU officer. Too bad. It would have been nice to add such a class act to his list of sexual conquests, but now she had become a mere liability.

The American's persistence surprised Stroski, to say the least. When he observed the job botched by his and the Brit's people at the hotel, and added the failure of the hit team at the airport to report in, Stroski realized this entire operation had become more trouble than it was worth. Now here was his head of security at his table in his club, leaning over to whisper in his ear of possible intruders through the roof entrance.

"It's probably the American," Carson Barbour told him.

"Take care of him," Stroski ordered his security chief.

The man had nodded and departed from the club through the same private entrance from which he'd entered. Stroski tried to enjoy the music and the girl who practically wriggled into his lap, but he couldn't push thoughts of the American from his mind.

Finally, Stroski left the table with Barbour in tow, and the two went to the control room where they had all the areas of the club under video and audio surveillance. There were cameras in the halls and cameras in each of the rooms on the second floor, part of which served as Stroski's quarters. He kept this place independent of the flat near the university—where allegedly he was enrolled as a full-time student—for those times when he stayed late at the club and didn't feel like traveling home in the early morning hours.

"Wow," Barbour said. "Quite impressive, all of this. How do you manage it on what I pay you?"

Stroski laughed. "You still don't get it, do you? What you pay me is very little in comparison to what I've made as chief recruiter for the Sevooborot."

He could tell the Brit forced a smile then. "So…you are not simply a paid informant as you originally led me to believe."

"I am a lot of things to a lot of people," Stroski said with smug confidence. "If others make certain assumptions about me, it is not up to me to dissuade them from such prejudice. As you well know, this can be quite an advantage to a businessman like me."

"You definitely caught me with my pants down."

"Never admit your weaknesses, Barbour. That itself is a sign of weakness."

Barbour kept his silence.

"What's the story?" Stroski asked the guard monitoring the cameras.

"The American's inside," the man replied. "He's taken out several of our people already."

"What?" Stroski could hardly believe his ears. "Where is he now?"

"I'm not sure," the man replied. "I believe he may be on the stairwell."

"You're not sure?" Stroski could feel his face flush. "What the hell do I pay you people for? Find him. Find him!"

"We don't have cameras in the stairwells, sir."

"Then send everybody we have to that area. Saturate the place, if you have to, but do *not* let that American into the main club."

"If he gets to ground level, it'll be bloody near impossible to stop him," Barbour pointed out.

Stroski pinned him with a furious glance, then whirled and left the control center. How could it have come to this? Where had he gone wrong? He certainly wouldn't have expected the American to come here. That was like a lamb walking into a den of wolves. Stroski's security had to easily number twenty guns, maybe more, not to mention the thirty or so reserve enlistees he could call in as reinforcement. That was the advantage to being a recruiter for an organization like the Sevooborot.

Well, the American might have been proficient but he couldn't remain concealed forever. They would find him sooner or later, and then they would destroy him.

After all, he wasn't invincible.

BOLAN STEPPED THROUGH the first-floor stairwell door to face four more security guards. He had obviously stepped into a hornet's nest. There was no way Club Volga would require this kind of security under normal circumstances. There was obviously more going on here than he'd originally been led to believe. Bolan hadn't intended to go up against the SMJ in force, particularly not on its own turf, but he maintained the best way to plug the leak that was Carson Barbour was still to hammer away at the group until its leader gave up. If nothing else, he'd be able to cripple its operations, a maneuver that might just give the JI reason to take pause and reconsider this alleged alliance.

The SMJ youths didn't seem overly surprised to see Bolan, although it was obvious his appearance through the stairwell door wasn't quite what they'd expected. The men fanned out—as best they could in the narrow hall—and reached for their slung submachine guns. Bolan brought his own weapon into a play a heartbeat sooner. He leveled the muzzle and triggered the first of two 3-round bursts.

Target one caught all three rounds in the face right as he tried to take to a knee and fire on Bolan. His head exploded in a red-gray mist. The second gunner took slugs in pelvis, stomach and chest, dancing under the impacts until he collapsed to the floor, dead. The third gunman managed to trigger two rounds but both ended up in the spine of his surviving comrade who had stepped into his line of fire. The delay caused by the incident cost the youth his life. Bolan dispatched him with a triburst that ripped through his belly.

The Executioner advanced down the hallway and could hear the thumping beat of music coming from beyond a door. The regular customers of Club Volga were innocents, people who knew nothing of the owner of the establishment or his reputation as top recruiter for the SMJ. Bolan didn't consider it acceptable to put them at risk; he'd have to try a different tactic.

Bolan whipped open the door. The club's seating was to his left and the bar occupied a space on a lighted platform across from him. Bolan looked to his right and spotted what he was looking for: the DJ booth. He moved to the door, gained entry with a single kick six inches below the handle and took the steps in two strides, leveling the FNC at the two surprised men charged with sound equipment.

"Kill the music and tell everyone the club's closed now," Bolan demanded, speaking Russian.

"On whose authority?" the man asked, looking Bolan up and down with skepticism.

The Executioner caught a movement in his peripheral vision and unleathered the Beretta. A security man had burst through the door and was advancing up the steps when Bolan shot him through the face. The man's body toppled backward and bounced down the steps.

Bolan returned his gaze to the DJ and with a cold smile replied, "Mine."

The man now apparently realized that wasn't a pop-gun in Bolan's hands and complied. A groan from the crowd reverberated up the steps into the otherwise soundproof booth. The other DJ started to reach for a switch and Bolan tracked on him with the FNC.

"Don't," Bolan said.

"It's the lights," the man replied.

Bolan shook his head slowly and the man moved his hand away, careful to keep both of them in sight. Neither had any problem believing the Executioner would cut them down in a moment if they made any sudden moves.

Bolan's eyes flicked through the wide, one-way glass once more and watched as people flocked toward the exit. It was early yet, so there weren't many club-goers. It wouldn't take long to clear the place. He indicated for the two men to get down on the floor, and once they obeyed he cinched their arms behind them with plastic riot cuffs he kept in a pouch on his web belt. Bolan then left the sound booth and made a beeline across the dance floor to the bar, which had also been evacuated. He unclipped a grenade from his web belt, primed the bomb and tossed it underhanded, then sprinted for the exit. He managed to make himself a part of the last wave of people as they pushed into the now crowded sidewalk just as the grenade blew.

Bolan moved to one side as people scattered to get away from the building. What few security people had been stationed at the front door could hardly maintain order among the chaos of some seventy frightened patrons. He watched with grim satisfaction as people continued to rush along the sidewalk or across the street to get as far away from the building as possible. Satisfied with the results, Bolan moved quickly down the sidewalk to his rental car, which he'd parked a block from the front door. He climbed behind the wheel and then brought the binoculars to his eyes so he could keep an eye on the activity out front. This blitz-play would shake things loose, of this much he was certain.

Now all he had to do was watch. And wait.

IT TOOK HIS QUARRY SURPRISINGLY longer to evacuate Club Volga than Bolan anticipated, but there was no mistaking the four large men who accompanied two smaller men from the club and rushed them into a waiting luxury sedan. One was tall, and through the binoculars Bolan could make out the profile: he recognized Carson Barbour from the description he'd obtained from Stony Man. The younger, dark-haired man didn't strike any chords in Bolan's memory, but he felt confident he was looking at none other than Olaf Stroski.

The vehicle lights came on a moment later and the sedan swung around in the street and headed straight toward him. Bolan slouched and waited until it sped past, then started his own car and laid in a pursuit course. When he reached the intersection where the sedan had turned, he stopped, flipped on his lights and allowed three cars to pass before making his own turn. Bolan looked at the dash clock. Nearly three hours remained before Rostov and Cherenko's train was scheduled to arrive. Assuming they were on time, Bolan was keeping to his schedule. As soon as he finished here, he'd have to call Grimaldi to find out how successful the pilot was in securing a helicopter. Such a task might prove difficult, but Bolan had total confidence Grimaldi could get it done. After all, the Diplomatic Security Service had significant resources from which to draw upon, and Bolan knew they could acquire those resources with one phone call.

The soldier kept a few cars between them, staying just far enough back not to appear as a threat. He wasn't worried about being spotted as much as what would happen if they made him as a tail. The driver might do something, try to bolt, and Bolan couldn't take that kind of risk in this traffic. Fortunately the pace had slowed to a crawl and the logjam along this main road allowed him to remain inconspicuous among the stream of cars and trucks.

It took almost fifteen minutes to get through the slow-moving line of vehicles, but eventually the traffic started to break apart and pretty soon they were leaving the city and heading toward the only major highway in and out of Murmansk. That's when Bolan realized his mistake. An SUV they had passed some minutes earlier but Bolan hadn't detected behind him met up with Stroski and Barbour at an intersection just before the ramp onto the highway. Bolan scanned the windshield and he could make out frantic, choppy movement inside. That brief moment of recognition saved Bolan's life. He scooped the satchel and FNC from the seat, opened the passenger side door and scrambled from the VW just as four men holding automatic rifles emerged from the SUV. A moment later, the air around him came alive with the buzz of metal fragments and whine of high-velocity rounds as the quartet opened up simultaneously on his position. The VW's body frame and windows shook under the violent assault. Bolan waited patiently, confident in the protection afforded by his car. His would-be assassins hadn't counted on the fact that because the VW was a diplomatic vehicle it sported a reinforced body and frame, and bulletproof glass.

Bolan waited for a lull in the firing, then answered with a volley of his own as he burst from cover, stock to shoulder, and sighted through the fixed sights of the FNC. His first short burst stitched one man from crotch to sternum. Another was changing out mags when the soldier took him with a burst to the head and splattered the top of the SUV with a gory wash of blood and brain matter.

Squealing tires drew his attention, and he turned in time to see the sedan lurch from the scene under smoking tires. Bolan knew if he lost track of Stroski and Barbour it would be almost impossible to pick up the trail again before Rostov and Cherenko arrived. He needed to change strategies and he needed to do it now. Bolan sighted on the driver's compartment of the sedan and squeezed off a sustained burst as he swept the windshield at a rate of 700 rounds per minute. He then punched through the grille with a second burst in an attempt to disable the vehicle before he jumped into the VW and put the vehicle in gear. Bolan tromped the accelerator in pursuit of the luxury sedan. A few more rounds slapped the side of the sedan with a dull rap before the VW moved out of range.

Bolan followed his quarry onto the highway and increased speed. A few marks along the windshield reduced visibility to a degree, but not so bad that Bolan couldn't operate the vehicle. The driver's-side windows, however, were about as transparent as stained glass. That made it impossible for Bolan to see the vehicle with its lights blacked out that pulled up next to him. Only the glint of a streetlight on the hood told the Executioner that more trouble had arrived.

He jerked reflexively when something struck the bulletproof glass and a moment later a small, hook-shaped object penetrated the window. The object seemed to expand and then the entire driver's-side window suddenly came away from the frame. A cold wind howled through the interior, and Bolan saw a dark-skinned man in a vehicle running parallel with the VW grin as he dropped the thin wire. In that moment, Bolan realized this new player had used some kind of grappler to penetrate the bulletproof glass and yank the entire unit from the window.

The man now raised a pistol and extended his arm out the window. Bolan swung the wheel to the left and slammed the vehicle into the SUV, causing the driver to veer onto the shoulder and scrape the driver's side against the concrete median dividing the four-lane highway. Bolan got back on track and considered these new arrivals. They didn't operate at all like the SMJ; Bolan knew professionals when he saw them, and these guys were hardcore through and through. Obviously they had realized that Bolan's vehicle was reinforced and recognized the need to improvise their engagement. That spoke volumes to Bolan, and the warrior had little doubt he'd come into his first contact of this mission with the Jemaah al-Islamiyah.

Bolan tried to maintain a lead on the SUV, but the vehicle had a more powerful engine and the pursuers quickly gained. He gritted his teeth as he tried to keep an eye on his quarry while keeping the SUV in check. As they rolled over a bridge that spanned the tributary that fed into the Barents Sea, Bolan saw the flash of headlights from two more vehicles swing onto his tail.

The Executioner hadn't counted on this kind of response—he'd obviously done a better job of shaking them up than originally anticipated.

The abrupt hammering into the tail of his sedan followed by a jerking slam from the driver's side created a fishtail from which even Bolan could not recover. The back end spun around and a black-ice patch did the rest. He heard a screech and the tearing of metal, and a moment later Bolan's stomach rolled as his sedan crashed through the thin guard-rail into open air and the nose tipped with the weight of the engine.

Bolan braced for impact as the vehicle crashed into the icy waters of the tributary.

CHAPTER THIRTEEN

Kisa Naryshkin could not believe her good fortune.

Not only did the train arrive at the station right on time, it took her only two minutes to find Leo and Sergei. She rushed into her boyfriend's arms and squeezed his neck so tightly that he wheezed. She didn't want to let go, but she knew she would have to put on a brave front and stifle any tears. She would have to be strong for Leo, for both of them really; she owed Cooper her life, as she did the lives of her mother and father, and he'd done so much for her. Now she would do something for him and see that Leo and Sergei were safely escorted back to the hotel.

"Oh, Leo!" she cried. "I have missed you so much."

"I have missed you," he said hoarsely.

She stepped back and studied him. He didn't look well. His haggard face and rumpled hair might only have been signs of tiredness, but he also stood slump-shouldered, and she could see he tried to hide the cough. She heard the deep, rumbling, seallike bark deep in his chest and rattled breathing, and she'd felt the heat of his flushed face against her own cheek. Sergei Cherenko had been right; her beloved Leo didn't look well.

"We need to get you to a doctor," she said.

"Later," he replied with a weak smile. "For now, we need to get away from here. As far and as fast as we can. There isn't any more time. We have to get out of this blasted place before the Sevooborot catch up to me.

"You no longer have to worry about that," Naryshkin said.

He furrowed his brow and looked at her sternly. "What are you talking about? I have killed one of them, and I know they murdered one of the American agents sent to meet us."

"They came after Papa and Mama, too," she said.

"What?" His face reddened with fury now, a more dangerous hue than the one left by his fever. "I will kill those bastards!"

"Shush!" Cherenko interjected, looking around wildly. The crowd seemed to be fading quickly and nobody appeared to take notice of them, but they figured they had only made it this far by being overly cautious. "Keep your voice down. You might attract unwanted attention."

"But don't you see?" Naryshkin said, clapping her hands. "That's what I'm trying to tell you both. You no longer have to worry. The American agent who saved me and brought me here to help find you. He is a good and strong man. And a brave one. He's here to help you."

"No...no." Rostov shook his head emphatically. "We can't put anybody else at risk."

"But you're the—"

"No more buts, Kisa!" Rostov snapped.

"Be quiet," Cherenko whispered again.

Rostov fired a dirty look at his friend, then put his arm around Naryshkin and steered her toward the exit. He shoved his hand in his pocket and withdrew a Makarov pistol. She knew it because her father had carried one very similar to it during his tenure with the GRU. He'd never offered any information on the gun or where he got it—she had noted how old it looked—so she never asked. Instead she inhaled sharply and looked at his features, which seemed cold and hard under the lights of the station. She shivered, an involuntary shudder really, but her Leo didn't seem to notice. There was a firm set to his mouth and his eyes looked beady as they shifted from one side to the other, alert for any sign of trouble. She couldn't really say she blamed him. It wasn't easy to leave, to swallow his pride and admit that he was afraid while the dogs of Hell hounded their every step. She wished there was something she might say to make Leo and Sergei change their minds about Cooper.

Now she felt bad having left Cooper in bed, not waking him to tell him where she had gone and what she planned. She'd actually expected to return before he awoke but now it didn't look like that would happen. Well, at least he knew what their plan was, so when he did awake he would know where to start looking for them.

Rostov said quietly over his shoulder to Cherenko, "Is everything in place?"

Cherenko nodded. "The boat will be waiting for us at Pier Nineteen in Kola, and will ferry us to Polyarnyy. From there we will board a freighter that leaves through Kola Bay and out to the Barents Sea. That should put us in Havesten by late tomorrow morning."

"And freedom, at last," Rostov replied.

"I cannot go with you," Naryshkin said.

"What?"

"I cannot go with you," she repeated. She stopped and shrugged her arm from Rostov's grip, and then turned to face the two young men. She put her hands on her hips. "This is crazy, Leo, and I want it to stop. Right now."

Rostov's jaw fell and his mouth was agape as he looked into her eyes. The young woman stood there and maintained her composure. In fact, she would stand there as long as it took to talk some sense into him. This really had become ridiculous, even bordering on insanity. Whatever possessed them to follow this crazy idea she would never know, but she knew the risks involved and there was no question in her mind they were safer with Cooper than out on their own.

"What do you mean, you aren't going with us?" Rostov said. "I'm telling you to come along, no, I'm ordering you to come with me. You're obviously not safe here."

Naryshkin maintained a posture of defiance and folded her arms. "No less safe than you. And I happen to trust Matt Cooper. I believe in him and I believe in you. And now I'm asking you to believe in *me*. To trust me just once, and believe that I know what I'm talking about."

"We don't have time for foolish games," Rostov replied with a dismissive wave.

"Oh, this is no game. Do you know what Cooper has been through? What *I've* been through? Eh? Do you, Leo? We've crossed half the country looking for you two. I've risked everything, my reputation as well as my life, to make no mention of considerable resources of my father to almost greater than he might bear, because I happen to think what you're doing is right. But if you do this you are betraying everything, *everything* that we've fought for and risked."

"I'm sorry if this disappoints you," Rostov replied, the bitterness evident in his tone. "Or if I haven't somehow lived up to some expectation you might have of me, Kisa. But the fact remains, this is my life." He gestured at Cherenko, adding, "And it's Sergei's life, too, and we happen to think we're right about this. And I'd be willing to bet that we know just a little bit more than this American of whom you seem recently enamored."

Naryshkin's disposition turned haughty. "I'm not smitten with him, if that's what you're suggesting. But I do believe he knows the best way to handle your defection."

Rostov shook his head. "We already tried it the Americans' way. You saw how it ended. I love you, but I do not have time for this. You either come with us or you don't, but I won't stand here arguing about it anymore. We're going to miss the boat."

Rostov turned on his heel and marched from the station, which was now fairly deserted. Cherenko studied her a moment, looked at his friend's retreating back, then looked at Naryshkin again before telling her, "He needs you, Kisa. I do not know how else to tell you this. He's sick, and I don't know how much longer I can care for him and myself, and manage to keep us alive. I'm tired."

The young woman looked at him for a long moment, then nodded. "I will go with you, then. At least I can keep an eye on the both of you."

With that, the two hurried to catch up to Rostov. But somewhere in the back of her mind, Naryshkin knew they hadn't seen the last of Matt Cooper. He would find them, to be sure, and certainly he would be able to convince Leo that he was able to help them. All she could do now was to go along with the men and hope that Cooper would wake soon and find the message she'd left.

Come soon, Cooper, she thought. Come soon.

BLACKNESS LIKE SWIRLING PATTERNS of ink turned navy-blue, then gray and then took shape through a blur of muted yellows and creams, until finally Mack Bolan opened his eyes—even that effort resulted in pain.

Bolan's first realization beyond that was the hard-hitting reality that every muscle in his body ached, which let him know he was still alive. The barrage of colors before his eyes began to disappear, although a gray haze remained around their periphery, and after taking stock of his physical being the Executioner found enough strength to sit up. He looked around and took in the surroundings: it was the hotel room.

But how the hell had he gotten here?

The Executioner searched his memory, but couldn't recall anything after the car went over the tributary. Then he looked down and noticed he was out of his blacksuit, which he finally found hanging on the curtain rod of the shower when he managed to get out of bed, and had been stripped to his skivvies. He noticed the large welts on the upper parts of both thighs, which he could only assume had come from the steering wheel when the vehicle impacted the water of the tributary. Bolan still couldn't remember much, although there were points that came flooding back in a rush. He knew as time went on that he'd probably remember more, but the cold water and the subsequent shock to his system had obviously left him with short-term memory loss. Bolan knew enough to realize it would all come back to him soon, so for the time being he wouldn't worry about it.

The blacksuit was still damp so Bolan opted for some warmer clothing—loose-fitting jeans, black sneakers and a heavy wool shirt. After a quick search he located the Beretta and Desert Eagle under the bed, both water-logged and already beginning to show surface rust. The extreme temperature changes coupled with the moisture played havoc on the alloy of gun metal. Bolan immediately stripped the Beretta, a mean task even for the warrior as his fingers still ached; probably from his exposure to the cold water. As he worked on the gun, it started coming back to him.

Bolan remembered the vehicle crashing through the guard rail and slamming into the surface ice of the tributary. He then recalled his thighs slammed into the steering wheel, and he marveled at the fact he hadn't broken both femurs and bled to death in an ice-water tomb. Bolan then remembered that the shock had nearly rendered him unconscious. The impact through the ice and into the water slowed the sinking enough that the cold water brought Bolan back to consciousness. He also remembered raising the steering wheel and using his combat knife to cut the seat belt before he exited the sedan through the open window.

Bolan wondered what might have happened if that window hadn't been yanked from the car by the JI terrorists. He considered the sheer irony of the enemy's actions, and decided that Fate smiled on him this time. They had attempted to murder him, but instead the one action intended to lead him to his death may well have spared him from it. Once he'd gotten clear and carefully dragged himself onto the ice and crawled some distance, Bolan figured he had to have made his way back to the hotel, although he didn't remember any of what had transpired after climbing from those icy waters. Then he remembered. Kisa Naryshkin!

Bolan stopped in midspray of nitro solvents and oil on the moving parts of the Beretta and looked around. Naryshkin wasn't here—hadn't been here since he awoke. Now the entirety of his mission came flooding back and he rose and began to search the room diligently. Eventually he spotted the note left on the bureau by the TV. In neat handwriting, she had written, "Matt, you arrived here half-past 9:00 or so, weak and chilled. Clothes hanging in washroom. Went to meet boys at train. Be back soon. Take care. All love—K."

The Executioner cursed himself. He was supposed to have protected her, and now he'd only put her in more danger. Bolan found his watch on the table and looked at it. It was reaching midnight. She should have returned hours ago. And with their car in the drink Bolan could only surmise she'd gone to the train station in a cab. Well, at least that wouldn't draw a lot of attention. But unless the train had arrived very late there was no explanation for why she hadn't returned by now. This didn't make a bit of sense.

Bolan dialed Grimaldi's number and the pilot answered on the first ring.

"It's me."

"Holy cripes! You okay, Sarge? I've been waiting hours for your call. Where are you?"

"Our hotel," Bolan replied. "Ran into some complications, and my tagalong's missing. She went to the train station without me and she's not back yet. Did you get the chopper?"

"Yeah," Grimaldi said. "At our disposal for the next twenty-four hours."

"Where is it?"

"Right here at the airport."

"Get her primed, Jack," Bolan said. "We have work to do."

ANATOLY SATYEV LISTENED with pleasure as Kovlun delivered his report.

The operation had been completed with total success and not a single casualty on their side. According to Kovlun, local law enforcement was still reeling from the sudden outbreak in gang violence with not a clue yet as to how to respond. This could only be good news for them and their future plans against the Americans. With any luck, they would have a complete fallout within the next twenty-four to thirty-six hours, at which point they would execute the final phase of their plan before packing up their operations and moving on to their next target.

After Satyev concluded his call, he proceeded downstairs to the operations center beneath his home in the private community nestled among the Sierra Vistas. The weather had become bitterly cold, something he didn't like much, and before long he knew he would have to move to the new location. For now, though, he would wait to see how things unfolded in Portland. The operations center was a feat of modern technology. A rack of cooled servers took up only a very small space at one end of the room, walled behind shatterproof glass and cooled by convection along special water pipes in the wall. A secondary unit then sucked the moisture from the convection cooling and provided the perfect environment for the sensitive electronics.

With this system attached to several personal computers in the main work area, along with a number of sixty-inch plasma monitors along one wall, Satyev was able to perform a vast number of communication and planning tasks. Not only did this complex electronics center allow him to speak with the various cells he had scattered in population centers throughout the country, Satyev could also conduct secure transmissions to other interests in and out of the nation. Buried deep among those transmissions were special communiqués to the variety of parties with whom he conducted regular business. They included arms dealers, gun runners, smugglers and assassination teams. There were former military commanders of the Soviet Bloc who now hid in locations ranging from Rio de Janeiro to London to even some places deep in Southeast Asia. Satyev had provided aid and comfort to many of those individuals and he liked to keep tabs on them, especially if he ever needed to call in a favor. It was this kind of network that allowed Satyev to maintain a watch on most parts of the world, and afforded him the resources that made him not only rich as a businessman but also as an information broker.

The information he read in this latest transmission had him seething. Why had it become so difficult to eliminate one American? His partners in the Jemaah al-

Islamiyah weren't happy with the latest situation and had finally decided to get their own people involved with putting this problem to bed. Apparently they hadn't been any more successful than the SMJ's goons. Not really all that surprising, although it irritated Satyev to no end. Now it was being left in his hands and the JI wanted results. They could go to hell. Colonel Anatoly Satyev didn't take orders from anyone, especially not Arab terrorists who provided substandard weapons for a job that required too many resources and too much complex planning for their simple minds to handle.

Nonetheless, Satyev had to admit this American who they had now identified by the name Matt Cooper—a name Satyev knew was all too likely to be an alias—had become a meddlesome pest. It would be best to deal swiftly with him now. Whatever had possessed Jurg to put this in the hands of an incompetent British agent he might never understand; he could be such a simpleton in matters such as these. This particular situation required the services of someone with a bit more stealth, a person who could operate with impunity and yet draw even the most efficient operatives into a trap like a black widow spider just awaiting her next meal.

Since their operation was under way, Rostov and Cherenko had become secondary considerations—as had the girl and her parents. Satyev could no longer worry about that. Their recent activities in Portland would undoubtedly attract the attention of a half dozen agencies, including whoever the American worked for. That meant they'd have to bring him back to this country in a hurry and eliminate him here. It would be eas-

ier on his own territory where the American would undoubtedly feel much more secure.

"Yes, I'm sure that's it," Satyev muttered to no one
as he picked up the phone. "Come, American…like a
lamb to the slaughter."

CHAPTER FOURTEEN

Captain Robin Tilburg squeezed the back of his neck and winced in pain.

His massage therapist had repeatedly told him he held most of his stress there, but Tilburg had never been cognizant of it until his wife recently talked him into going to such a person, so he didn't really know where else to hold it. He could have used a massage right there, but he knew that wasn't going to happen any time soon. As head of the Portland Joint Gang Task Force, it was Tilburg's responsibility to pull out the stops, call in the cavalry and get to work on this latest fiasco.

Fiasco. That was a damned understatement. This was a downright travesty and Tilburg didn't even know where to start. First, the leader of the Bloods and the two women closest to him get wasted right in front of God and country, and then not even a few minutes later more 18th Street bangers slide into Medford's single, largest source of legitimate income and shoot up the place, along with a whole bunch of people in it, like someone had posted a television commercial that gangland style killings were going to be free this week.

Yeah, this is all he needed.

This would be a great addition to all his stress, which included a wife who wasn't sleeping with him right now and a daughter away at college who couldn't seem to abstain from sleeping with every guy she encountered, so he'd been told. Not to mention his high-school-age boy who dressed in Goth fashion, wore a lip ring and went out on his sixteenth birthday to one of the local tattoo parlors on the south side—a place Tilburg had expressly forbidden him to go, *ever,* for any reason—and got the symbol of a punk rock band emblazoned across his back. When Tilburg saw it, he'd gone nearly postal on the kid and threatened to remove the thing via the new rotary sander he'd received that previous Christmas. Hence, his wife no longer wanted to sleep with him until he took it back.

Tilburg refused.

So now he sat in his office and looked over the paperwork already stacked three inches thick that included seventeen homicides related to this latest outbreak of violence, and somewhere on the order of about seventy thousand dollars in property damage.

"Seventy grand?" he asked Squad Sergeant Rick Niesewand.

Niesewand, a cop with more than ten years of experience and a former member of the Bloods, nodded as he pulled a toothpick from his mouth. "And counting, Captain. Those are just the estimates from the club. We're going to have to wait for an appraisal on that Hummer Medford arrived in."

Tilburg turned his attention to his second in command, Lieutenant Roger Brothers. Brothers was a no-nonsense man who'd come up through the academy with Tilburg and didn't put up with any bull. Brothers knew the city and its suburbs intimately, as well as all the gangs and their members. He'd been decorated time and again for averting more gangland wars than any cop in Portland history, perhaps even that of the country, and he was chief liaison to the federal task force.

"Roger, what's your take on this? Are we looking at a war?"

"It's possible, Rob," Brothers said. "It's hard to put your finger on something like this. But you can be sure whatever the Bloods decide to do, it won't take them long. They'll rally for a meeting soon enough, and you can be sure if they decide to retaliate, which I can just about guarantee they will, we're going to have a disaster on our hands."

Tilburg grabbed his neck again and shook his head. "I don't get it. There's been a truce between these gangs going on what…three years?"

Brothers nodded. "At least."

"So why all of a sudden does the 18th Street go loco on them? There has to be more to this than what we're seeing."

"Maybe it's a message," one of the other sergeants selected.

"Then that's a hell of a message," Niesewand countered. "I mean, look, we don't have the first clue what might have caused this, and it seems too important for us to start guessing."

"What do you suggest, Sarge?" Tilburg asked.

"I suggest we start with the facts, sir, and see where it takes us. First, we know the only point here wasn't to kill Luther Medford, otherwise there wouldn't have been any need for hitting the club. We also know the particular way in which they did these hits seems a little out of school for them."

"How so?"

"Well, for one thing," Brothers cut in, "they used some pretty hefty hardware. From what the few witnesses we found were able to describe, these weren't modified Tech-9s in the hands of our shooters. They were using Uzi machine pistols and submachine guns. Foreign submachine guns, no less."

Tilburg nodded. "Which they could only have obtained from a major arms supplier."

"And that takes a lot of cash," Niesewand said. "They wouldn't have spent that kind of money lightly, even if they had it."

"You think somebody else may be involved?" Tilburg asked.

Brothers shrugged and looked past Tilburg with an almost absent expression. "Maybe…possibly. Hell, I don't know, Rob! None of this is going to be easy to piece together." He waved at the stack of folders. "We got nearly twenty dead people, and I don't know to Christ how many more at the hospital in various conditions, including some critical who may not make it through the night. Which will only up the homicide number."

"So where do we go, then?" Tilburg said, rising and pacing behind his desk. "I'm willing to take any suggestions."

"For the moment," Niesewand said, "I think we ought to prepare for the worst, Cap. If the Bloods decide to retaliate, Lieu's right. They'll do it quick and hard. We need to get somebody on the inside now and try to get them to hold off until we've had a chance to look at this."

"And you think they'll go for it?"

"I can't possibly know until we try."

"I'm not sure that's a good idea," Brothers said.

Tilburg looked at his long-time friend. "Why not?"

"Because, Rob, this is serious shit. There were cops crawling through that place, and we couldn't do a damn thing to save Luther Medford or his kin. Not to mention that by the time we got to that club the doers were all long gone. And let's not forget that we've been watching the build-up of 18th Street in their crews for years and we did very little to stop it."

"How are we going to stop recruitment other than putting the recruiters in lockup?" Tilburg protested. "And even then they got ten more to pop up in their place."

"That's not the Bloods' problem as far as they're concerned," he said. "That's for Whitey to figure out and they don't care about our problems."

Tilburg looked to Niesewand for support, but all he got was a shrug with a "what can I say" expression that said Brothers spoke the unadulterated truth. Tilburg knew that already but he didn't want to hear it, really. Again, though, that wasn't the problem of his men to work out, it was his, and basically they didn't give a damn about his problems. His job was to lead by example and provide the best solutions possible to stem the tide of gang violence and their organized crime activities, since everyone in the room knew they sure as hell couldn't put an end to it.

"So we might be faced with a full-blown war," Tilburg said. He sighed heavily and added, "All right,

Niesewand, let's see if you can get a meet with whoever's up for Medford's spot. And you, Roger, I want you to take as many from the squad as possible and distribute them at every major 18th Street outlet you can. Maybe we can stop any other problems before they get started that way."

Tilburg didn't really believe that, but he could hope it showed some good faith on their part. Still, something told him that this was only the beginning of what would turn out to be a very long morning. Already the press was outside and hounding for a statement from anyone on the violence that had been perpetrated across the city the previous evening. There was a lot to answer for, and everyone from the mayor on down had been ringing his phone this morning and demanding answers pretty. What the hell could he tell them? Tilburg didn't know any more than anyone else at the moment, and the best he could say was he was on it and they would have an answer as soon as humanly possible.

As the men filed out, the phone on Tilburg's desk rang again. He looked at it, tempted not to answer, but then called for the last man out to close the door behind him before he sat and lifted the receiver from its cradle.

"Portland Gang Crimes, Captain Tilburg speaking."

"Captain Tilburg?" a gruff voice replied. "My name's Hal Brognola. I'm with the Justice Department. I'm calling to find out what the hell happened."

Great. Another big shot who wanted to get in on the game. What the hell did these Feds think he was running here? He had enough problems baby-sitting the candy asses they had assigned locally to his task force, never mind he didn't need a bigger problem from some bureaucrat in Washington, D.C., who was compiling statistics for just another Senate oversight committee on the terrible aspects of violence and crime by inner-city youth. Tilburg had never been much for politics, and he especially hated nosey ass-kissers like this Brognola guy who hid behind a tin badge while he and his men did all the real work.

"Listen, Brognola," Tilburg said. "No offense, but we're pretty damn busy here right now and I don't have time—"

"Make time," the guy cut in. "You can start by listening very carefully to what I'm about to tell you. I know how it might look there, and I know you probably think I'm just another blow-hard pansy Fed from Wonderland here to tread on your toes. That about size it up for you?"

Tilburg kept quiet.

"I'll take that as a yes," Brognola said. "And if you want to know the truth, I don't have any patience for guys like that, either. But you can bet your ass I'm not the type. I've been in the thick of stuff and I know what you're faced with. And I'm calling to let you know you're not alone. So let me help."

Tilburg cleared his throat and said, "Fine. That it?"

"No," Brognola replied. "You should also know that I've had some people looking at the angles here, and there's no way the 18th Street did this."

Now he had Tilburg's attention. "Really? And just who *is* behind it?"

"I don't know yet for sure, but there are some things I'd like to lay out for you. And if you're willing, I want to send someone I think can help. Someone who is uniquely qualified to take real action, who won't be tied down with rules and red tape. You interested?"

"I'm all ears," Tilburg replied.

EVEN AS JACK GRIMALDI positioned the chopper for an approach to land on the deck of the freighter, permission he'd been granted by the captain over ship-to-shore communications, the touchdown would still be precarious. Especially if the approach of lights from a smaller craft were any indication. When they were hovering about twenty feet above the topside markers of the deck that were kept on hand in the event of a medical emergency requiring air transport, the Stony Man pilot pointed in the direction of approaching lights.

Mack Bolan studied them briefly and nodded acknowledgment. There wasn't anything he could do about them if they were enemy, and he hoped he could retrieve the three little fugitives and get airborne before they encountered any more trouble. The Executioner had run out of time and patience—his mission had gone in more bad directions than he originally anticipated—and he didn't wish to exacerbate the situation by putting the entire freighter crew at risk from wholesale slaughter by Arab terrorists or young Russian revolutionaries. He would deal with them, whoever they might be, when or if they posed a threat to the retrieval or his mission. For now, he needed to concentrate on the task at hand.

"Put us down, Jack," Bolan said, and Grimaldi complied.

The four men who greeted the Executioner on deck were burly, their bodies only that much larger wrapped in padded fleece coats and fur headgear. Bolan flashed his diplomatic credentials at the one who appeared to be the leader and the two had a brief, shouted exchange before the man led him up a narrow set of steps to the bridge. It was comparatively warmer there, and Bolan caught a whiff of the pipe tobacco that left the entire area smelling a bit like burned apples before he actually saw the captain, who yanked a pipe from his mouth.

In a cloud of smoke, he looked at the credentials a minute, then eyed Bolan suspiciously.

"Permission to come aboard," Bolan said.

The captain smiled briefly, then in English asked, "You are with the American Diplomatic Service?"

Bolan nodded. "I'm told your destination is Norway, Captain."

The officer nodded, looked at the men who had formed a semicircle around Bolan and returned the Executioner's credentials. "I'm sure you understand when I say that I don't see how that should be any concern of yours, sir."

Okay. This was the situation he'd hoped he wouldn't face, which now had Bolan thinking furiously. He could have conjured a cover story, but he didn't think this man would be much interested in hearing some cockamamie excuse. Besides, he was walking on thin ice as it was, and it wouldn't do to tell a fish story if he wanted their exchange to be based on good faith. In fact, the captain had surely received his money for Rostov, Cherenko and Naryshkin's passage to Havesten, which according to harbor authority was on the books as their port of destination. And like most sea captains, this man had likely built his reputation on being a man of his word. In many respects, a good number of freighter captains treated their ships like little countries, sanctuaries really, floating havens where the poor and weary and oppressed could find both amnesty and anonymity.

"You're right," Bolan said. "It's not. And since you were good enough to grant me permission to land on your ship, I won't sit here and feed you a comfortable lie. You don't strike me as the kind of man who'd believe it anyway."

That brought a broader smile to the officer's lips. "I'm sure you right."

"The truth is that the three people you have on board have been mercilessly hunted for the past month by members of Sevooborot Molodjozhny. You know this organization?"

The captain nodded curtly.

"I was sent by the American government to offer them escort to the United States in safety."

"And how do I know you are not part of this plot?" the captain asked.

"Because it would be stupid of me to land my helicopter on your ship with no guarantees of safely leaving in it. Not to mention there's a distinct possibility that a ship approaching you right now has armed aggressors aboard who would think nothing of shooting up your ship, up to and including sinking her, for the purpose of killing these three people. So you see, Captain, I'm the only chance they have of getting them out of here alive, and your only chance of keeping your ship above water."

For a long time the captain said nothing, rather he just looked at Bolan with a studious gaze. The Executioner couldn't be sure the man had bought one single word, but the most he could do at this stage of the game was tell the truth. If he had any hope whatsoever of getting all three of his charges safely off this ship and back to America, now was his moment. He'd take them by force, if necessary, but he didn't want to go to that level if he didn't have to.

One of the crewmen at the helm spoke rapidly at the captain in Russian, and pointed at one of the instrument panels.

The captain stopped to study the instrumentation a moment, then looked at his men who had escorted Bolan to the bridge. "Take him to the berth where our guests are quartered. Make sure you do not let him out of your sight. When you find the men and the girl, escort all of them to their chopper." He looked Bolan in the eye now. "I don't know why you would bring this trouble to my ship, but I believe what you have said. What protection, then, I have afforded to my passengers extends to all of them. I hope I will not regret it."

Bolan extended his hand and they shook. "You won't, Captain. And if it's any consolation, I plan to leave a little surprise you can drop in on your friends if you wish."

"I don't wish, sir," the captain said with a haughty shove of the pipe between his teeth. "This is not a ship of war."

Bolan looked around and said, "No. But she's a fine ship and I'd hate to see anything bad happen to her."

The captain stared at him a moment longer, then nodded to his men. Bolan took that on cue, tossed a casual salute at the captain and accompanied his escort off the bridge. It took them nearly five minutes to reach the berthing area, and Bolan could hear the numbers ticking down inside his head. They wouldn't have much time left to get to the chopper and take off. Bolan could only hope that the satchel of high explosives could be put to good use. Whatever happened, the captain was experienced leading a cargo freighter not a battleship. They wouldn't stand a chance against a group of heavily armed terrorists.

One of the men stopped in front of a door and beat on it. The echo of flesh against the door reverberated through the narrow hold. A moment later the door opened to reveal the face Bolan recognized as belonging to Sergei Cherenko.

"Yes?" he said.

"My name's Cooper," Bolan replied. "I'm here to help you."

Kisa Naryshkin stepped into view next to Cherenko a moment later, a bit out of breath. "Matt! I'm so glad you found us. Leo needs your help."

"What's wrong?" Bolan said, pushing his way past them into the cabin.

"He's sick," she replied. "Really, really sick."

Indeed, Rostov didn't look good. He was coughing and delirious, his face flushed and the skin on his arms pale. His entire body was soaked with sweat, and he was muttering something Bolan couldn't even understand.

"His condition has grown worse in the past few hours," Cherenko said.

Bolan nodded and stepped forward to lift Rostov easily off the bunk. As he turned to leave, he said to their escorts, "We need to move. Now."

Nobody argued with him.

CHAPTER FIFTEEN

As Grimaldi helped Bolan load Rostov's feverish body onto the chopper, the Executioner realized they wouldn't be able to leave without encountering whoever was on the approaching boat.

Whether they were from the SMJ or JI didn't make much difference at that point, since Bolan had no intention of leaving a group of unarmed crew members to defend the freighter. He thought that perhaps if they saw the chopper taking off, the enemy would simply give up the idea of even attempting to board the freighter, but he dismissed the idea. Even if the crew didn't know anything about Matt Cooper, it didn't mean the enemy wouldn't try to find it out, and once they did that, they certainly couldn't leave witnesses.

Once Rostov was aboard, Bolan grabbed the satchel of plastic explosives Grimaldi had brought from their plane and jumped from the chopper. He ran across the deck with several of the captain's beefy crewmen on his heels. Bolan ignored them and ran to the edge of the freighter. The small motorcraft closed rapidly, and he could barely distinguish the outlines of about a half dozen armed men standing on her prow.

A thick hand encircled Bolan's arm, but he shrugged it off and fixed the burly man who had grabbed him with a harsh gaze. The guy stepped back a respectful distance as Bolan gestured to the nearing boat. The man looked in that direction, looked into Bolan's eyes and then at the bag he carried. Finally he nodded. The Executioner knelt and flipped open the top of the satchel. Inside were twenty-four quarter-pound sticks neatly packaged into six, one-pound bundles. Six pounds of C-4 would be more than enough to do the job.

The Executioner finished priming the explosives, then crouched and in Russian ordered the crew members to make themselves scarce. He couldn't be absolutely certain they had seen him from that distance, but he would just have to take that chance. If there was any possibility at all they might attempt to board the freighter, Bolan wasn't going to give them the opportunity. The headset he wore that kept him in constant contact with Grimaldi signaled him with a light beep.

Bolan keyed the transmitter clipped to his belt. "Go, Eagle."

"Striker, I'm starting up now. Where away?"

"Taking care of a little problem," Bolan replied. "Look for me as soon as you hear the big boom."

"Roger that," Grimaldi replied.

Bolan hunched more as the sound of the boat motor reached his ears. His eyes looked to either side for any sign of the crew, but they had obviously taken his advice and gotten clear of the hot zone. A remote possibility existed that the approaching gunners might gain access to the ship, although Bolan planned do everything he could to thwart a boarding attempt. If he played this one right, and with correct timing, the enemy would never know what hit them.

Bolan gritted his teeth when he saw the wink of muzzle-flashes and heard the sound of rounds as they glanced off the iron frame of the freighter just below where he crouched. So they had seen him—probably watching activity on the ship through a night-vision scope. The Executioner hadn't considered that possibility, and once more he knew that couldn't be the handiwork of SMJ's inexperienced crews. These were professional terrorists.

Bolan raced across the deck, the Desert Eagle in his fist and triggering rounds in the general direction of the terrorists. The motor launch turned out to be a bit larger than the Executioner had estimated but still well within range of the heavy Magnum rounds. As the motor died out and the boat coasted toward the freighter, Bolan ducked to avoid a maelstrom of hot lead directed at him. He hit the deck and rolled from the railing when he realized the motor launch would eventually reach a point close enough to the ship that would effectively eliminate their field of fire. Now Bolan only had to ensure he timed his own offensive in such a way the explosion didn't rip a hole in the side of the freighter.

He got to his feet, charged to the side and saw that the boat had rolled to within twenty-five yards. The Executioner ran parallel to the railing until he reached a spot directly above the boat, leaned over the side and released the satchel in a silent, casual throw. He withdrew the antenna of the remote detonator with his teeth, hit the deck and triggered the switch. For a moment nothing happened and then suddenly the night erupted in a fireball that rolled into the sky, high above the top deck. Bolan watched with grim satisfaction as flaming metal and wood rained upon the surrounding sea, many of the flames doused instantly by crashing waves of icy, northern waters. Bolan climbed to his feet and took a look over the side. Very little remained of the forward part of the boat and the back end, now awash in flame, had tipped upward and would soon slip beneath the surface and sink to its final resting place some seven hundred feet below.

The Executioner looked for bodies but saw none.

Bolan turned from the railing and jogged toward the helicopter. Soon they would be airborne and headed for home. They didn't have time to get Rostov to a hospital—Bolan would have to give him first aid aboard the plane. He climbed into the chopper with a hand from Cherenko and slammed the door, watching the freighter captain who stood on the bridge and waved at him. Bolan nodded in gratitude. There were people he *could* trust, who realized that there may be more at stake than what showed on the surface. The captain of this ship had demonstrated that today.

ONCE THEY HAD TRANSFERRED to the plane and were clear of Russian airspace, Bolan went about the work of tending to Leonid Rostov.

Stony Man's Learjet 36A sported a combat medipouch with fairly advanced medical equipment. It sported an automated external defibrillator, field surgical kits comprised of varied surgical tools and even shelters that could be built into a mobile surgical station. One large bag contained antibiotics and intravenous solutions, along with ample supplies of morphine,

Valium and even drugs that could immobilize combative patients. While the majority of the equipment at Bolan's disposal had been designed more to treat battle wounds, it contained a box with drugs needed to treat everything from common colds to cardiac arrest.

Rostov had not been initially conscious enough to receive any drugs by mouth, so all Bolan could do was contact Stony Man and get Calvin James on the phone, a member of the elite Phoenix Force and its combat medic.

"Give me some idea of his present condition, Striker," James said.

"He's not in good shape, Cal," Bolan replied. "It looks like maybe this is a long-term thing he's fighting, like maybe an infection or disease that's started to enter advanced stages."

"That could be," James replied. "But it will take a doctor to diagnose any such conditions and since we have no way of running the tests necessary, all I can do is talk you through treating the signs and symptoms as they present themselves."

"Understood." Bolan took a deep breath, and said, "Okay, he's pale in the body but his face is flushed. Feels like he's running a pretty high fever. Cherenko tells me he's also had a cough about a week now, but it sounds like maybe congestion has moved to his lower lungs. He isn't coughing much, but when he does it sounds like a seal barking."

"Any wheezes?"

"Not really," Bolan replied. "I'd describe it more like a rattle or buzz saw."

"All right, that would indicate he has lower airway challenge. Pinch the skin somewhere on him, like around the neck or forearm. Tell me what you see."

Bolan did and replied, "It's very slow in returning to normal position."

"Okay, that's called tenting and it means he's very dehydrated. Since he's not conscious enough to take in water, you'll have to start an IV line."

"No problem. It's been a while, but I can do it."

"Remind me to give all of you guys a refresher course on combat medicine, Striker," James said. "Okay, I'll walk you through it anyway."

For the next ten minutes, James helped Bolan through applying a tourniquet, prepping the IV bag of Lactated Ringer's solution and tubing and finding a vein. In no time, the Executioner had an IV line in Rostov, secured and flowing freely.

"You should give him an initial bolus of 500 cc's," James said. "That's half the bag. After that, you turn the clamp until you've titrated for effect. How much you think he weighs?"

"Buck-fifty."

"Okay, in his case then I'd say about 250 cc's an hour over say the next twelve hours, or until you get stateside, whichever comes first. But whatever you do don't give him more than that. We don't want to overhydrate the poor kid or we could send him into hypernatremic hypovolemia."

"I won't even ask what that is. How many drops a minute are we talking?" Bolan asked.

"I'm figuring about one drop a second, give or take. Also, only give him one bag of that LR, and then switch over to the 0.9% normal saline. He should be coming around in the next half hour or so, and when he does I'd go ahead and give him some aspirin by mouth. Along with the IV that will help to cut the fever. And if you want, it might be good to hang a 250 mil bag of the D5W. Just piggyback it into that needle port on the other IV line and set it at half the drop rate of the other IV. A little sugar sure couldn't hurt the guy and it will help push the medicine into his cells faster."

"Got it," Bolan replied. "Hey, Cal, thanks for the assist."

"Any time, Striker. Just get back here in one piece."

"Roger that."

Bolan disconnected the call and then went about the process James had suggested. When he'd completed the work, he covered Rostov with a pair of heavy wool blankets and then took a seat in the main forward area where he could keep an eye on Rostov. Cherenko and Naryshkin were seated next to each other, talking in whispers, but they clammed up when Bolan sat close to them. For a moment the Executioner wondered why the attempt at secrecy but then realized in many respects he was an outsider where it concerned Cherenko. He'd won Naryshkin's trust, but it didn't seem that was enough for Cherenko and under the circumstances Bolan couldn't say he blamed the guy. Still, Cherenko had information vital to the security of the country and Bolan didn't have time to walk on broken eggshells.

Time to get down to brass tacks.

Bolan leaned forward and extended a handshake to Cherenko. "My name's Cooper. I work for the United States government."

Cherenko took the gesture with hesitation, his eyes watching Bolan with suspicion.

Bolan decided to try something else. "Kisa, why don't you go sit by Leo, talk to him. It might help him to wake up sooner."

The young woman looked at Cherenko, resting a hand on his arm, but he nodded at her and she left them facing each other.

"I know you've had a rough time of it," Bolan said. "I'm not here to make trouble for you. But my government has kept its end of the bargain, and now it's time for you guys to reciprocate."

Cherenko nodded. "It is true that we agreed to help. But you must understand that we are not in your country yet, and there is still a chance that those inside the Sevooborot can find us and kill us."

"Not unless they're equipped with the ability to shoot down a jet over international waters," Bolan replied.

"What's to stop you from dumping me out the door once I've told you what you want to know?"

"To what end? Listen, Sergei, I have no stake in seeing either your or Rostov dead. In fact, I made a promise to Kisa's father that I'd see to it she was returned unharmed. I've traveled halfway across the world to find you two, and risked considerably more to keep you alive. Why would I go through all that just to kill you?"

Cherenko didn't have an answer for that, which is exactly what Bolan expected. Finally he broke down and began to spill it. "Some months ago, Leo came to me and told me of a meeting between himself and some of the other members from our base of operations in Moscow. He said that there was some discussion about a deal that had been brokered between a former Soviet army officer and Islamic terrorists that would supply us with updated weapons and training, along with a place to hide if pursued by police during an operation."

"In return for what?" Bolan asked.

"We were to smuggle our veteran members into America for several specific operations. We were never privy to the details. Leo and I thought about volunteering to go. That is, until he met Kisa. That's when she talked him out of remaining with the Sevooborot."

"Did you decide to get out, too?"

Cherenko sighed. "Leo and I have been friends for a long time. We went to school together, we lived together in the same drafty apartment building on the outskirts of Moscow. We attended the same college, although we did not realize at the time what a turn our education would ultimately take."

"Your English is amazing," Bolan interjected.

"This should be of no surprise," Cherenko said. "We had volunteered for this and we spent many hours studying English. Like I say, we were prepared to go on the mission until Leo met Kisa. And then everything changed. It was then that she convinced him to defect to your country, to seek refuge in America in exchange for information on the operation. It was only by accident that we found out the Arabs were actually the Jemaah al-Islamiyah. And once we understood that, and our own people knew we had this information, that's when our lives became forfeit.

"At first, Leo tried to talk them out of it. He tried to convince them that the Islamic extremists had nothing to offer, that they would never look past the abuses on so many of their kind by other militant groups, the fascists and supremacists who were beating up Arabs in the colleges and burning down their homes. But the leaders wouldn't listen to him. They told him to shut his mouth or leave, although it's clear now they never had any intention of letting him out of the Sevooborot alive."

Bolan nodded in understanding. "So as soon as he told them he was going to leave, they tried to kill him."

"I don't know who actually ordered it," he said. "Half of those friendly to us said they thought it was the leadership in Moscow, the other half thought the Jemaah al-Islamiyah was behind it. Whatever." Cherenko waved it away. "The point was that we knew our lives wouldn't be worth the paper on which our names were written unless we found a way out. And right away."

"So that's when Kisa stepped in and used her connections to make contact with the U.S. government."

Cherenko nodded.

It all made sense. The only problem was they couldn't have foreseen that the British agent who was liaison between them might actually be on the JI's payroll. However, Bolan decided not to mention this fact. He had finally managed to get Cherenko at ease, which led to him feeling comfortable enough to talk. To make it known they'd been betrayed by Barbour wouldn't serve any purpose; it might even drive Cherenko to clam up.

"So you say a former Soviet officer brokered this deal between the Sevooborot and JI." When Cherenko nodded, Bolan said, "Did you get any names?"

"I do not know who it was that actually made the deal, but as we got close to completing our training for the mission in America, we were told we would report to a man named Jurg Kovlun."

Bolan filed the name for later reference. Kovlun was one of the men Brognola had mentioned, which meant Stony Man was much closer to unraveling this mystery than they thought. And with the Executioner having really shaken things up Russia, putting both the Sevooborot and JI on the defensive, he knew the pressure would roll onto the heads of the operatives in the U.S. and they would start rushing to complete the operation. That would give Bolan the advantage, since it was always easier to take the fight to the enemy when he could put them on the defensive and keep them there. It also reduced the chances of innocent bystanders getting in the way, because Bolan could decide where and when it was best to hit the enemy.

"So Kovlun or somebody associated with him makes this deal. What exactly were you supposed to be doing in the States?"

"Part of the time we would be training members in American gangs how to operate the weapons supplied by the JI," he said. "The rest of the time, we would assist the squad leaders with setting up similar cells in other American cities."

"Where were you supposed to start?"

"Portland, Oregon."

Okay, so it made sense. Stir up rival gangs and create chaos among the larger cities in the U.S. It made perfect sense, especially with the rising tide of gang violence and its prevalence in organized crime. And it wasn't the first time terrorists had attempted to use the ills of American society against its citizens. Poverty and social depravity had always been tools wielded by those bent on destroying a society. They worked on corrupting the target's infrastructure in a way similar to Bolan's method of sowing strife within the highest power structures of the Mafia, a technique that proved quite effective in helping to bring the Mob to its knees. It wasn't a new story and it implied tactics Bolan knew exactly how to counteract.

Yeah, he'd played that game before.

But the Executioner was about to bring a new batch of rules to the table.

Total war.

CHAPTER SIXTEEN

Captain Robin Tilburg would have liked to hear better news from Staff Sergeant Rick Niesewand, but instead he heard the news he'd expected to hear.

"The Bloods said there's no way in hell they'll call a truce," Niesewand reported. "I begged and pleaded with them to give us a chance to figure this out, that we had good information the 18th Street didn't do this at all, and that someone was trying to incite them to start an all-out gang war."

"They didn't believe you," Lieutenant Brothers concluded.

Niesewand exchanged looks with his lieutenant and captain grimly, then frowned and shook his head.

"Don't let it worry you, Rick," Tilburg finally said. "I don't think if God himself walked in there and told them it was bogus that they'd stop this. For the Bloods, this comes down to a matter of honor and nothing more."

"What about this guy from the DOJ, this... What ya say his name was?" Brothers asked. "Brognola?"

Tilburg nodded.

"What's his take on this thing?"

"Well, this morning he told me that they suspected a Russian war criminal here in the United States illegally. Some guy that flew the coop after the fall of the Soviet Union, a guy by the name of—" he stopped to find the file on his desk with paperwork faxed by Brognola "—uh yeah, here it is, guy named Satyev. Anatoly Satyev, former colonel overseeing special operations in the Soviet army."

"Good God," Brothers said. "Why the hell would this guy want to start a gang war in Portland?"

Tilburg frowned. "Well, Brognola gave me some mumbo-jumbo about how some of the information is classified, but I guess this is some plot that's possibly been hatched by an Islamic terrorist group, although he wouldn't say which one."

"So what are we supposed to do with that, Captain?" Niesewand asked. "Sit on our hands and wait?"

"Not exactly," Tilburg replied. "Apparently Brognola has someone he's sending to help out. A specialist of some sort."

"Oh, great," Brothers replied. "That's all we need is some candy-ass analyst from the Feds in here trying to tell us what we already know, or give us the latest psychological profile on gang leaders!"

Tilburg raised his eyebrows and then looked at the other sergeants. "You guys want to give me and Roger a minute here?"

The sergeants looked at each other and then filed out of the room, leaving the two officers. They had their orders and they really didn't need to sit around the station anyway. They had enough work ahead of them and getting their units on the street would be a priority now. Until this specialist arrived, Tilburg needed to keep the press and the brass at arm's length until he could sort out some of this mess. They also had plenty of homicides to work. The mayor and chief of police had already advised Tilburg he could have all the support staff and overtime he wanted, but that didn't make the work any easier. They had to follow procedure on every single one of those cases because the family of every victim would demand justice as if *their* case were the only one the department had to work.

"All right, Roger," Tilburg said. "The last fucking thing I need right now is to have us divided about the support this Brognola's offered to help us. So in the future, if you want to pop off with any discontent then I'd prefer you do it when it's just you and me, and not in front of the guys we're asking to lead our troops on the front lines. Got it?"

Brothers nodded once, then sighed. "You're right, Rob. I was being an asshole and you didn't deserve that. Won't happen again."

"Fine." Tilburg leaned back in his chair and folded his arms. "Now, we've been friends a long time, and I value your opinion…as a friend and a cop. So, speak your piece."

"All right, Rob, here it is. We need to jump on this thing now before it bites us in the ass."

"I think it's a little bit late for that," Tilburg countered, "seeing as how it already seems to have bitten us in the ass, Roger."

"That's not what I'm talking about. What I mean is, I don't think we should wait for the Feds because while we're waiting on them to actually *do* something, the heavy stuff could go down and we'll have more bodies. Now, I'm not against seeing a few less gangbangers buy the farm. As you know, most of them aren't long for this world anyway once they get into gangs, and I don't think any of us will get too broken up about it if there's a few less in the city by close of business tonight. But the fact remains we just can't sit on our hands and wait for FBI or DHS or whoever to respond. We need to get in front of this thing right now, Rob, before we lose complete control. Once the war starts out there on the streets, it'll be next to impossible to stop it."

"Aside from the political nightmare this is creating for the people I answer to," Tilburg said, "and the dangers of using force to repel a full-scale gang war, I can't add blatant disobedience to my list of sins. You have to understand that."

"What I understand is that we have nothing to lose by taking this into our hands and delivering some asskicking of our own. Maybe that will diffuse the situation. At best, it will at least deter it for a bit and give you some time to think up a better plan."

For a long time Tilburg looked at his friend. He trusted Brothers with his life, would trust him in the heat of things if it came right down to it. But Brothers was still a man of action, and as such he didn't always think clearly before acting. He tended to work from the gut, like any good street cop, which made him an excellent policeman where it concerned gangs. Those same traits, though, made him only an average officer and leader, something that Tilburg's superiors had noted. That had not only kept him from promotions but made it so half a dozen other captains in the division wouldn't touch him.

"I'm sorry, Roger," Tilburg finally said. "I understand what you're saying but it's too risky."

"Damn it, Rob!" Brothers slammed his fist on Tilburg's desk. "You're making a mistake here. We can't—"

A steady rap at the door interrupted them, and Tilburg looked toward the door with irritation, at first. And then he saw the man standing there, tall and muscular with dark hair and dressed in unmarked, black fatigues. Brognola hadn't given him any description of Matt Cooper but Tilburg didn't need one. Something about the way the guy stood there, the way he carried himself, told Tilburg all he needed to know. This was a guy who could command people, a leader among leaders, and as Tilburg gestured for the guy to enter he could feel the aura of confidence that came through that door with the man. It was strong and intense, as intense as the blue eyes that seemed to take in the room with a single glance.

"Captain Tilburg?" the man said, stepping forward and offering a hand. "Matt Cooper."

Tilburg rose and shook the guy's hand. Firm grip. Not hard or clammy—just a firm, dry grasp that spoke of considerable power. Tilburg had always believed he could tell something about a guy based just on his handshake, and Cooper proved no exception.

"Pleasure," Tilburg said. He gestured toward Brothers and introduced them. The men shook hands, and Tilburg watched carefully as his friend sized up their new arrival. They would be working closely with each other, and Tilburg didn't want any sort of trouble. He could see from Brothers's expression alone, though, that he'd be watching Cooper. He didn't plan to give this guy an inch until Cooper did or said something to prove he wasn't just another bureaucrat.

"Have a seat," Tilburg said. Once they were comfortable and Bolan had declined an offer for coffee, Tilburg continued, "I spoke with Mr. Hal Brognola in Washington. He spoke very highly of you. Said you could help us."

Bolan tendered a quick smile. "Hal's usually right about these things."

Tilburg reserved comment to that. "I was just listening to Lieutenant Brothers here who was telling me he'd prefer I sanction an offensive strategy."

"He's right."

"Come again?" Tilburg inquired.

"My plan is to get in front of this immediately," Bolan replied. "We don't have time for games. If you want to avert a full-scale gang war, we need to find out where the real operatives are holed up and cripple them before it gets worse. With luck, that'll give us enough to expose the threat for what it is and avert a bloodbath."

Tilburg could feel his jaw drop as he looked at Brothers, who wore a similar expression of surprise. Brothers sat back slowly in his chair and folded his arms, never taking his eyes off Bolan. For a moment nobody said anything. The silence was enough to evidence that Bolan had made a good first impression on both of them.

This guy wasn't what Tilburg had expected and he could tell that Brothers was thinking the exact same way. Maybe Brognola had told the truth; maybe the guy they'd sent could help them after all; maybe they still had something to hold on to, after all.

Something called hope.

WAR EVERLASTING HAD TAUGHT the Executioner many important lessons. One of them involved drafting a schedule that directly interfered with the opponent's timetable. If intelligence indicated the enemy would likely do something at a certain time, then Bolan realized the value of acting before that could happen. In other words, hit them before they could hit you, act on some piece of information before they could act on it. Inevitably, that strategy would send them running for cover, desirous of the chance to come up with a countermove. Like a game of chess, war was really nothing more than moves and countermoves, and the victor usually turned out to be the one who could lay down an offense that would make the enemy shift their time and resources to counteract that play.

They'd refueled in Greenland and the Northwest Territories, then did a plane change in Anchorage before moving on to Seattle where Bolan delivered Rostov, Cherenko and Naryshkin into the protective custody of U.S. Marshals. They would stand watch over Rostov in the hospital and the other two at a safehouse. Cherenko would feed information to Bolan as he went, and the Executioner could focus on developing a battle strategy that would offset the plans of Kovlun and Satyev. Both, he now figured, had a hand in this plot.

It was nearing 1830 hours local time when Bolan rapped on the door of Captain Robin Tilburg's office. He'd received a full brief from Brognola during the short hop from Seattle to Portland. The slaying of dozens of innocent people was something he'd wanted desperately to avoid, but the mission in Russia had taken some bad turns. But he was here now, and he could act before any more bystanders got killed, or gangs started shooting up the streets. Bolan noted the surprise on the faces of both cops when he announced his agreement with Lieutenant Brothers.

Tilburg finally said, "Okay, I'm more than happy to concede the point now that I have two informed opinions suggesting the same thing. But I think I should let you know here and now I'm not keen about freelancers operating on my streets. You want to take the fight to these terrorists, then I say more power to you, but you'd best understand my first responsibility is to the safety of our citizens."

Bolan's eyes narrowed. "So is mine, Tilburg."

"Let me put this another way, just so we understand each other. You want to start some suck-head plays you run them by me first. Don't think you can go off half-cocked and start blowing shit up and shooting gang members dead without involving me and my team."

"I'm not going to endanger your citizens," Bolan said. "But I need freedom to operate. I can't go checking with you every time I follow up on a lead or conduct a hard target contact. Now I'll be more than happy to keep you posted, but I run the operation my way, and you give me total authority to position your team as support when and how needed."

"How do I know you're the best man for the job?" Tilburg asked.

Bolan frowned. "I don't normally offer to do this, but I could have someone from the Oval Office call and confirm it for you."

That brought a measure of silence to the room before Tilburg finally nodded, "All right, it's a deal. But one more dead bystander and I shut you down."

Bolan nodded.

"Good. So what do you have in mind here?"

"Well, I have intelligence that indicates automatic weapons were used at both scenes."

Brothers nodded. "Yeah, we've started looking at that angle, as well. We've decided to assume the hardware used had to come from foreign gunrunners, maybe OC out of Mexico, possibly even a terrorist network."

"Jemaah al-Islamiyah, to be exact," Bolan replied.

"Say what?"

"JI is a radical group of terrorists based in Southeast Asia, specifically Indonesia, Malaysia and the Philippines. Two former members of the Soviet army brokered a deal with the JI to spread gang violence in at least a dozen major U.S. cities in return for support of their own goals, which are yet unknown to us. We think the plot was originally masterminded by a former Russian colonel named Anatoly Satyev. I believe Satyev may be manipulating a guy who used to work for him, one Jurg Kovlun. Kovlun's a hard case, former Spetsnaz commando. It seems these two figured this little plan of theirs would create enough unrest to turn Homeland Security's focus to internal threats, thereby taking some of the heat and resources off the international terror network. They decided to use a Russian militant youth organization known as the SMJ to train these gangs in the use of weapons and terrorist tactics to minimize any connection between these activities and Islamic radicals within the JI."

Tilburg's voice was a bare whisper as he replied, "God save us all."

"Sounds like your people are off to a good start in your analysis," Bolan continued. "You're thinking right about it anyway. The only way to track down Kovlun and Satyev is through the Russian SMJ recruits who are training them, and the only way you find them is to follow the guns. And seeing as the gangs here in Portland would pretty much have a stranglehold on any gunrunning activities, I need to know who just might have the connections to pipeline that kind of major hardware through this city."

"That's easy," Brothers said. "The Kent brothers, Marvin and Divan Kent. And here's the odd thing about that, Cooper. Those guys worked for Luther Medford, the head of the Bloods who was assassinated by the 18th Street guns…or, whoever the hell it actually was who did this."

Bolan nodded. "That's just the kind of thing Kovlun and Satyev would look at. They'd have no qualms about paying good money to the locals. Where do we find these Kent brothers?"

"They're gone," Tilburg said. "According to what we've determined, they flew out together on a plane for the Bahamas late last night."

"And probably paid to do it so we couldn't connect them to the guns. They have any known associates you could grab up?"

Tilburg looked at Brothers who said, "I know of only one guy. Willie Harris. You can find him over on Fifteenth Street normally. He owns a little pawn shop there, but we think that's probably a front for the interference he runs between the Kent brothers and potential buyers."

"Can you show me where this pawn shop is at?"

"I'll do you one better," Brothers replied. "I'll take you there personally."

Bolan shook his head. "This is one of those times we need to tread softly and carry a big stick. The magic kind that nobody can see. We send a bunch of cops over there, and Harris will either run or shut down entirely. We can't afford that. It's our only connection to finding out who the Kent brothers distributed the weapons to."

"What if he won't tell you?"

"He'll tell me," Bolan replied. "It's my experience that if nothing else, he'll have a name."

"Is that enough?" Tilburg asked.

"Usually."

It sure enough would be, if Bolan asked the right questions. After all, a name led to a situation, a situation to a time and place. If Harris knew anything at all about the business the Kent brothers did in Portland, Bolan would exploit that information to its maximum yield. The soldier bet it would be enough to pin down where the most likely point of operation was for Kovlun and Satyev. And with that, Bolan could pen them in and hit them hard before they even knew he was on to them. From there, he could only hope he knocked enough pieces off the board that Satyev or Kovlun wouldn't play anymore. And if not, then he'd use whatever resources remained to track Kovlun and Satyev to their home turf and deliver a final punch that would surely end the operation before it got off the ground. Yeah, once more the Executioner had all he needed to bring this mission to a close. He had a name: Willie Harris.

CHAPTER SEVENTEEN

It didn't take Mack Bolan long to retrieve the information he sought. He found Willie Harris at the pawn shop, just as Brothers had predicted, and by applying just the right pressure in his questioning, the Executioner came away with information on which he could act. Bolan didn't want to involve the cops in this one, although he knew he probably didn't have much of a choice. He'd given his word to Tilburg and he meant to keep it. That didn't mean he couldn't check it out first, and so that fact had brought him to a swanky chain hotel in an uptown section of Portland. A quick check with the desk clerk confirmed every room in the place booked—probably all the people in for the jazz festival—but nobody under the name Harris had given Bolan: Lisanne Ruemont.

Ruemont was a professional escort and met a lot of interesting people. She knew just about everybody who was anybody in Portland since she'd worked several years as a street hooker before "going legit" with the escort service; or at least that was the story Willie Harris had relayed to the Executioner.

Bolan now waited in the semicrowded lobby of the hotel. Ruemont didn't keep a room here but this was a pretty busy time for escorts, it being the start of the weekend. The phone attendant at the escort place had become so irritated when Bolan kept repeatedly insisting that Lisanne was the only one who would do to accompany him to a nonexistent party that she finally hung up on him, and when he called back to demand some justice the manager came on the phone. Then Bolan went to work on him and eventually the manager gave up that Ruemont was working at this hotel, and if he really wanted her that bad to see if he could buy her from the guy who'd picked her up, just as long as he promised not to start trouble or to tell the client—some rich hoity-toity from out of town—that he'd told Bolan where to find them. The soldier then checked with the desk clerk to find out Mr. Leonard Wachovia had not yet left his suite, and would Bolan like to have him rung up. He politely informed the desk clerk he was a little early and would simply wait for Wachovia to come down. Then he took a seat in the lounge, a place that afforded him a perfect view of both main entrances, and pretended to be involved in yesterday's newspaper.

Bolan didn't have to wait long before a woman matching Harris's detailed description walked through the door in high heels. She went directly to the main desk, and Bolan watched as she leaned close to talk with the clerk. The two chatted a minute like old friends, much to the chagrin of the growing line of clientele waiting for service, and then with a final titter of conversation and a giggle, the clerk handed over a room key card. The Executioner figured it was to the suite of one Leonard Wachovia, so he rose and casually followed Ruemont to the elevators.

Bolan made sure he got on the same one as her. Fortunately they were alone so the Executioner had time to make his play. There were always right moments and wrong moments to implement a plan, and oftentimes the thing that separated the novice from the expert came down to two things: patience and timing. All too often, the novice would jump the gun and act too soon in their haste to accomplish the objective, thus missing some important detail or blowing their cover. Many people could sense nervousness and suspicion in others, and this would even more true of a streetwise person such as Ruemont.

Bolan watched to see which button she pressed, noting the level coincided with Wachovia's room number, and then excused himself as he stepped in front of her and pushed a button for two levels above it. He then leaned casually against the wall, giving her a fair amount of room, and looked at his watch as if he were late for some engagement. He considered speaking to her but decided against it—that would put her on guard. He didn't even want her to think he had any interest in her.

The elevator dinged to a stop and the doors swept open a moment later. She stepped into the hall and turned immediately to her left. Bolan let the doors start to close, then at the last minute stuck his hand between them to engage the safety bumpers. They slid aside obediently, and Bolan stepped into the hallway and watched Ruemont's shapely form retreat to a door at the end of the hallway. Bolan padded down the hall after her, cautious to stay against one wall to lessen the chance she'd catch a glimpse of him in her peripheral vision. As he got closer he watched her knock twice on the door, then slide the key card into the lock. There was a whir and click, and as she pulled on the handle and started to push inward, Bolan made his move.

The Executioner rushed the open door and pushed through behind her. He grabbed her by the waist as he came through the doorway and steered her farther into the room while simultaneously slamming the door behind him. Ruemont emitted a soft cry as she staggered against the couch, but seemed to quickly recover and turned to reach for something in her purse. Bolan figured she might go for a weapon, and although he wasn't sure what kind he had planned to be ready for just such a move. When Ruemont produced a small black canister Bolan slapped it out of her hand with a left backswing as his right went for the Beretta 93-R nestled in shoulder leather beneath his jacket. He pointed the pistol at a portly, gray-haired man who emerged from the bedroom in nothing but black socks, underwear and a pleated white tux shirt with sock suspenders.

"Keep your hands visible," Bolan told the man.

Wachovia did as ordered.

Ruemont now wheeled and tried to flee but Bolan caught her foot, tripping her and sending her lithe form sprawling on the couch. The Executioner moved quickly to the phone and pulled the cord from the back of the base, then ordered Wachovia to go into the bedroom suite and do the same while he watched. When the man complied, Bolan directed him to sit in the dining area, palms flat on the table.

"I have no issues with you, mister," Bolan stated. "And I'm sorry about the extremism, but I'm sure you've seen the news about the massacre last night."

Wachovia nodded.

Bolan jabbed a thumb at Ruemont and said, "Your girlfriend here is partly responsible for that, so I need to talk to her, and this is the only chance I have. As soon as she provides the information I'm looking for, I walk out of here and you can go about your business. You understand?"

"I get it," he said, looking at Ruemont with some measure of distaste now evident in his expression.

The Executioner nodded, holstered his pistol and turned to study Ruemont. He folded his arms, put one foot on the coffee table and leaned closer to Ruemont with an icy-eyed expression of malevolence—she returned his gaze with stony-faced silence. Tough gal, no doubt about it, but Bolan was tougher and had gone against much tougher people than her. Despite Ruemont's experience she was just a very small fish in a very big pond, and she probably didn't feel she owed much allegiance to the Kent brothers. Well, he'd know soon enough where Lisanne Ruemont's loyalties lay.

"A few months back you helped a guy make a connection with Marvin and Divan Kent," Bolan began. "This guy was tall, in good physical condition and spoke with a Russian accent. He probably gave you a cover, but his real name is Jurg Kovlun."

Ruemont's mouth parted just slightly as if she might say something, but then she simply licked her lips before closing them. Bolan could see the wheels turning. She might figure this was some kind of test, that maybe he'd been sent by the Kents to see if she'd talk out of turn. He had to find some leverage and he thought he knew what he could use to get it.

"You might think it's better to keep your mouth shut," Bolan said. "Maybe ask for a lawyer. The problem is,

I'm not a cop, and my interests in your little shenanigans are the least of my worries. But I do know some cops who would be very interested in your activities, maybe stir up some trouble within the escort service you're working for. That would put you over real well with your boss, wouldn't it? Might cut into your living, too."

"Is that a threat?" she asked in a husky voice with a tone that dripped defiance. "Because I'm not really scared."

"I don't need to threaten you," Bolan said. "All I have to do is make a phone call and you and all your girlfriends are out of business. Not to mention your life won't be worth a spit once the Kent boys find out their key go-between has been busted. Especially when the word gets out you'll be looking to make a deal to avoid prosecution by blabbing everything you know about their arms running. You'll be so unpopular you'll have to leave town the same day." Bolan concluded his spiel with a frosty smile.

"Asshole," Ruemont finally swore.

"My fight's not with you," Bolan said. "In fact, I can forget your name altogether if you just level with me. I'm giving you a chance to get out of this with your head still attached to your body, lady. Take the offer."

For a long time she didn't say anything, but Bolan knew his ruse had worked. Of course, he wouldn't have made good on the threat, but Ruemont didn't know that. The Executioner had never been into sacrificing others to the jackals of the world, no matter how they conducted their personal lives. Bolan had never deemed his work as that of a judge or a jury. The rules of humankind had been laid down long ago.

"What do you want to know?" she asked.

"The Russian, Kovlun. You met with him?"

"Yeah, we had a romp. A few romps, actually. He liked sex. That was obvious."

"Did you hook him up with the Kent brothers?"

She shrugged and reached for her purse. As Bolan's hand wavered over the pistol she said, "I just want a cigarette." Bolan studied her a moment, then nodded. When she had a smoke lit, she took a deep drag and let it out noisily. She continued, "Actually, I did the deal for Divan. He wanted to get his hooks into the guy right away."

"Why?"

"I don't know," she said evenly. "But I figured it was important because Divan told me to do whatever I could to land the guy. He's only ever done that with a few guys, and every time I found out later it was because there was lots of money involved. So this time, I learned my lesson and held out for a larger cut."

"What about your customer? You ever try to roll *him* for something extra?"

She nodded. "He wouldn't budge, the cold bastard. He had money, though. He reeked of money."

"How so?"

"He wore nice clothes, expensive designer jeans and sweaters, had a Rolex watch, that kind of stuff."

"You seem to know your way around the ones with cash," Bolan observed.

She laughed around another drag of her cigarette and her eyes flicked to Wachovia before returning to Bolan. "In my business, you learn real quick to tell the difference between who has the money and who just pretends they have it, honey. You know the old saying—'The only difference between the men and the boys…'"

She didn't have to finish her statement—Bolan knew the saying and he nodded as much. "So you didn't do any snooping?"

"Once," she said. "He had some credit cards, lots of cash. One weird thing, though. He always chose to pay me in traveler's checks, small denominations. I never could figure out why, but that didn't much matter. I have quite a few connections in the local hotels. I could always find someone to cash them and waive the fees, so it never really bothered me that much. I just thought it was strange."

The Executioner didn't. He knew exactly the reason but he didn't feel like getting into that with her at the moment. "What about these little rendezvous? You always meet at the same place?"

She nodded. "Yeah, a nice restaurant over on Harbor Way, inside a cozy little hotel called the Riverview Stay."

Bolan was familiar with the area from his previous visits to Portland. The hotel was among many upscale businesses that ran along the banks of the Willamette River and catered to mostly a touristy clientele. It wasn't that crowded this time of year, although some of the attractions like the jazz festival would have seen a rush in terms of general congestion and populace. It would serve as a perfect place for Kovlun and his goons to fit in among the crowd.

"All right," Bolan replied. "You bought yourself a reprieve. Come on, pick up your stuff and let's go."

Ruemont looked surprised. "Where?"

"Portland police headquarters," Bolan said, extending a hand and wrapping it around her elbow.

"What the hell are you talking about?" she demanded. "You said you weren't a cop!"

"I'm not."

"So why you hauling me down to the police station like some perp?"

"Because you obviously have a lot of information about the Kent brothers and their operations. And the authorities are very interested in shutting down the pipeline of guns coming into this city so nothing like what happened last night ever happens again." In a more even tone, Bolan added, "So grab your purse and let's go."

Wachovia jumped to his feet. "Wait one damn minute! I already paid for her company!"

Bolan pinned him with a level stare. "Then maybe you ought to lodge a complaint with the customer service department. I'm sure they'll be happy to refund your money."

Wachovia looked like he wanted to say something else but wisely kept his mouth shut.

"WE APPRECIATE YOU bringing her in like this, Cooper," Tilburg said.

"Yeah," Brothers added. "That's quite a bit of police-work on your part. Sure you don't want a job?"

"I'll pass," the Executioner replied with a grin. "I think she can give you enough to shut down any more business by the Kent brothers. If they have the corner on the market like you've said they do, this'll take a big chunk of the work off your plates. Not to mention you'll be able to take Harris out of the loop, too."

"Well," Tilburg replied, "it won't get the guns off the streets that are currently out there, but it will be some time before we have to worry about new ones coming in. And Ruemont's testimony in court might just be enough to get extradition warrants for Marvin and Divan Kent, have them brought back here for prosecution."

"Shouldn't be a problem," Brothers said. "So what other tricks you got up your sleeve, Cooper?"

"Ruemont said she met with Kovlun about a half dozen times over the past few months," Bolan replied. "Apparently he has a soft spot for the opposite sex. Made it sound like he was pretty insatiable. But he always initiated the meets by placing a call directly to her."

Brothers frowned in puzzlement. "He didn't use the escort service?"

"No." The Executioner shook his head. "And it sounds like he paid her well enough in traveler's checks that she decided to keep it under wraps and not let her employer onto the little side gig she ran with him."

"Travelers checks," Tilburg said. "Is that significant?"

Bolan nodded. "A large number of terrorist organizations operate using them, primarily because most of their cash has to be converted to U.S. currency when they get new arrivals in the States. A large amount of foreign currency being traded in for U.S. denominations is logged."

Brothers nodded his understanding. "They do that to cut down on money-laundering scams."

"Right," Bolan said. "But if they use foreign dollars to purchase traveler's checks in U.S. denominations, nobody gets the least bit suspicious because the travelers checks aren't really negotiable to foreign currencies. And the serial numbers on each one have pretty much eliminated counterfeiting."

"Hence, federal agencies don't look hard at anyone cashing them here in the States," Tilburg concluded.

Bolan nodded. "Right."

"That's all well and good, but I don't see how it's going to help us," commented Staff Sergeant Rick Niesewand, who'd been assigned to assist Bolan with follow-ups.

"By itself, it doesn't help much at all. But knowing he used them to pay her, coupled with his regular calls to her when he was feeling amorous, will help me narrow down possible locations he'll operate out of. And that's where your guys come in."

"How?" Tilburg asked.

"Ruemont said Kovlun always initiated contact with her," he said. "I'm guessing he did that by calling her cell phone. I doubt a woman with her smarts would've given her home number to anybody. Her cell phone was logged in with her personal possessions when you booked her. I need to borrow it for a short time. I have connections who can track the number or numbers Kovlun called her from and triangulate his position to within a half mile."

"Okay, but where do the traveler's checks come in?" Brothers inquired.

"If he used them with her, chances are good he or his associates used them at other places. Once we pinpoint the source location of his phone calls to her, your men can start a canvas to find out where else they've been used."

"And eventually that will lead us their base of operations," Tilburg concluded.

Bolan smiled. "Right on."

"Then what?" Brothers said. "I mean, once we find Kovlun's base, what do we do from there?"

"That," the Executioner replied, "you'll leave to me."

CHAPTER EIGHTEEN

"The operation is set to commence at midnight," Jurg Kovlun told Anatoly Satyev. "At least, that's when my spies have informed me the official declaration of war against the 18th Street will be made by the Bloods."

"Excellent," Satyev replied. "Make sure that nothing goes wrong. You did an excellent job with the first operation and I'm confident you'll handle this one with the same care."

"I will."

"Keep me posted," Satyev said, then disconnected the call.

Kovlun held the phone a moment and then slowly dropped it into the cradle. The thumping music annoyed him, had given him a bit of a headache, but he couldn't really get away from it. Kovlun turned to watch as young women, more full-figured than they had a right to be at their tender ages, jerked and gyrated in time to the beat. Their hips swayed and their breasts rode waves in time to movements—as if mesmerized by the electronic dance music like a cobra to a snake charmer's pipe—and Kovlun felt a sweet, sickly ball form in his belly as the urge for female companionship tugged at his groin.

Kovlun pushed those thoughts to the back of his mind. There would be time enough for that once he'd completed this phase of the mission. If all went according to plan, this would be the last thing he would need to do before he could make some decisions on his own direction. He'd thought for some time of returning to the Mother Country for a while, but he couldn't be sure the police weren't still looking for him. He'd been gone nearly ten years, though, and nobody could actually prove his involvement in the deaths of dissidents.

Kovlun had to wonder some at the irony of all this. At one time he'd served the Soviet army, sworn to defend the ways of communism and the social stability it brought, and yet he could do nothing when the citizens rebelled in their decision for change. He had acted on his oath, unswerving in his duty to protect a way of life, but in the end the people had not only treated him like a criminal but chased him out of his own country. The fact he had to seek refuge in a country he once considered an enemy still burned like a hot coal in his gut, and one day he would revel in seeing her great cities fall. Let them declare martial law in America one time and see what happened; it would be total anarchy.

Kovlun's only real problem with this operation, however, was dealing with the Jemaah al-Islamiyah. He didn't like Arab terrorist organizations—never had liked them—and he didn't agree with the slaughter of innocents on September 11, 2001, or any of the other attacks. The terrorists of the world had been as violent against his own people as Russia's enemies. They thought only of their way of life, and cared nothing for those who deviated from it whatever their nationality, ethnic origin or creed. As a member of Spetsnaz, Kovlun had been taught how to counteract terrorist groups, and that had included training on why terrorists operated as they did and the reasons behind many of their actions. Kovlun learned that terrorists were equal-opportunity killers, and he found their activities distasteful.

When all was said and done, he could have a clear conscience in the fact that it had never been his idea to work with them in the beginning. This entire affiliation was the mastermind of the colonel's, and the sooner Kovlun could get out from under Satyev's thumb the better he would feel. Until that time, though, he would have to keep his mouth shut and do as he was told, aware that if this plan failed it would fall on *his* head, not Anatoly Satyev's.

Kovlun couldn't take the throbbing in his temples anymore. The pain of the headache had started in the top of his head until it grew and worked its way along the sides and behind his eyes. Now the bright sparkles of light had begun, and Kovlun knew if he didn't step out of the club for at least a minute or two his head would simply build up so much pressure inside it would explode. He didn't see much purpose in suffering a brain aneurysm or some other malady just for this crap. Kovlun wound his way through the club until he found Pilkin and Briansky, and gestured for them to accompany him through the rear exit.

Once they were outside, Kovlun lit a cigarette. The three men huddled close together for warmth, the door into the club propped open slightly, the beat of the music still audible over the cold wind that blew across the river. Kovlun shivered a bit, but he didn't react quite as violently as his lieutenants, who were visibly affected by the change of climate. Kovlun had trained in the most bleak, frigid and remote regions of the world but he realized St. Petersburg was probably the coldest area his men had encountered. To Kovlun it was almost downright balmy, although he had discovered his acclimation to the cold wasn't what it had once been.

"I spoke with the colonel," Kovlun told them. "He is very pleased that the first phase of the operation went so well. I told him about the announcement of war tonight by the Bloods. Are your men ready?"

Pilkin nodded and let out a gust of smoke through chattering teeth. "They are ready, Comrade."

Kovlun now noticed Briansky seemed a bit fidgety. "Something on your mind, Aleks?"

Briansky, who didn't smoke, took a quick pull from his cola—which wasn't mixed with any alcohol since they were set to begin operations in a few hours—replied, "I was wondering if you had told the colonel yet of your intent to leave once this phase of our plans is complete."

"No," Kovlun replied with a shake of his head. "Why do you ask?"

"I must be honest, Comrade, in asking you to consider taking me with you in wherever you decide to go."

Kovlun cocked his head. He hadn't seen *that* coming at all. He'd always wondered about Briansky, a young man who had come to him unkempt and somewhat directionless, but they had connected almost immediately when Kovlun began to exploit Briansky's uncanny talents with firearms. They had built somewhat of a kinship over the time they worked together, and now Kovlun considered the fact he'd worked with Pilkin and Briansky for a couple of years. He'd forged bonds with these men without even realizing it.

"I see," Kovlun finally replied. He looked at Pilkin. "You feel the same way, Mikhail?"

Pilkin's eyes shifted between his two friends for a time, and then he lowered his head and nodded slightly.

"But unlike Aleks, you feel you're betraying the Sevooborot."

"No," Pilkin replied. "I am simply concerned what the colonel might do when you inform him of your desire to leave the business and make your own way, and that you plan to take two men who he has spent considerable money to train along with you for the ride."

"There is no need for you to worry about that," Kovlun said. "I can handle the colonel. He is an excellent businessman and honorable in his political convictions, but he lacks the tactical vision necessary to execute any plans of consequence. I, on the other hand, am more calculating and have a long-range plan I think will bring both stability and prosperity to our cause. And if you choose to go with me, then I can only promise I shall compensate you appropriately for your allegiance."

"How much?" Pilkin asked.

This caused Kovlun to laugh. "Ah, Mikhail, always the opportunist."

"Of course," Pilkin said with a shrug, as if it should have been of no consequence or surprise to them.

"I don't yet know exactly how much," Kovlun said. "But you can rest assured that it will be much more than your current compensation."

That answer seemed to satisfy the two men so they turned back to the discussion of their current operation.

"Once the Bloods declare war, they will not wait to hit the 18th Street's major money-making operations," Kovlun told them, "I've arranged for operators among our Islamic contacts to be ready with the guns they promised. Your only requirement for that part of the mission will be to supply the weapons as promised and on time, Mikhail. Then join me at the warehouse with your team after you've secured delivery of the arms cache."

Pilkin nodded.

Kovlun looked at Briansky now. "Once the Bloods make their move, you will need to have your trainees in position to counterattack. My spies tell me they have already learned the Bloods' primary targets will be the house of the 18th Street leader and a warehouse he owns that is packed with crates of designer knockoffs. You will lead the counterreactionary force at the 18th Street leader's house. This should be no trouble for you and your men. I will lead the detachment assigned to raze that warehouse, personally. When the shooting ends, we will have destroyed the 18th Street merchandise, and there will be plenty of dead gang members on both sides. This should be adequate enough to fuel a war that will become unstoppable for the police. As soon as we've finished our mission, we will then pack up and head for Los Angeles. By 4:00 a.m. tomorrow, I want everyone moved out so that there isn't so much as a trace we were ever here, that we even existed. Am I clear?"

The two men nodded and Kovlun dismissed them, at which point both made quickly for the door and the warmth of the club interior. Kovlun decided to stay there and smoke another cigarette. His headache had started to subside and he didn't wish to go back to the torture. He thought for a moment about calling the woman he knew only as Lisanne. After all, it was still several hours before midnight came around and he was definitely feeling the need to feed his sexual appetite. He thought better of it, though, as Colonel Satyev had indicated he had a "special operative" in Portland to support their efforts, which made Kovlun wonder if that was another way of saying he had a spy watching them. In either case, it didn't matter. In a few hours they would accomplish their final operational objectives and then Jurg Kovlun would finally be free.

Free to begin his own war, to forge the New Soviet Empire.

USING INFORMATION FROM THE SIM card inside Lisanne Ruemont's phone, Aaron Kurtzman was able to give Bolan and the Portland teams a one-square-mile area to sweep, a one-third of which included warehouses and factories. The Executioner knew Kovlun wouldn't pick any such places because they were too obvious. His operations would be headquartered out of a local business, one that ideally drew major crowds. In many respects, it seemed to be the modus operandi of the SMJ. Bolan thought on how unique this mission had been in contrast to many others. He'd never thought of himself much like a cop—although he considered them brothers on the same side—but this particular mission had forced him to operate much that way. He'd used informants, criminal forensics and evidence, not to mention some good old-fashioned witness intimidation, to evaluate gangland activities that would eventually bring him information on Russian militants and terrorists. What made it all the more fantastic was that Kovlun and Satyev had done most of the work themselves by electing to use an American criminal element that hadn't ever proved itself that adept to keeping secrets.

As soon as he had the information, Tilburg ordered his men to work. Bolan kept in contact with the units by cellular phone and before long they had a list of seven places where not only had traveler's checks been used, but most of the proprietors had been able to pull Kovlun out of a photo lineup or described him to detail.

"We're close now, Hal," Bolan told the Stony Man chief from the cell phone as he drove around along the streets of the canvas zone. "I can feel it."

"That's good news, Striker. Anything else I can do to help?"

"Not right at the moment. I have to admit, this Captain Tilburg runs a pretty impressive operation."

Brognola grunted. "Yeah. And it always helps when you get some federal monies thrown your way."

"You mean the task force," Bolan said.

"Correct."

"Well, I think I'll have this nailed down before the night's through," Bolan said and then he heard his call sign over the radio. "That's my cue. I'll get back with you as soon as I know something. Out, here."

Bolan picked up the radio. "This is Raven." The code name he'd been given by Tilburg for his unique dress in the black fatigues with no visible insignia.

"We may have trouble brewing," Brothers replied. "Just got news the Bloods are gathering at a number of undisclosed locations in force. Word from one of our CI's is that the war kicks off at midnight."

Bolan looked at his watch: just past 2300, which gave him almost no time to find Kovlun's operation and shut it down. That didn't even account for getting the proof they needed to avert this war. The Bloods knew only one thing, and that was Luther Medford was dead and the 18th Street had done the killing right on national television. Not to mention the financial cut into their profits by the shooting at one of the hottest clubs in Portland. With fourteen homicides and the damage done at that scene, the club wouldn't be opening anytime soon. And how could anyone ever feel safe going back there anyway?

No, Bolan knew what this meant. They had failed to avert a disaster and now he was duty-bound to take whatever steps were necessary to neutralize the aggressors. This wasn't a matter of sides anymore; it was plainly a matter of practicality. Bolan knew he couldn't convince the Bloods to stand down unless he got the two leaders together in the same room. He could figure only one way to do that. Snatch up the new leader of the Bloods and arrange a meeting with 18th Street's top dog.

"Understood," Bolan said. "Keep up with the canvas, and I'll join you as soon—"

Something spiderwebbed the right side of the windshield and suddenly Bolan's entire view ahead transformed into a bright wash of red-orange flame. The Executioner pumped his brakes and swerved to the right, gritting his teeth as the rental car scraped against a row of parked cars with a noise that resembled fingernails on a blackboard. Bolan's vehicle finally careened off the tail of an SUV just as a second object smashed through the back window, bounced off the rear seat and dropped to the back floorboard. A moment later the entire rear seats burst into flame and Bolan could smell the harsh, biting odor of gasoline. His car had now become a rolling hazard of flame and would soon erupt into a fireball. Bolan realized he could do only one thing to protect innocents from danger and still avoid being immolated.

The flames grew rapidly and the intensity of heat with them as the warrior whipped the wheel at the next intersection and increased speed. The Willamette River loomed ahead. Bolan felt like a fire-breathing dragon sat on his shoulder, and leaning forward in the seat did little to ease his discomfort. Some of the flame along the windshield had dissipated, but blue-white patches still burned along the hood as the paint bubbled and gave way to the intense heat of the gasoline vapors. Bolan considered rolling down his window to vent the smoke but realized that would only feed the inferno. He felt something at his elbow and risked a glance to see flames now licking through the material of the front seat. In the next moment, he knew his own body would be on fire.

The chain-link gate surrounding the entrance to a pier proved no match for Bolan's sedan, which the speedometer pegged at doing better than 80 mph. Bolan waited until the last possible minute, ensuring he had a free shot to the water, and then bailed from the vehicle. This time he had no desire to take a swim in the chilled, swift-moving waters of Portland's premier river. Bolan's body hit the macadam hard and he rolled to help absorb the impact, ending in a kneeling position in time to see his now fully engulfed sedan plunge off the end of the pier.

The vehicle had barely started its downward slide, the flames dying under the torrent of water saturating the interior, when Bolan heard the crunch of tires on gravel. He turned to see an onyx-black Buick sedan roar through the opening Bolan had made in the chain-link gate and bear down on him. The soldier jumped to his feet and rushed for the cover of a concrete light stanchion. He reached it in time to avoid being run down, then dashed from cover and headed for open ground while the driver of the sedan had to brake and get turned around.

Racing for the perimeter, Bolan glanced once behind him to see the Buick now in pursuit. He couldn't figure who would be trying to kill him, but it didn't seem they planned to give up easily. Bolan reached the chain-link fence. He went up and over with the grace of a gazelle, threw his body over the top as the barbed wire tore hungrily at his sleeves and dropped the ten feet to the other side with a graceful landing. The Executioner unleathered his Beretta 93-R as he turned and rushed for the cover of some nearby buildings. If he could get his pursuers to chase him into the labyrinth of structures, he might find a place to set up an ambush.

Bolan reached the courtyard and turned to see the sedan had made its way out of the pier lot and screeched tires on a path up the street that took it parallel with him. At one point, the window on the passenger side came down and Bolan caught the glint of light on metal. A millisecond following that the area around him came alive with sparks as bullets chewed near his heels like the snapping of a ravenous dog.

And with each passing second the shots drew closer.

CHAPTER NINETEEN

The enemy had come to him with no thought of taking prisoners, and Mack Bolan decided he would be happy to reciprocate. He continued up the sidewalk until he reached the cover of a building that stood between him and the vehicle on the street. The building looked onto a square courtyard formed by its proximity with other buildings, all of which looked onto the pier and river. Bolan thought maybe he'd backed himself into a corner when he noticed a small gap between the buildings. He rushed to it and thrashed among hedges in the dark as he wound his way through a maze that eventually brought him onto a cross street on the back side of the business complex.

Bolan took position and waited in the shadows for the enemy vehicle. A minute passed before it appeared and turned the corner less than twenty feet from where he crouched. The Executioner allowed the Buick to cruise past his location very slowly, then sprinted from cover and pursued on foot, careful to approach in the blind spot. When he reached the back door, Bolan grabbed the handle and pulled it open. An Arab in dark clothing looked at him with surprise a moment before the warrior reached in, grabbed a fistful of collar and yanked hard. The guy rolled out of the vehicle and struck his head on the concrete as Bolan jumped inside to take his place.

The driver leaned on the brakes instead of gunning it to get away, a mistake for his partner in the backseat opposite Bolan who tried to bring an Uzi into play. The Executioner shoved the SMG aside just as the hardman triggered a short burst. The rounds cut through the leather and foam seat and into the back of the front passenger. Bolan raised his pistol and triggered a single round that entered the gunner's forehead and exited the back of his head with enough force to shatter the door window, taking blood, bone and gray matter with it.

That left the driver. Bolan swung the barrel of the pistol to the front seat and stuck the muzzle against the man's head. The guy let out a small cry as the hot metal touched his scalp. He wore a neatly trimmed beard and glasses, and looked to be in his early twenties. By his dress and features, Bolan couldn't see how this crew could have been mistaken as rival members of the 18th Street gang by anyone in the Bloods. This was the type of thing he'd expect only from the JI, and he planned to work this fact to his advantage.

"I won't bother to ask if you speak English," Bolan said. "I know your masters train you to speak it fluently before sending you into the country. Now put the car in Park and kill the engine."

The man didn't move for a moment. Bolan almost could see the wheels turning in the guy's head via the rearview mirror. Common sense had to have prevailed, however, because he finally complied with Bolan's instructions.

"Who sent you? Was it Kovlun?" The man didn't say anything, so Bolan tapped the back of his head with the Beretta for emphasis. "My patience is wearing thin. I know about Kovlun and Satyev, and I know about your plans to destabilize gangs here in America. The only thing that's left, then, is whether you feel it's worth your life to protect these people. Your friends are dead and very soon this plot by the Islamic jihad will be defunct. That means the only thing left for you to decide is if you want to walk here and now or hold out for the losing team."

"How do I know you won't kill me if I talk?" the man asked, with only the barest trace of a Middle Eastern accent.

"Because I'm not a murderer," Bolan replied.

"I have murdered nobody. All I do, I do in the name of God."

"Whatever. My advice is that you turn yourself around while you still can." Bolan leaned closer to the man and hissed, "Because if you decide to get on the wrong side of me, I can guarantee you a brand-new kind of hell. So decide. Now."

"Okay, okay," he said. "What do you want to know?"

"Who sent you?" Bolan asked. "Kovlun or Satyev?"

"I don't know," the man replied quickly. "Our orders come by special courier. We got an envelope with your name and description in it. You were not difficult to find."

The fact he kept his eyes on Bolan and there was no change in the inflection of his voice told the soldier that the guy had likely told him the truth.

"The Bloods are going to declare war at midnight," Bolan said. "What does Kovlun have planned?"

"I don't know this Kovlun you talk about," the man replied.

Bolan again didn't note any deception in the man's answer, but it told him what he needed to know. This was either a case of the tail wagging the dog or Satyev and Kovlun weren't operating on the same levels. Bolan told the man, "Okay, get out."

The man looked surprised. "Y-you will not kill me?"

"I already said I wouldn't. Out."

The man got out of the car and Bolan escorted him across the street. Traffic was nonexistent in this part of town, since it was mostly factories and dockside areas. Very few businesses here catered to tourists, and there were no residential areas to speak of. Bolan made the guy lie on the sidewalk with his hands behind him. He snapped two pairs of plastic riot cuffs around his wrists and attached the other ends to a parking meter. He then positioned a third pair around the man's feet, bent his legs back and hog-tied him to the pole by intertwining the feet cuffs with those around his hands.

Bolan returned to the Buick. He dragged out the bodies of the other three and dumped them near the prisoner, then, as he headed back to the car to fire up the engine and get away from there as fast as possible, told the man, "I'll send someone to pick you up soon."

This hadn't gone down at all like Bolan initially thought it would. He figured Kovlun found out about his involvement, tracked his flight from Russia and sent a band of SMJ goons to finish him off once and for all. Instead he was finding quite the opposite. Since the start of his mission, the attacks by both sides had been mostly random and disorganized, as if more than one pilot was at the helm. Something had happened that transcended the original deal between the SMJ and the Jemaah al-Islamiyah, and Bolan was betting he knew what.

The Executioner reached into the breast pocket of his fatigues and withdrew his cell phone. He called the number of the operator at the PPD headquarters and requested a direct patch to Brothers's unit, which had been cruising the canvas area along with a dozen or so other squads.

"Cooper," Brothers said. "You okay? We've been calling you on the radio for the last five minutes."

"I'm fine," Bolan said. "Ran into a bit of trouble with some of our friends in the JI." He gave Brothers the general location where he'd left the terrorist prisoner. "What else do you know?"

"We caught a break," Brothers replied. "That's why we were trying to contact you. Apparently, witnesses have said they know of a club where they see Kovlun regularly. It was just like you said, a rave down close to the river. Lots of crowds and lots of young people."

"Makes sense," Bolan replied. "Mixing their crews into something like that would give Kovlun and the SMJ the ability to remain inconspicuous."

"Well, we couldn't raise you so I sent all our units to that location, including SWAT."

"Call them off," Bolan said. "You don't know what you're dealing with yet."

"Cooper, this is Tilburg." Apparently the captain had joined Brothers. "We can't wait on this. We need to shut it down before the gangs go to war."

"That's the whole point, Tilburg," Bolan replied. "They want you to do that. In fact, I think they're counting on you to do that. If you send your men in there, you'll be wasting your time and resources."

"Averting a gang war could hardly be classified as a waste of time, Cooper," Tilburg replied.

"You said you were going to trust me," Bolan protested. "So trust me on this one. You need to pull back."

"No," Tilburg said with a finality in his tone that implied he had no intention of changing his mind. "We need to move. Now clear this channel, we're going to emergency communications only."

Bolan didn't reply, he simply disconnected the cell phone call. There was no way he could convince Tilburg and his men that they were playing right into Satyev's plans. Bolan understood it all too well. All these small attacks, the sending of the Kent brothers on the plane, the use of traveler's checks—all of it had been in the plans of the designer from the beginning. Satyev would never have implemented this kind of operation without accounting for every move on the part of the enemy. He was a military tactician, as was Kovlun, and had learned the nuances of war. The things they had encountered up to this point were planted to act as diversions, and even the Executioner had nearly played into the hand.

While the police threw all of their efforts into finding Kovlun and his people, the war would start and Kovlun's teams would fan the flames by providing the Bloods with something to fight against. So while Portland's finest were raiding clubs that will undoubtedly be empty, or least no longer in use by the SMJ's goons, the Bloods would be hitting targets across town in 18th Street territory—an area nowhere near the canvas zone—with Kovlun holding the match that would light a powder keg.

Bolan dialed the number to Stony Man and Kurtzman answered. "Bear, it's Striker. Things went south with Portland PD. I need you to get into their system and get me some intelligence."

"No problem," Kurtzman replied. "I went forward with creating the interface as soon as Hal told me you'd be working with them. What do you need?"

"In the Gang Task Force's database they have files on a gang called 18th Street."

Bolan heard the clack of keys being rattled at a rate so fast it sounded almost as if one uniform noise. A moment later Kurtzman said, "Got it here. What do you need?"

"Name of their leader and a last known address."

"Leader's name is Javier Villar." Kurtzman gave him the address.

"Got it," Bolan said. "And pass a message to Hal for me. Let him know that Satyev's been using decoys to draw Tilburg's people offside. And I think Kovlun doesn't know anything about it."

"Looks like maybe Kovlun's marching to a different tune, eh?"

"Looks like," Bolan replied. "And they're leading Tilburg's people around by the nose. I almost fell for it until an anonymous party sent a JI hit team to take me out."

"Okay," Kurtzman said. "But I don't get the connection."

"It's simple," Bolan replied. "Kovlun probably didn't figure me to be any sort of a real threat. Everything they initiated back in Russia was based solely on their desire to eliminate Rostov and Cherenko. But once Satyev learned I was here and working with the cops, I became a potential threat."

"I get it now," Kurtzman said. "Satyev sees his deal's being threatened, so he puts a bug in the ear of the JI, and they rub you out before we realize he's had you and the task force chasing your tails."

"Right," Bolan says. "Meanwhile it's business as usual for Kovlun, who obviously has no idea I'm even here."

"It wouldn't be in Satyev's best interests to tell him."

"Right again."

"That's sharp thinking, Striker," Kurtzman said. "And I understand your concern that this puts Portland PD on a dead-end trail. I'll let Hal know. Maybe he can make some calls, shake down a few of Tilburg's highers-ups."

"Let's hope so," Bolan said. "Or we're going to have a lot more dead, and there's a good chance some police officers will be among them."

"So you figure they'll try to take out the head of 18th Street?"

"It only makes sense," Bolan replied. "The official declaration of war kicks off in less than thirty minutes. They'll want justice for Luther Medford. Gang thinking has always been along the lines of an eye for an eye. I think the fireworks will start right away, and that means one of the things the Bloods attempt is a hit on Villar."

"Sure, but I'm betting 18th Street knows that. Don't you think they'll move Villar to protect him?"

"Most likely," Bolan said. "And I'm sure the Bloods understand that, too. But I don't think the SMJ will figure it that way. They'll want men in place to make it look good. Remember, they're doing this for show. They don't have a stake in either side winning, only in keeping both sides in the fight."

"So you're hoping to get there first to neutralize the situation."

"Yeah, but it's not the situation I plan to neutralize," the Executioner replied. "It's the SMJ."

BOLAN DROVE TO Villar's neighborhood, a posh suburb bordering the west side of Portland, and parked his car two blocks from the 18th Street leader's house.

He went EVA with only the Beretta and Desert Eagle as companions, and one of the Uzis provided courtesy of the JI, since the heavier weapons he'd brought now rested at the bottom of the Willamette River. Bolan packed all the spare clips he could in the various pockets of his fatigues and located an alley that ran between the residences along that block. He could only guess that Kovlun's men were already in position, waiting for the Bloods to arrive. Bolan knew that Villar and his people would have abandoned the residence as soon as they received word Medford had been gunned down.

In one respect, it surprised Bolan the 18th Street hadn't tried to contact the Bloods, let them know they didn't have anything to do with it, but then he realized they probably wouldn't have bothered. There's no way they would believe 18th Street innocent of the crime, especially since Kovlun's people had gone to great lengths in ensuring their people committed their atrocities in public view while wearing 18th Street colors. That was the one thing those who didn't fight in the trenches every day failed to realize—the precarious and uneasy peace that existed between gangs could fall apart at any moment. Although gangs these days were interested more in making money than in violence, there were still rites of initiation that were just as public and violent as they had once been. It was more important gang members be good earners than soldiers. The highest gang leadership had come to learn that in a capitalist America, the more money they made the more powerful their gang would become, and the more influence it would have on the decision-makers.

These days, gangs had become the new organized crime to the point the federal government could now put gang members on trial for racketeering violations. That had been somewhat of a deterrent for the less powerful gangs in suburban areas, but most large cities in America were still replete with gang violence and activities. That's when men like Bolan were the only answer. But this new threat went far beyond anyone's biggest nightmare. Now there were Islamic terrorists putting weapons in the hands of gang members, spurring them on to cross territorial lines and bringing war to their own streets.

The Executioner vowed to make sure that didn't happen. Ever.

Bolan made his way down the alley until he came on Villar's house. A ten-foot-high wall topped with barbed wire ringed the estate, and Bolan noted cameras at each corner. He walked along the rear wall until he came to a wrought-iron gate nearly as high as the wall. Bolan noticed the gate sat ajar, and he had to lean in to find the metal still hot around a section where the lock had been cut away by an acetylene torch. Bolan was careful not to touch the hot metal as he squeezed through the opening and crouched just inside. His eyes had adjusted to the gloom. The house was fully lit—probably an attempt to make it look occupied—but Bolan detected no signs of life. If people waited inside the house, they had chosen to remain concealed.

Bolan rose and started forward but froze in his tracks at the first sign of movement. He crouched and watched with interest as two men burst from a hedge bordering the property and dashed across lawn until they reached a small retaining wall near the massive back patio. Bolan thought about hitting them there but decided to wait for their next move. He didn't wait long. Several more pairs of SMJ soldiers followed suit, each in classic fire team movement, and congregated at the wall.

Obviously they had designated this as a rally point.

Bolan considered his options as he watched the unit of eight leave cover and make for the rear doors. The Executioner marveled that the SMJ gunners would have been sloppy enough not to cover their flanks, although he wasn't going to look a gift horse in the mouth. He supposed it shouldn't have surprised him. Kovlun's people hadn't figured anyone would be around to stop them, especially since they were assuming the cops were on the other side of the city and probably had already hit the club. Bolan could see the expressions on their faces when Tilburg's people realized the SMJ had duped them.

Well, they had refused to listen to him and there wasn't anything he could do about it now.

As soon as the first SMJ force made entry to the house, a second team of four congregated at the patio wall, obviously waiting for some arranged signal. Bolan decided it wouldn't be wise to wait any longer. If he was going to hit them, it had to be now and it had to be fast. Bolan glanced at his watch and realized the irony of the moment as he noted it was seconds before midnight. He jumped to his feet and sprinted across the massive lawn directly for the enemy's position, Uzi held low and at the ready.

Yeah, war had just been declared all right.

The Executioner's war.

CHAPTER TWENTY

The SMJ fire team whirled on hearing Bolan's approach, but the gunners were unprepared for the encounter.

Bolan triggered a short burst from the Uzi when he got within ten yards of the group, drilling one gunner through the chest. The impact knocked him off his feet and slammed him into a dormant flower bed behind the retaining wall the crew had used as cover. The remaining trio fired on Bolan, but he'd already changed direction and fired again, three rounds cutting through the stomach of one opponent while a fourth cored the side of an SMJ soldier's neck.

Bolan shoulder-rolled to cover behind an inert fountain as the last gunner opened up on full-auto. Rounds buzzed over his head while others chipped pieces of decorative stone from the fountain. Bolan rolled clear on the other side on one knee, leveled the Uzi and triggered a reply that chopped the man's belly to shreds. The man subsequently spun and triggered a few shots skyward before collapsing to the manicured lawn.

The Executioner regained his feet and sprinted up the flagstone steps to the sliding back door where the first fire team had made entry. He had nearly reached it when one of the enemy gunners appeared in the doorway. The youth looked a bit surprised, probably expecting to see his comrades standing over the bleeding bodies of members from the Bloods instead of the specterlike form of the Executioner heading toward him with determined fury. That brief pause cost the young militant his life as Bolan dispatched him with a short burst from the Uzi. Three rounds slammed into his chest and drove the gunner into the drywall behind him with enough force to crack it. He slid to the floor, leaving a messy streak of blood in his wake.

Bolan stuck his head through the doorway and looked in both directions on an empty hallway. He waited a moment and listened, conscious the others might be setting up an ambush. After nearly a minute he stepped inside, then closed and secured the sliding door behind him. He didn't intend for any of them to get away. The only people leaving this house alive were innocent bystanders and Bolan. The SMJ had signed its death warrant by coming here. The Executioner lifted a radio from the body of the SMJ hood, then proceeded silently along the hallway, Uzi held at the ready. He stopped every so often and detected the patter of feet on the floors above. The SMJ fire team had spread out and was obviously conducting a room-by-room search. Bolan surmised they wouldn't find anything.

He wondered for a moment why they hadn't called to check on their compatriots, but then he remembered that these were young militants with little experience. They had expected to go up against the Bloods, which means they had expected potential losses. Bolan had noticed that SMJ youths were wearing 18th Street colors, although he couldn't figure how they expected to be convincing since none of them looked Hispanic. Then again, they only needed to make it appear as if they were from the rival gang; their plans didn't require them to be more convincing than that. If the Bloods believed they were fighting rival gangbangers, that was enough for Kovlun's people to achieve their ends. After that, it became the JI's problem.

A voice came over the radio in Russian, apparently demanding some sort of update. So they hadn't gone to such levels of detail as speaking in Spanish or English. It would also be less likely someone would know what they were saying in the event law enforcement or ham radio enthusiasts happened upon their frequency. It would sound like so much babble, kids goofing around, and they wouldn't pay it much mind. Who would suspect Russian militants conducting operations against gangs in urban America? The very idea would have seemed ludicrous, which only spoke of the rather ingenious plan Satyev had put together for the JI.

Bolan continued down the hallway until he reached a break that opened onto a large entertainment room. He spotted a pinball machine against one wall and a massive 102-inch plasma television mounted above the mantel of a fireplace. There was also a complex computer system, along with plenty of leather seating. The decor itself spoke to the Hispanic origins of its owner.

The soldier swept the room with the muzzle of the Uzi before proceeding. He was halfway across the massive room when he heard the thunderous hammer of footfalls on stairs to his left. Bolan knelt and raised the

Uzi to eye level, cheek pressed to the receiver and the wire stock tight against his shoulder. An SMJ soldier rounded the corner a moment later and raised his own weapon, but Bolan easily had the drop on him. The Executioner triggered a short burst that blew the youth's skull apart and dumped him on his back. Bolan rose and gave the body only a cursory glance as he stepped past, careful not to step in the pool of blood rapidly collecting around the corpse.

He started with a count of twelve and within two minutes he had reduced their force by fifty percent. Bolan felt a pang of regret in one sense; these SMJ inductees were nowhere near equally matched with a soldier of Bolan's experience and caliber. The Executioner counted one measure of thanks in that they weren't any younger than this, although teenagers with guns were no less dangerous than adults. Still, he didn't want the deaths of such young people on his conscience, regardless of the fact they had made their decision the moment they decided to fight for an ideal that had long passed with history. Bolan tried not to take it personally. This was self-defense by means of tactical offense, and it was necessary to diffuse a situation that could potentially lead to bloodshed on a massive scale. What angered Bolan was that many of these impressionable young people were victims themselves—victims of the venom and ideology of men like Kovlun and Satyev.

Bolan reached the stairs and hit the second floor at full speed, aware the gunfire inside the house would draw the remaining SMJ gunners to investigate. One pair burst through a door at the far end of the hallway and immediately triggered their SMGs. Bolan went prone and rolled in time to avoid the angry buzz of rounds that burned the air where he'd stood a moment before. He reached a closed door, tried the handle and found it locked, then put his foot to it. The door gave and Bolan made it inside as a fresh maelstrom of lead chewed up the floor and wall.

The soldier waited for a lull in the fire, then leaned out and spotted the pair attempting to reload. He raised the Uzi and triggered a burst that caught one across the knees. The guy dropped his weapon and collapsed to the carpet, writhing and screaming in pain as he tried to stem the torrent of blood that flowed from the bullet wounds. The second youth managed to get a magazine into the well of his SMG before Bolan caught him with a 4-round sweep from belly to throat. The target's weapon sprang from his fingers, his body stiffened and he toppled prone to the floor with a heavy thud.

Bolan whirled as two more SMJ gunmen rushed down the steps and burst onto the second-floor landing. Their weapons were held at the ready, but they hadn't expected to become engaged with a formidable enemy like Bolan. The Executioner brushed the trigger of the Uzi once more and hammered the pair with a sustained burst, sweeping them with a shower of hot lead. The heat and smells of burned gunpowder blasted up into his face with the proximity of the weapon, and Bolan's ears rang with reports as flame spit from the muzzle and the 9 mm slugs ripped through flesh, bone and tissue. The pair danced under the assault like puppets on strings and crumpled to the floor when the hammer locked back on an empty chamber.

Bolan tossed the spent weapon and drew the .44 Magnum Desert Eagle as he got to his feet. He stepped over the bodies and headed up the stairs to the top floor. It didn't take long to find the last two SMJ gunners. They tried to ambush him by waiting until he walked down the hallway before they emerged from behind closed doors, but they failed to time it correctly. Bolan heard the first door open behind him, turned and knelt. The SMJ gunner stepped into the hall and raised his weapon just as the second door opened and his partner jumped into the fray. He also jumped right into the line of his comrade's fire, and the rounds meant for Bolan were absorbed by his overeager enemy, giving the warrior enough time to raise his pistol and deliver a double tap to the shooter's chest. Twin rounds of .300-grain hardball blew the SMJ hood's chest wide open and the back pressure collapsed both lungs. The gunner fell to the carpet with a final gurgle of life.

As Bolan got slowly to his feet he heard the screech of vehicles outside. He rushed back to the stairs and descended to the midflight landing where a small, crescent-shaped window afforded a view onto the street below. An angry swarm of black combatants wearing the colors of the Bloods piled from an assortment of vehicles and made their way up the drive behind what looked like an armored SUV. The lead vehicle plowed through the wrought-iron front gate and roared up the drive with a plethora of foot soldiers bringing up the rear.

Time to go.

Bolan descended the steps and retreated via the same back entrance through which he'd gained egress. Hopefully, he'd accounted for all of Kovlun's goons. The Bloods would be very surprised to find the job they had hoped to do was already done for them to a degree, and maybe—just maybe—that would give them enough pause to consider what might be happening. If nothing else, Bolan had bought himself time enough to finish what the SMJ and JI had started. Bolan knew it would be impossible for the Bloods and 18th Street to do battle if they never came into contact with each other. And if good fortune would smile on Mack Bolan just a little bit longer, the conflict would stop here in Portland and go no further.

All he needed was a little more time.

CAPTAIN ROBIN TILBURG couldn't believe his hard luck.

Once the teams were in position, Tilburg gave the order and every member of the gang task force—along with a dozen or so uniforms and a fully equipped SWAT unit—entered the rave club and contained the young rabble-rousers without firing a single shot. Eventually they found a hidden entrance leading to the basement where they discovered a comprehensive armory, firing range, bunks, recreation area and even a full kitchen. There was plenty of evidence to point to the fact Jurg Kovlun had set up shop here, but it looked as if the place had been abandoned.

"How long ago?" he asked Brothers as they sent most of the party-goers home to their parents, keeping a select few in custody for further questioning.

"Difficult to say," Brothers said. "Could've been a few hours, could've been a month."

"No clues as to what they might have in mind?"

"Not a thing, Rob," Brothers had said. "I'm sorry. If it's okay with you, I'm going to head down to HQ and see to the processing of the few we have in custody."

After Brothers had left, Tilburg leaned against his

unmarked police unit and folded his arms as he looked over the front of the club. Finally he slammed his fist into his palm and cursed. He knew it was his own damn fault. Cooper had tried to warn him this was a dead end but he'd refused to listen. Now they were up a creek without a paddle and the trouble was only starting. Already he could hear calls over the radio asking for any available units to respond to reports of gunfire at a residence on the west side of town on the border of Portland and the suburbs. Tilburg knew the neighborhood: 18th Street territory.

He reached through the open window of his unit and grabbed the radio microphone. "Dispatch, this is Tilburg. I want a report of what's going on there as soon as possible."

"Roger that, Two-David-Six," the dispatcher's voice replied crisply.

Tilburg threw the radio microphone on the seat with a disgusted wheeze and turned to see a black, late-model Buick winding its way through the parade of squad cars and unmarked units scattered along the street for half a block in either direction. He didn't recognize the vehicle, but he sure as hell recognized the driver when his head appeared over the top of the sedan.

"Cooper!" he shouted. "Where the hell've *you* been?"

"Didn't find anything, did you?" Bolan asked.

"No," Tilburg said as he shoved his hands into the pockets of his police-issue jacket to keep them warm. "Why?"

"Because I just left the house where your guys are headed. They're not going to find anything but about a dozen dead terrorists."

"Oh, really? How do you know that?"

"Better you don't know," Bolan replied as he stopped to stand in front of Tilburg.

The big cop looked his ally in the eyes and scowled. At first he'd taken a bit of a shine to Cooper, but now he was starting to dislike the guy.

"This shouldn't have gone down like this," Tilburg said.

"You're right."

"You know, Cooper, at first I thought we really had something when you cracked Harris to get to Ruemont and brought back a witness who could lock up a whole bunch of bad guys in this city. But since you arrived the body count has nearly doubled. I got a guy locked up down at the station who isn't even from this country, three more just like him who are taking up space at a morgue that's already filled to capacity. Now you tell me I got twelve more homicides just waiting in the heart of 18th Street territory. I thought you were here to help me on this stuff, goddamn it!"

Bolan's eyes narrowed. "You finished?"

"Hardly," Tilburg replied with a snort. He looked around Bolan and made a show of studying the Buick. "And that's not one of ours. Where the hell's the police vehicle we loaned you?"

"At the bottom of the river a few blocks from here. I owe you a new car."

"Yeah, well *some*-damn-body sure as hell owes us a new car," Tilburg said. "It isn't coming out of my budget. This little stunt's already costing the department a fortune."

"Don't be a bureaucrat, Captain," Bolan replied. "It's not in your nature."

"How the hell would you know my nature?"

Bolan smiled. "Simple. You're a cop, through-and-through. I read your file before I ever showed up. Your bosses downtown couldn't have picked a better man to lead this task force. You've single-handedly kept the peace here for the past few years between two rival gangs, something I know couldn't have been easy. And whether you believe it or not, I *am* here to help you."

Tilburg cocked his head and looked at Bolan out of the corner of his eye as he wiped a hand across his mouth. Finally he looked at the ground, shook his head with a husky laugh and pulled a pack of cigarettes from his coat. He tapped one out, offered one to Bolan who declined, and then fired it up and noisily let go with gust a smoke.

"I don't know how the hell I get into these things. All right… Tell me what you know."

"All of what we've been doing, the whole wild-goose chase we went on and the JI assassins sent to hit me, they were all for the purpose of stalling. It wouldn't surprise me if the hit wasn't even a ruse. And I'm guessing that what happened in 18th Street territory isn't the last we'll hear of it."

"How do you figure?"

"You didn't find them here," Bolan said.

"No." Tilburg shook his head as he took a drag, and then replied, "We didn't find squat. They were using the basement of this club as a base of operations. They had full gun range and quarters underneath the place. The works, really. But we didn't find a damn thing in the way of information. Brothers isn't even sure how long they've been gone."

"I wouldn't guess more than a few hours. How many do you think the place could hold?"

"At least forty, maybe more if they packed it in tight."

"And since there are only about a dozen accounted for we know of," Bolan said, "that leaves another thirty or so unaccounted for."

"You think you know where they might be operating?"

"I don't have a clue," Bolan replied truthfully. "But I'm fairly confident that none of it up until this point had been the real design behind this. I think Anatoly Satyev is manipulating Jurg Kovlun and his trainees to meet his own purposes and interests. I think Kovlun suspects this, and I believe once he completes this operation he may go rogue."

"Then what do you think Satyev really wants?"

"I'm not sure about that yet, but I'm sure it has something to do with JI, as I'm equally confident we need to be ready wherever Kovlun's people strike next. We can't afford to let them leave this city intact. That'll force me into a two-front war, and as I'm sure you can guess there's very little to be gained in that kind of fight. Especially for the good guys."

Tilburg nodded. "Hell, I may not approve of your methods, but I can't argue the fact it sounds like you're speaking from experience. You really *have* been around the block a few times, haven't you?"

Bolan nodded. "I've had my fair share of this business."

"So you say we wait?"

"Yeah. We wait."

CHAPTER TWENTY-ONE

Anatoly Satyev slammed the handset into the cradle of the telephone and cursed.

While the majority of his plans to divert the attention of the authorities had worked so far, the American managed to escape from the hit team the JI had sent after Satyev advised them of the threat he believed Matt Cooper posed. That wasn't good, especially in light of the fact that somewhere out there Leonid Rostov and Sergei Cherenko were still alive. In fact, they were probably pouring their weak and pathetic hearts out to American officials, telling them everything they knew about the Sevooborot and the operations Satyev had planned in America.

But that thought didn't disgust him half as much as the idea that Kovlun had plans to step out on him once the operation had been completed in Portland. The news he'd just heard from Mikhail Pilkin made him wonder who the real traitors in the organization were. Pilkin had sworn his allegiance to Satyev, even offered to kill Kovlun when the time was right, but not cheaply.

Pilkin had demanded payment of one million U.S. dollars in small notes, deliverable on confirmation of Kovlun's death. What's worse, Satyev had actually agreed to pay the bloodsucking opportunist.

Oh, Jurg, where did I go wrong with you? he thought.

It was a good thing Satyev had developed a policy early in his career with the Soviet army not to trust anyone, and that included the people working for him, especially the people working for him. This new development would require action on his part, but since Kovlun seemed to have the majority of manpower under his control and some time would pass before Pilkin eliminated him, Satyev would have to rely on the JI's assistance. They wouldn't be happy when they got the report that four of their best men had failed. It was neither cheap nor easy to smuggle operatives into the country since the increased security, and the loss in resources every time one of their men fell could be felt, even by an organization that enjoyed funding by al Qaeda.

Well, he couldn't do anything about it now. His partnership with the JI had become precarious, at best, and he knew he'd have to sever that relationship as soon as possible. It had no longer become profitable for him to continue his operations. A transfer to his residence on Catalina Island would be in order soon enough, although not until he'd concluded his meeting with representatives from the JI. Even now, they were on their way and would arrive very soon. It would be the first and only time, if Satyev had anything to say about it, that they would conduct their business dealings in person.

Satyev had never wanted this meeting to begin with. He preferred to let others represent his interests, while he carefully guided them behind the scenes, and maintain the aura of mystery. Unfortunately the leader of the terrorist cell representing the JI's interests here in the United States didn't feel that way, and so they had finally come to the decision after Satyev's call advising they needed to eliminate Matt Cooper, that it was time for a personal meeting. Satyev took a small measure of comfort that they were able to conduct the meeting at his home, although he wasn't sure he liked the idea of the JI knowing where he lived. Not that he couldn't pack up and move to a more secure location on a moment's notice.

For the moment, he would remain where he was if for no other reason than to maintain appearances.

One of the housemen rapped on the door of his study before stepping in and announcing his guests had arrived. Satyev acknowledged him and asked the men be shown into his study and he would join them shortly. When he had departed, Satyev returned his attention to his computer and drafted a quick message that would transmit encoded to Pilkin's cell phone. It was an order to proceed with the plan they had discussed at the right time, with additional instructions to see what he could find out about the location of Rostov and Cherenko. At this point, it never hurt to have an insurance policy.

His work completed, Satyev then proceeded to the study where several men waited. A couple were dressed in plain, dark suits and carried themselves in such a way that Satyev knew they were security for the man who had seated himself on an ornate settee. This man carried himself quite differently, the air of authority seeming to rise off him like a bad odor. His eyes were intensely dark and his hair as black as night, set into a medium, almost bronzelike complexion. He wore slacks and a button shirt open at the collar over a wiry body. His hands were unusually large and despite the power he wielded, not to mention his obvious distaste for any ethnicity or way of life other than his own, he managed to demonstrate a smile of goodwill on seeing Satyev enter the room.

Satyev stepped forward and extended a hand. "Nurjaman al-Habshi. It is a pleasure to meet you."

"Colonel Satyev," al-Habshi replied in flawless English, as they had agreed to speak in a neutral tongue. He stood and shook Satyev's hand. "Indeed, I am honored to meet you, as well. Our contacts in Russia speak very highly of your efforts to assist the jihad."

"Please, sit," Satyev said, and he gestured toward the settee. Satyev took a wingback chair directly across from the settee that purposely sat higher than any other chair in the parlor. He wanted to establish psychological dominance immediately, and he'd read somewhere this was one of the ways to do it. "Would you like something to drink?"

"Coffee, if you please."

"And for your men?" After al-Habshi shook his head, Satyev gestured to a waiting servant who departed hastily to do his bidding.

"This reminds me, that your men required my bodyguards to hand over their sidearms before they would permit us entry," al-Habshi said. "I was wondering why you would do this. After all, I had understood that we were building a relationship of trust here."

"And so we are," Satyev said. "Do not take this personally, Mr. al-Habshi. But I do not permit anyone to enter my house with a firearm other than my security staff. I detest the things, really."

Al-Habshi's smile was crafty at best. "A surprise, to be sure, coming from a military man."

"Do you know what I did in the Soviet army?" Satyev asked, but then quickly followed with, "But of course you do. What a foolish question. I'm sure you know just about everything there is to know about me by now."

Al-Habshi inclined his head.

Satyev continued, "Then you know that I was in logistics and intelligence. I did no real fighting, although I have fully trained in a martial arts known as *sambo*, and I am quite proficient with firearms. I do, however, believe in a philosophy of nonviolence to achieve most ends."

"A worthwhile goal," al-Habshi replied, "if somewhat of a lofty one. Oh, I mean no offense. But after many years spent in this country I have come to believe that what we set out to do, and the reasons for which we do it, are almost never what we end up achieving."

"It's strange you should say that," Satyev replied. "Considering that your particular religion is one whose beliefs are founded on matters of faith and optimism."

"Believing in God does not necessarily mean one cannot be a realist."

"And that is what you consider yourself? A realist?"

"Let us just say, Colonel, that I consider myself to be a practical man on certain matters. Take our relationship, for example. While I tell you that our contacts speak highly of you, I know you are not a man of purely altruistic objectives. I know that deep in your soul you have your own goals and desires, and that it is quite unlikely you would not hesitate to cut my throat right here in order to achieve them if times required it.

"Ah, I see you look surprised. That's good. That tells me my assumptions were correct. It's quite all right, though. Your secret is safe with me. To be completely honest, I do not care what your plans are for the future or your objectives, as long as you do nothing to interfere with our plans to destabilize the West. You can become dictator, even emperor, over a new communist Russia if that is your desire. In fact, such a relationship would then benefit the Jemaah al-Islamiyah even more. However, I cannot ignore the recent and most disturbing reports I have received regarding your operations in Portland."

Satyev crossed his legs and folded his arms. "And what reports, might I ask, are those?"

"I have heard we lost our men who I sent to eliminate the American, this Matt Cooper." When Satyev stiffened, al-Habshi continued quickly, "Oh, don't let it trouble you. It was my decision to send them to do your dirty work. I would not have done this if I weren't prepared to lose them."

"Your professionalism in this matter is appreciable."

"Maybe," al-Habshi replied. The arrival of the coffee interrupted their conversation and so they turned to small talk while the maid served them. Once she'd left the room, al-Habshi continued, "What's happened in Portland seems to indicate to us that you no longer have control of the situation."

"That seems rather presumptuous of you."

"Does it?" Al-Habshi sipped at his coffee, nodded with satisfaction. "This is quite delicious. An Indochinese blend if I'm not mistaken."

"Yes. I acquired it especially for this occasion as I knew you would appreciate it."

Al-Habshi inclined his head in way of thanks. "Perhaps you disagree with me regarding the current situation in Portland. But it will surprise you also to know that I've heard this American took out more than a dozen of your men. One of my own is in police custody, which will now require me to expose our potential operations in that area by sending an attorney to represent him. If we cannot free him through the legal system, we will have to employ…well, let us say more tried methods of retrieval. We stand to be put at considerable inconvenience for this."

The news of a dozen or more of the trainees being killed troubled Satyev, but he knew he couldn't show the smallest sign of weakness. He had to pretend he knew about this and act as if he'd almost expected losses. Like Nurjaman al-Habshi, he had to understand that he couldn't send armed militants to a job without accepting the fact that losses were an all too real possibility. Although he hadn't quite expected to come up against a man like Matt Cooper. Kovlun had trained his people to fight against young gangbangers and police, not a highly trained commando with specialized equipment, resources and significant firepower at his disposal.

"It seems from what happened first in Murmansk, and now in Portland, that this American operative has become a source of trouble for us. It's no longer feasible to continue with the operations until he is dealt with. So, it shall become our first and only objective to eliminate this Cooper before we can allow you to proceed to the other locations. In the meantime, you need to take care of the internal problems with your organization. You have a bit of a mess among your ranks, or at least it seems that way to us, and I want it handled."

Satyev didn't know what to say to that. How the hell could al-Habshi have known about Kovlun's intent to cut and run unless they had spies inside the training units? So the JI had put a Russian informant on their payroll, perhaps more than one. Obviously, since they knew about some of Kovlun's people getting killed and Satyev didn't. Why hadn't Pilkin reported this to him?

"What about Rostov and Cherenko?" Satyev asked. "They still have information about this operation."

"That is not our problem," al-Habshi said. "It's up to you to deal with that. Our part will be to assassinate Cooper. Nothing more. We have met all of our other obligations to you. In fact, I view this particular item with the American as a simple favor, a gesture of good faith between us."

"Very well. I will take care of our issues immediately. In fact, I've already taken steps to make sure this is handled."

"Good." Al-Habshi stood and extended his hand. "Then I'm sure you'll understand that I must be going now. But it has been a pleasure meeting you. I look forward to a prosperous business relationship."

Satyev rose and took the man's hand again. "You cannot stay and eat? I have arranged for supper, albeit a very late one."

Al-Habshi shook his head. "I have a strict dietary regimen. A calling of my duties to Islam."

Satyev escorted his guest to the door and as it opened, al-Habshi turned to him and said, "I have your assurances you will clear up the matters on your end?"

"Of course."

"That's fine. I feel as if we have reached a new level in our relationship, and I would not want to have to report to my superiors that your performance doesn't indicate you are keeping your end of the bargain."

"Forgive me for saying so, but that sounds a little like a threat."

"Does it?" Al-Habshi shook his head and smiled. "I certainly did not mean for it to sound like that, Colonel. I was merely attempting to state the facts of the matter. Like you, I believe in maintaining forthrightness and honesty in my business dealings. It is never intended to be personal."

Satyev smiled, doing as much as he could to keep the friendliness in it. He didn't like al-Habshi. He hardly knew the guy and he didn't like him; he didn't like the man's condescending tone and he didn't like his implications. His original assessment that the relationship had become a matter of some inconvenience weighed heavily on his mind. There wouldn't be any easy way to break it off, Satyev knew, but it would have to be done. There were certainly other ways to accomplish his overall objectives—he didn't need the Jemaah al-Islamiyah's help do to that any more than he needed Kovlun. In fact, Anatoly Satyev didn't need anyone. He could easily complete this on his own.

"I will keep that in mind," Satyev told him, and he didn't even bother to show al-Habshi personally to the door, instead assigning the task to his bodyguards.

Once they were gone, Satyev retreated to his study. He needed to think, and that was the one place where he could think most clearly. He lit a cigarette, poured himself a drink from a snifter of cognac and sat at his desk for a time. At last, after running it through his mind, he knew what he had to do. To protect his assets he would need trained professionals. There was only one person who could provide them, and while he knew Pilkin would probably double his price for the effort, the shift in the balance of power would be the only way he could protect his investments.

Satyev picked up the phone and dialed Pilkin's number. It rang twice before he answered.

"Are you alone?" Satyev asked.

"No."

"Get somewhere you can talk and call me back."

"Understood," Pilkin replied and hung up.

Five minutes passed, ten minutes, and finally the phone on his desk rang—a personal number he'd given to only a few.

"I'm alone," Pilkin said.

"We have a problem. I just met with the JI's representative and they're starting to get restless. They know about our little problem internally, which tells me they have a spy in your midst. Do you have any idea who it might be?"

"Perhaps," Pilkin replied. "Although I cannot be totally sure of it."

"Well, then, you need to get sure. Understand? If we don't shut down their network inside our people soon, we're going to have many more problems to deal with. They no longer wish for us to proceed, which means I need to use the teams for other, more important efforts."

"Such as?"

"We need to locate Rostov and Cherenko."

"They're here?"

"Yes," Satyev replied. "The American named Cooper managed to get out them out of Russia and back here to the United States. I'm putting my connections to work now to figure out where he might have secured them."

"But I thought that our people were going to make sure he didn't leave alive."

"Well, they obviously failed!" Satyev realized he was letting the stress get to him, showing his irritation to the hired help, and that was never good for a leader. He had to keep himself under control at all times if he wanted to instill confidence in his followers. "But we shall not fail. The JI have promised to eliminate Cooper, but they have indicated the traitors are *my* problem. Therefore, that makes them *your* problem."

"So our other mission has been deferred."

"For the time being. We must take care of Rostov and Cherenko first. They know too much to be left alive."

"Okay. You know, of course, this will cost you more. Our original agreement did not stipulate I would have to take leadership of the team."

"I'm willing to triple the original offer. No more."

"Three million? I believe that's fair."

"You're a blood-sucking pig, Mikhail." Satyev spit.

"Maybe so, Colonel," Pilkin replied with a short laugh. "But you must admit that I know how to get results. Much better results than Jurg has brought you."

"Just make sure that you take care of that problem, too," Satyev reminded him. "And I want a full report every four hours."

"That seems a bit much, Colonel. If you don't mind my saying."

"I do mind. You're being paid plenty to take care of this, Mikhail. And if you are successful, and you *will* be successful, there are other opportunities to be had."

Satyev knew how to sweeten the pot. Mikhail Pilkin might have been purely mercenary in his dealings with his countrymen, but he got the picture. Other opportunities spelled more money, and that's what motivated Pilkin. In some respects, that made him much easier to control than Kovlun had ever been. He was younger, more impressionable and idealistic, and yet less prone to buy into all the propaganda that his peers seemed to eat up. A surprise, considering the Sevooborot was all Pilkin had ever really known.

"I understand, Colonel. You have my assurances I will have a complete resolution to your problems within twenty-four hours."

"I look forward to it," Satyev replied.

CHAPTER TWENTY-TWO

"That's it," Mack Bolan announced.

Tilburg looked at the Executioner with a modicum of surprise etched into his expression. "The security company reporting suspicious activity at a warehouse?"

Bolan nodded. "That's what we've been waiting for."

"How do you know?"

"I know," Bolan replied as he headed toward the Buick.

"Hold up a minute," Tilburg said. "I'll come with you."

"No dice, Captain," Bolan replied. "I have to go it alone on this one."

"Nobody *has* to go it alone, Cooper," Tilburg said. He reached through the window of his squad car, popped the trunk and withdrew a pair of police-issued Colt AR-15A3 Tactical Carbine rifles. Bolan recognized the weapon instantly, with its telescopic butt that could adjust to four positions and sixteen-inch heavy barrel. Unlike the civil variant that chambered .223 Remington, the AR-15A3 fired 5.56 mm in M193 ball ammunition or NATO SS109, either of which would prove more than adequate for the job at hand.

"We'll need to stop by the armory and get some spare ammo for this," Tilburg said, gesturing with one of the AR-15A3s.

"I can see I'm not going to talk you out of this," Bolan said as he climbed behind the Buick's wheel and Tilburg took shotgun seat.

"Not on your life."

Bolan started the engine with a grin and said, "All right, but don't forget what happened the last time you wouldn't listen to me."

"Listen, Cooper, I was wrong about before and I apologize. I've known some men like you. Not many, but I've known them and I understand them."

"That right?"

"Yeah," he said. "I served with plenty of them in the Marine Corps. Even was one myself in the mideighties."

"Where'd you serve?"

"Beirut," Tilburg replied. "So I know a fighter when I see one, and you're about the biggest recruiting poster candidate for urban commandos I've ever come across. Probably in all my years of police work. But I screwed up here and I feel a measure of personal responsibility. So I want to make it right, see, and I figure the best way I can do that is to kick ass and take names. Portland's *my* city. Christ, I grew up here. I just want to make a difference."

Tilburg was right about one thing: Bolan didn't usually let the boys in blue play tagalong on most missions. But he saw something in Robin Tilburg, and he realized the guy had just as much right to get into the thick of it as Bolan. He had a job to do, a city to protect, and he'd just figured out that Bolan was going wherever the action was, the only real place to make a difference. The Executioner wouldn't have let anybody stop him from doing that any more than he didn't have a right to stop Tilburg from fulfilling whatever he considered his destiny.

"Okay," Bolan said, raising a hand. "You've made your case."

"Glad to hear it."

"As long as you realize we play by my rules on this," Bolan said. "It's not likely I'm going there to arrest anybody. Understand that if you don't understand anything else, Tilburg. I'm going there to finish these guys. Period."

"I understand. Why do you think I brought the rifles?"

A bulletin came over the radio from one of the stationary units watching a Bloods hangout. Fifteen or so of the Bloods crew had left in vehicles that appeared to be headed in the general direction of the warehouse.

"Looks like you were right," Tilburg said. He held the portable radio close to his mouth and said, "Two-David-Six to Dispatch, all units should hold position. Do not, I repeat *do not* engage hostiles until I've arrived."

There was a moment of silence, then, "Two-David-Six, assistant chief is requesting you give him a twenty-one to advise the reason for holding up response."

"Because I'm the head of the gang task force and this is a gang-related incident, which makes me the incident commander. And I don't have my phone with me, so advise the assistant chief I can't twenty-one him. Now give the order."

As the dispatcher replied in the affirmative and gave the order to stand down, Tilburg muttered, "I'll probably lose my badge over this."

"Probably," Bolan said.

"But it takes more courage to do what's right than what the bureaucrats tell me to do. Bunch of wiseass politicians sitting behind their desks, thinking they can solve all this city's problems by waving some sort of magic wand at it. And all the criminals do is take that wand, break it over their knees and shove the pieces up the collective asses of our department."

Bolan cast a sideways glance at Tilburg. "There's an image."

Tilburg snorted. "It's true. I'm tired of sitting on my hands like a frightened hen while these guys chew up everything that's important to me. The punk rockers have already corrupted my son, and God knows what my daughter might be into these days at her college campus."

Bolan could hear that same ideology in the voice of another man, one he'd known long ago; one who had come home from the war in Southeast Asia to find the Mafia corrupting everything he'd ever known. One young, idealistic Army sniper who decided to take his own stand by laying down one war to pick up another that needed fighting—a war nobody else seemed willing to fight. So yeah, Bolan could understand a guy like Tilburg because he'd been one himself. And though the years might have matured him some— hell, the years had matured him a lot—and that man had learned a lot of important lessons, the rules hadn't changed one bit.

Mack Bolan still did what he did out of necessity.

He did it out of duty.

The news of Aleksander Briansky's death at the warehouse hadn't set well with Mikhail Pilkin.

In his mind, Jurg Kovlun was entirely to blame for Briansky's death. The guy was an arms specialist, not a soldier, and Kovlun had no business sending him to the house of the Hispanic gang leader. It should have been Pilkin who went there. Then Briansky would be alive right now, as would Pilkin, and the American would be dead—and Kovlun would have been sitting on the money promised him. Now, instead of fortune and a chance to rest, Pilkin had two things to worry about: the assassination of Jurg Kovlun and tracking down those traitors to the Sevooborot. Pilkin had to admit he felt some anticipation at the prospect of wiping Kovlun from existence. The guy had never really belonged to the Sevooborot; he always carried an air of superiority whenever he dealt with underlings, especially Pilkin and Briansky, talking down to them like they were incapable of conjuring an original thought between them.

Now, Kovlun's arrogance had led to Briansky's death and the loss of a dozen revolutionaries, a waste of life and talent that Pilkin could not and would not let go unpunished. Besides, Pilkin knew—as he felt pretty certain Satyev did—that any more foul-ups by Kovlun might very well lead to his own death. He couldn't afford to take that chance. Kovlun suffered from the biggest problem for any leader: megalomania coated by a delusion of invincibility. That's exactly the kind of thinking that had gotten Briansky killed and would surely get Pilkin dead, too, if he didn't act now.

Pilkin had ridden in silence for most of the trip from the rendezvous point where they took delivery of the arms cache to the warehouse where Kovlun awaited his arrival. During the transit, he wondered whether Kovlun had yet heard about the defeat at the house. Probably not: he'd insisted on maintaining communications silence during the operations, another silly gesture in his attempt to appear like he knew what he was doing. Communications were a critical part of any team operation. Pilkin knew this. Why didn't Kovlun?

Pilkin directed the convoy to park on the abandoned street two blocks from the warehouse.

"But this isn't the assigned rally point," his driver said. "We were supposed to park on the next block over."

Pilkin looked at the youth and demanded, "Who's in charge here?"

The young man's eyes grew, the whites visible in the semidarkness of the car. He stammered, "You are, sir."

"That's right. And did I ask for your opinion?"

"No, sir."

"Then shut up and park here."

When the convoy was stopped, Pilkin got out of the sedan and stepped back to the large panel truck they had used for the operation at the club. He hammered his fist against its side twice, then once, and the back door swung open a moment later. Nearly twenty armed recruits jumped from the back, toting a variety of SMGs and assault rifles. They hit the ground with admirable enthusiasm and the slap of their boot soles on concrete coupled with the clatter of the firepower they wielded caused Pilkin's face to flush with excitement. In just a few hours he would not only command a crack fighting unit of Russian Sevooborot—youths who were becoming men and would answer to him as their captain—but he would have three million in U.S. dollars to sustain a more customizable lifestyle.

"Let's go," he said. "Comrade Kovlun awaits our assistance!"

The revolutionaries turned on their heels and began to sprint for their assigned positions. Once the men had dispersed, Pilkin sauntered back to the sedan. He climbed into the front seat and ordered the driver to take him to a secondary access road by the warehouse. After they arrived, Pilkin ordered the young man to wait there with the engine running and do nothing except wait for his return, along with orders to contact Colonel Satyev in the event he didn't return.

"If I'm not back within thirty minutes, you know what to do."

The young man nodded, then Pilkin left him to join Kovlun at the designated rendezvous point. Kovlun was there with only two other men from his squad, watching the area ahead through infrared binoculars. Pilkin mused that Kovlun was behaving as if some kind of major skirmish were about to occur. They were going to shoot some black American gangbangers, not repel an invading force of tanks. Actually, they weren't even going to do that. Colonel Satyev's orders had been clear. Eliminating Kovlun and finding the traitors Rostov and Cherenko had become the priorities.

Kovlun never took his eyes from the binoculars as he asked, "You received the weapons?"

"Yes," Pilkin replied.

"And they were in good condition?"

"As near as I could tell, they completed the order," Pilkin replied. "I cannot yet attest to their condition."

Kovlun lowered the binoculars. "I'm sure Aleks will do a thorough inspection before issuing them."

Pilkin thought about replying to the contrary but he

decided to hold his tongue. What he wanted most to do was to draw his pistol right there and put a bullet in Kovlun's smirking face, but he knew the opportune time would present itself soon enough, and that time wasn't quite yet. Kovlun would soon send his two men to penetrate the warehouse and torch the place, but they still had a few minutes before that could happen.

"I wonder how the operation is going at the 18th Street leader's house."

"I do not know," Pilkin lied. "I wish we had a way to communicate with them and ask."

Kovlun looked sharply at him. "You do not approve of my tactics regarding communications silence?"

"It is not up to me to approve or disapprove of your tactics, Comrade," Pilkin replied, choosing his words carefully.

"You're right," Kovlun said, sneering. "It's not."

Kovlun's attitude made it all that more difficult for Pilkin not to kill him right there. He looked at the two men who waited for Kovlun's order to move out and wondered what they might do if he decided to make such a move. He also couldn't help but wonder if Kovlun had always spoken to him that way, but he'd been mandated up until now to act in a subservient role. In either case, it didn't really matter because Kovlun would be dead in a very short time, and the entire point would become moot.

Kovlun looked at his watch and then turned to the two Sevooborot youths and nodded. They rose without a sound, broke the crest of the high weeds in which they had taken cover and sprinted toward the warehouse. One carried a pair of bolt cutters for gaining access to the warehouse. Kovlun had equipped the other with a few incendiary grenades that Pilkin knew, when placed carefully for maximizing spread, would act as the chief catalyst of a full-scale war between the Bloods and 18th Street gang. Kovlun watched the two through the binoculars as they became mere shadowy outlines in the darkness to Pilkin.

With Kovlun's mind focused on the retreating SMJ soldiers, Pilkin saw his opportunity. Slowly, silently, he reached beneath his jacket and slid the German-made P9 pistol from its holster. He'd come to appreciate this weapon because it was compact but effective. Pilkin wouldn't necessarily have classified himself as a fan of German engineering, but they surely knew how to make guns, a talent they had demonstrated since the advent of World War I, and Pilkin was about to demonstrate his talent for using them. He moved forward and pressed the muzzle of the weapon against the back of Kovlun's head, about two inches above the base of his skull.

"Don't move," he whispered.

Kovlun let the binoculars fall and raised his hands, his voice barely its own whisper as he said, "What is this, Mikhail?"

Pilkin seemed almost amused by the question, and quipped, "Well, I think we would call it an assassination."

"You have betrayed the Sevooborot?"

"Not at all," Pilkin said as he leaned close. "I have betrayed *you*."

"And why, may I ask?"

"There are many reasons, I suppose, not the least of which is that your incompetence has led to the death of one of my few friends."

"What the hell are you talking about?" Kovlun squealed. "I *am* one of your friends."

"No, you are a superior. And that means you could never possibly be my friend."

"You're insane."

That made Pilkin chuckle. "Hardly. In fact, I don't think I've ever been more sane and clear about anything before. You sent poor Aleks into that death trap, and because of your incompetence he is now dead. Oh, that's right, don't look quite so surprised. I just heard that the American, that damned American you were supposed to make sure didn't leave the Mother Country alive, showed up at Villar's estate and killed Aleks right along with his entire crew. As if that isn't enough, I then find out that you were obviously planning to leave the Sevooborot without even telling Colonel Satyev. I thought you would do the honorable thing, but I must have been crazy at that particular time to believe you would actually be man enough to declare your intentions."

"What does that have to do with you?"

"What does it have to do with me?" Pilkin echoed. "What does it have to do with me? You see, that's just like you, Jurg. You think of nobody but yourself. What do you suppose would have happened if we left to work with you and the colonel got word of our intentions? He would have hunted you down like a dog and killed you, and Aleks and I would have died right along beside you. But instead, the colonel has wised up and asked me to save him the trouble by killing you here and now."

"So, it's Satyev behind this."

"Yes," Pilkin replied.

"How much did he offer you Mikhail? Huh?" Kovlun snarled. "Tell me that much, at least. How much did he offer you to kill me?"

"One million U.S. dollars."

"Is that all? You're pathetic. I can offer you five times that amount, easily. Ten times that amount, if you wish."

"The offer is tempting except for one thing, Jurg. I don't like you... I have never liked you. From the day we met you've treated me with arrogance and indifference, making it clear that you were some great soldier of the Spetsnaz while I was nothing. You acted as if I were scum under your shoe, a minor irritation. Well, here is something you might not remember. While you were hiding after the rebellion, my father was risking his life to put food in the mouths of his entire family. The Sevooborot gave him everything and asked for nothing more in return than the one thing you cannot buy. Loyalty."

"That's a laugh," Kovlun snapped. "You've just shown that your own loyalty is for sale."

"No, Jurg, that's what you fail to understand. My loyalty is not for sale. But my services are, and the colonel seems quite appreciative of them."

"That's where you're mistaken, Mikhail. The colonel despises and looks down on even me, and I am a trained professional who served under him in the Soviet army. What do you surmise, then, that he thinks about a young, smart-mouthed revolutionary filled with grand schemes of being the richest and most powerful crime czar in Russia? No, Mikhail, it is you who are mistaken about a great many things. And if you pull that trigger, you will only be selling your soul to a man who thumbs his nose at your kind and looks on you with a disdain ten times that of what you perceive I do."

"Perhaps," Pilkin replied. "But, then, at least with him I know where I stand."

And with that, Pilkin squeezed the trigger.

The report from his weapon drowned in the cacophony of autofire and explosions that ripped open the night like a thunderstorm. Pilkin looked toward the warehouse as Kovlun's body slumped forward to the ground. Everywhere he could see muzzle-flashes light up the night, winking from the various areas where his men had concealed themselves. The sudden violence took Pilkin utterly by surprise, and all he could do was wonder what had happened to turn the entire area into a battleground.

Yes, it was almost like hell itself had arrived.

CHAPTER TWENTY-THREE

Mack Bolan waited and watched in the shadows as a pair of armed men left the concealment of a field of tall, dry weeds and headed for the rear of the warehouse. He'd insisted on reconnoitering the area first, and Tilburg was damned glad because a few blocks over they rolled past a vehicle parked at the curb, engine idling, with a lone driver waiting. Behind the sedan they saw a panel van that Tilburg had remarked matched the description of the one seen at the club slaughter the previous evening. That left no doubt in Bolan's mind they'd made the right connection. Tilburg had radioed dispatch and advised taking down the drivers of both vehicles on his signal.

Now the Executioner lay across the Buick, his upper torso against the roof with the back window supporting his legs, and pressed his check against the cold, hard plastic of the AR-15A3's stock. The lights of the warehouse parking lot provided minimal illumination, and Bolan wished right about then he'd brought the PSG-1 sniper rifle stored in the armament compartment aboard

Stony Man's Learjet. Well, not much he could do about it now—he would have to work with what he had. Beside, if he had brought the rifle it would have met the same fate as the FNC now engulfed by tons of river water. Bolan tracked the movement of the pair through the sights, waited until they crossed under the light of the back door. There was no wind to speak of, so at his estimated sixty yards the shot wouldn't be tough. Bolan pressed the stock of the rifle tighter against his shoulder, took a deep breath, let half out and squeezed the trigger. The rifle produced a sharp crack as the 5.56 mm M193 hardball round left the muzzle at a velocity of 975 meters per second. Bolan couldn't see details but there was no mistaking the explosive force of the red mist that splattered across the metal door of the warehouse where they had planned to make their entry. Even as the first body fell, Bolan tracked on the second one and got him with a hastier shot through the spine that slammed the hood into the concrete wall of the warehouse.

Bolan rolled from the roof of the vehicle to land on his feet, the AR-15A3 in tow, and keyed up his radio. "That's it."

Tilburg was on the other end and clicked an acknowledgment before switching from the tactical band assigned to the task force and back to the main channel to order the squads to converge on the warehouse. Simultaneously, another half dozen units were assigned to pull over the Bloods bangers on their way to the warehouse. Bolan had to admit that he wouldn't have been able to avert the crisis if he hadn't accepted Tilburg's help. Whether the country knew it or not, they owed a debt to the Portland police.

Bolan jumped into the Buick, put it in gear and tromped the accelerator. The vehicle lurched from its cover behind a large garbage bin in an adjacent parking lot as Bolan picked up speed to give himself a bit of running room. He angled across the deserted lot and crashed through a wooden barricade that had been put up to separate that lot from the warehouse owned by 18th Street. Bolan got his vehicle up to the front door and squealed to a stop so his vehicle acted as a block of the front entrance. The warrior went EVA through the passenger side door as a dozen or so muzzle-flashes began to wink from various points of cover along the perimeter of the warehouse. Yeah, just like Villar's estate, the Sevooborot had lain in wait for the Bloods to show up and would have cut the unsuspecting gang members to ribbons.

Bolan took cover behind the Buick and began to return fire. A few gunners charged from the woods to attempt to get closer, but they were hardly a match for the unerring accuracy of Bolan's marksmanship. One burst from concealment behind a hedge lining one of the administration buildings near the warehouse and tried to flank Bolan but instead got a pair of slugs through the belly for his effort. A second gunner charged head-on with a crazed shout, apparently under the misconception he was bulletproof, and Bolan took him when he was still more than thirty yards from the Executioner's position.

During a lull in the firing, Bolan heard the sound of a door opening behind him and turned to look into a pair of crinkly eyes peering back at him over the barrel of a pistol. "Just hold it there, big feller."

An older black man with salt-and-pepper hair cut short stood there in the light gray and red patches of his uniform, which hung a bit loose on him. Bolan surmised he was probably the person who had called in the suspicious activity to begin with. His hand shook just slightly as he tried to aim steadily at Bolan. The fact the old man had him at gunpoint didn't concern Bolan nearly as much as the fact he was standing visible, a silhouette backlit by the interior, and a target ripe for the picking by blood-hungry Sevooborot troops.

"Get down!" Bolan ordered him.

"You just—"

The Executioner sprang into action, throwing his hand to deflect the pistol upward as he wrapped his free muscular arm around the guy's legs behind the knees. He tugged hard while simultaneously swinging his legs around front of him in a sitting position to help break the security guard's fall. It wasn't a moment too soon as the air where the guard had stood came alive with high-velocity rounds. The plate-glass windows of the front entry gave way under the onslaught and rained shards of jagged, heavy glass on the pair. One fell, and its jagged edge neatly cut through the sleeve of Bolan's fatigue blouse and left a deep gouge in the fleshy portion of his shoulder.

Bolan bit back pain and folded his body over the guard to protect him. When the glass ceased flying, the Executioner grabbed a fistful of the guard's shirt collar, got on his knees and dragged the guy inside the building. He then leaned out and snatched the AR-15A3 he'd left in the exterior entryway. The door closed slowly, its upper window essentially decimated under the destruction that the Sevooborot had just rained on him. Bolan counted it good fortune they both hadn't died under that last barrage.

The guard shook and looked at Bolan, terror evident in his eyes. "I—I thought y-you were—"

"I know what you thought. Can you stand?"

The man nodded and climbed to his feet as Bolan scanned the parking lot. In the dim gloom cast by overhead lights, the Executioner could see at least half a dozen shapes headed for them. This hadn't been exactly what he had planned, but he couldn't count the number of times he'd been on missions where things hadn't gone his way. No point in getting worked up about it now. He would adapt to the situation as it unfolded.

Once Bolan got under the guy's shoulder to steady him, the guard asked, "Where's my gun?"

Bolan turned to see the weapon lying outside the door. The Sevooborot troops were close now, and there wasn't time to risk going for the weapon. Bolan advised the man not to worry about it and the two made their way deeper into the warehouse. They passed an open office door from which a voice on the radio announced what sounded like some kind of sporting event. Bolan and the guard continued past the office until they reached a set of doors that turned out to be restrooms for men and women.

"What's your name, friend?" Bolan asked.

"Melvin," he replied. "Melvin Sampson."

Bolan released his arm and stepped back. His takedown had only stunned Sampson for a minute, and the guy looked able to stand on his own two feet. Bolan reached to his shoulder holster and drew the Beretta 93-R. After verifying the selector switch was set to single shot, he pressed the handle of the weapon into Sampson's right palm, keeping the muzzle at a respectable distance from his body.

"Here," Bolan told him. "Now first thing is, don't shoot me. I'm on your side. Second, this is a single action, semiautomatic 9 mm pistol. You have a full clip of fifteen rounds, and the safety's off with one in the pipe. You ever fire a semiauto before?"

Sampson nodded with a glint of ferocity in his eyes, and executed a snappy salute. "Yes, sir. Shot plenty. Twenty years security police, United States Air Force, retired."

"Glad to hear it." Bolan pointed toward the front entrance. "There are at least a dozen Russian terrorists out there armed with automatic weapons who intend to kill me and burn this place to the ground. They're not really interested in you, but they won't hesitate for a moment to kill you if get in their way. So I'm leaving you that pistol strictly for self-defense. Understand?"

Sampson nodded.

"All right," Bolan said as he pointed to doors at the end of the hall. "I assume that's the entrance to the warehouse. But right above us I noticed some windows from the outside. What's up there?"

"Just offices, mostly."

"I saw lights. Are they occupied?"

"Well, the cleaning crew is up there."

"At one o'clock in the morning?"

"That's when they always come," Sampson said matter-of-factly. "Every Friday night, er, well, I guess it's more like Saturday morning."

"Okay, I get the idea," Bolan replied quickly. "Now listen to me. I want you to get up there and get the cleaning people into a safe place."

"Okay, but what're you gonna do, mister?"

"I'm going to draw them away from you."

"Sounds dangerous."

"Story of my life," Bolan said. "Now head out."

Sampson tossed another salute, then did an about-face and headed toward a flight of stairs that led to the second floor. Bolan then took up a position behind a water fountain, crouched and waited. At first he saw nothing from that position but eventually human shadows spanned across the door, growing smaller as the crew of gunners got nearer. Bolan pressed the butt of the AR-15A3 tight against his shoulder, closed one eye and acquired a target through the sight. The outline of an enemy gunman fell across the interior door.

Bolan squeezed off a shot. The glass shattered and the black, shadowy form dropped instantly to the linoleum of the foyer. Almost instantly the hallway came alive with a chorus of autofire and a volley of rounds burned the air, most coming nowhere near Bolan's position. A few ricocheted off the polished floor near his feet, and one even thwacked into the sheeting of the fountain but had to have been trapped by either its internal workings or the concrete block walls. Bolan flipped to 3-shot bursts and triggered a couple replies before breaking cover and heading for the doors of the warehouse. He needed to take the advantage, and there was only one way he knew how to do that in the confines of his environment.

The Executioner would get to higher ground.

"BREAK OFF! BREAK OFF!" Pilkin screamed into the radio, but it was too late.

He'd watched helplessly as both of the men sent to torch the building were cut down by an unknown sharpshooter. Then a half minute later a lone sedan screamed across the parking lot and disappeared from sight in front of the warehouse. That's when the shooting really started, and by the time he realized his teams had engaged some sort of enemy it was much too late to stop them. Only a select few would hear the order above the wave of shooting. It sounded like they were battling with an army, but Pilkin couldn't make out anything beyond that since he couldn't see. Pilkin stopped for a moment, stared at the back of Kovlun's head and the rapidly pooling blood that leaked out around where he lay. He looked helplessly toward the warehouse one last time and then scrambled to his feet. He turned and started for the sedan, stopped on afterthought and went back to Kovlun's body. He snapped a couple of pictures using the digital camera built into his phone—Colonel Satyev would probably require proof before paying him—and then crunched along the thick dry weeds until he reached the street.

The radio crackled, then a voice came through clearly. It was one of the team leaders requesting orders. Pilkin stopped, put the radio close to his lips and ordered the team leader to pull his men back to the rally point. Two of three team leaders acknowledged, and Pilkin set into a jog down a narrow alley on the backside of the warehouse district in the direction from which he'd come. Their mission had completely fallen apart; just another testament to the sore incompetence of Kovlun's leadership.

Pilkin reached the rally point to find the drivers of the panel truck and his sedan still there, waiting patiently for him. The driver of the sedan was outside the vehicle, leaned against his door and smoking a cigarette. What a dimwit! He was supposed to have waited *inside* the damn car, and here he stood in plain view in the early hours of the morning, smoking. Why didn't

the moron just wave a big neon flag at the nearest police car as it drove by to announce he was there?

"Get in the car!" Pilkin snapped when he got within
speaking distance.

The driver flicked away his cigarette, opened the
door and nervously jumped behind the wheel as Pilkin
proceeded to the panel truck, opened the back and
waited for his teams to arrive. It didn't take them long.
Within a minute they emerged from the darkness of an
abandoned gravel lot and rushed across the street, jump-
ing aboard the panel truck in groups of two and three.
As soon as they were inside, Pilkin closed and secured
the doors, then hurried to the sedan.

"Let's go," he ordered the driver.

The man dropped the shift into gear and started to
pull out when the flashing strobes of red and blue from
every angle of the street lit up the night, followed by
the sounds of sirens and car doors being opened. Then
a voice came over a loudspeaker, and although Pilkin
couldn't make out the words he understood the intent.
So they had set a trap for him, or rather for Kovlun, and
Pilkin had walked right into it. Well, there was no way
he wasn't going to collect his money for the risks he'd
invested, and there was sure as hell no way he would
allow them to take him alive.

Pilkin ordered the driver to break through the block-
ade of cars on the street. At first the youth opened his
mouth to argue, but the thought quickly evaporated
when Pilkin stuck the muzzle of his pistol an inch from
his eye and repeated the order. The youth tromped the
accelerator pedal and tried to smash through the cor-
don of squad cars, but it didn't do much more than

mash the front end of the vehicle and send smoke from the tires as they spun uselessly against the pavement.

The windshield spiderwebbed and Pilkin knew it was time to go. He whipped the door open and tumbled from the vehicle, P9 in hand. Pilkin rose and began to fire in the direction of the police cars. He couldn't see much due to the glare of their spotlights, but he managed to take out one of them in a fantastic display of sparks before something cut through his chest, burning like a hot poker. And then suddenly he couldn't breathe and he watched helplessly as he vomited a torrent of blood, and then he felt another burn cut through his chest, and then another through his gut. And another.

And then Mikhail Pilkin sensed his body falling, and darkness folded around him like the arms of a mother cradling her baby. Sweet, yes, sweet darkness. Then nothing…

KISA NARYSHKIN AWOKE with a start, awash in a sense of utter dread.

Her body dripped with sweat, bed sheets soaked, and it took her a moment to move past the terror and take in the surroundings of her bedroom at the safehouse. Her next thoughts were of her beloved Leo and the pain he had to be suffering. When Cooper finally got him to a hospital, the doctors hadn't delivered the best news. Fortunately, they had gotten Leo to a hospital just in time. A few more hours and he might have been lost. Still, the diagnosis had surprised all of them, even Matt Cooper: he had a strain of pulmonary fibrosis. The first pronouncement by the doctors had made Naryshkin angry. There was no way he could have such a horrible disease—he'd always been rather healthy. And while the doctors admitted seeing a late-stage onset like this wasn't common, it wasn't entirely unheard-of, either. And then she realized that Leo was only a few years older than her, twenty-six, so he wasn't really that old.

"I want to take him back to Russia," Naryshkin had told Bolan. "My father will help take care of him. We know the finest physicians in the entire world."

"We'll see, Kisa," Bolan said. "I can't make any promises."

"That's what you *usually* say, Matt," she had replied, but he'd just smiled at her.

Now she couldn't sleep, thoughts of the possibility he would never be able to return to Russia rushing through her mind. Finally she pulled back the covers, swung her feet over the edge and tucked them into slippers Cooper had bought for her in the hospital gift shop. She couldn't sleep, not with this endless parade of doubts and fears marching through her mind, so she crossed the room and went out the door. It opened onto a hallway, one side of which was lined with a banister that overlooked a living area below. She peered over the railing and saw the two U.S. Marshals assigned to protect her seated on chairs and engrossed in the television. Naryshkin walked down the hallway to Sergei Cherenko's room. She hated to disturb him, but she really needed someone to talk to, another Russian who could understand her and her need for comfort; besides, Sergei was Leo's friend, too.

The young woman knocked lightly at the door, then a little louder, but nobody answered—probably exhausted, poor thing. Maybe she should have waited until morning but she just couldn't. She tried the door handle and found it unlocked; she opened the door just enough to poke her head inside. A pile of rumpled covers were visible. She called Sergei's name in a tight whisper, then louder, but he didn't stir. Finally she slipped inside the room and closed the door behind her before walking over to the bed. She shook the lump but still no response. At last, she clicked on the lamp next to the bed and threw back the covers.

Empty!

Naryshkin let out a cry, then turned and rushed out to the hallway. She leaned over the banister and called to the marshals. They were out of their seats and charging up the stairwell in a moment.

"What's wrong?" one of them demanded when they had reached the landing.

She pointed toward Cherenko's room. "Sergei, he's gone. I went to talk to him and…he's just gone!"

The man's partner rushed to investigate while the other guy went down the hall to the bathroom. The door was wide open but he flipped on the light to check anyway. He returned to Kisa's side and his partnered joined them a moment later with a shake of his head.

The guy whipped out a cell phone and said, "This is Williamson. Get me the SAIC of the day. We have a missing witness."

CHAPTER TWENTY-FOUR

Mack Bolan lay concealed atop a dusty, canvas tarp strewed over a stack of crates. The position afforded him a perfect view of the entrance to the warehouse below, arrayed before him without a single obstacle in his line of sight. It would be like shooting fish in a barrel.

The first gunner appeared through the door, which opened with a squeak of hinges, alerting Bolan his prey had arrived. A pair of Sevooborot hoods toting semiauto machine guns passed through the opening and fanned out, sweeping the aisles in front of them. Neither of the crew bothered to look overhead for their enemy, which only reinforced to Bolan that whoever had trained them hadn't done that well. Two more gunners came through after them, followed by another four. The Executioner waited, watching for any additional troops, but none arrived.

The Executioner took a deep breath and went on the offensive. The key to an assault where an enemy outnumbered the soldier by eight to one was firing as much to create confusion as for hit effect. Bolan took the latter group first, then, which would cause the two point units to turn away from the line of fire initially, presenting stationary targets he could pick off at leisure. The first burst he fired was sustained, hammering the tight-knit quartet on rear guard with a merciless barrage. The first gunner was stitched crotch to sternum and slammed into the unyielding wall near the doors; the second man's head exploded under the impact of high-velocity rounds that slammed the gunner's corpse into his comrade. The third was tripped up by the assault and dropped his weapon, throwing his arms over his head. Bolan passed over him at the last moment—he wasn't going to shoot a defenseless youth who barely knew how to respond to the kind of punishment Bolan was doling out. The last man responded with considerable skill, rolling to avoid being ventilated by the Executioner's fire. Bolan led the gunner and caught him as he came out of the roll and swept his weapon into target acquisition. Twin rounds struck the guy in the chest and spun him into a nearby crate.

The point teams had done just as Bolan predicted and turned to watch the devastation unfold on their rear. One gunner managed to spot him from his position well above them and bring his weapon to bear. He triggered a short burst that chewed up the crate, several rounds skimming dangerously close over Bolan's head. The soldier leaned into the stock of his rifle, clenched his teeth as he aimed through the sight and squeezed off a 3-round reply. The slugs opened a gap in the guy's stomach and he dropped his weapon as a piece of his bowels protruded from the opening.

The remaining three Russians raced for cover behind

crates, and Bolan rolled from his perch and dropped to a lower set of crates below him, confident he'd exhausted the high ground resource. Bolan stepped off the crates and dropped to the concrete floor. He slipped down a passageway between rows of stacked crates and crouched in the darkness. Now began the game of cat-and-mouse. Two of the Sevooborot gunners broke cover and headed down the main thoroughfare, then made their way up the side passage in an attempt to flank him. As they did, they passed right by Bolan's hiding spot. The soldier emerged from the shadows, walked down the aisle and stepped into the light, now positioned to their rear. Without a sound he dispatched them with a sweeping burst.

Bolan wheeled and advanced toward the front doors where the remaining enemy gunner waited, but when he rounded the corner with weapon held at the ready he saw a pair of legs protruding from behind a crate. The Executioner advanced with caution, the AR-15A3 held at the ready. As he got close he saw the edge of a blood pool. The evidence of high-velocity splatter against the edge of the crate told him all he needed to know. Bolan found the young man's corpse, back propped against the crate, with a pistol in the left hand and a good part of the right side of its head missing. Bolan's eyes narrowed. The kid couldn't have been more than twenty or twenty-one, another young victim of the worst humankind had to offer. He should have been at home in Russia, attending college, instead of here fighting for a shameful and hopeless cause dreamed up by maniacs like Kovlun and Satyev.

The sound of stifled sobs brought Bolan to the here and now, and he whirled toward the source of the sound.

His eyes scanned the shadows near the wall until he spotted the shaking, crouched form of the gunner who had earlier thrown his hands over his head and run. Bolan stepped up to him. The young man looked up and Bolan gauged the tear-rimmed eyes that peered at him. There was no threat there and no sign of deception; just the fear and heartache of a young man whose innocence had been snatched from him way too early in life. Bolan reached for him but he shied away, so he had to extend his arm to get a hand around the kid's arm and haul him to his feet. He relieved him quickly of his knife and sidearm, then bound his hands behind him with riot cuffs.

He escorted the youth into the hall and sat him against the wall, then turned up the volume on his radio, adjusted it to the gang task force tactical frequency and keyed up. "Cooper to Tilburg. You read?"

"Roger that," Tilburg's voice came back.

"What's your status?"

"All clear. We got damn near the whole lot of 'em, Cooper."

"Nice work. Any sign of Kovlun?"

"Negative. We had to take out two who tried to break through our roadblock, but neither of them matches Kovlun's description. We also nabbed a couple dozen of their shooters without having to fire a shot."

"And the Bloods?"

"Stopped them cold, too. And no casualties on our side," Tilburg replied.

"All right. I have one prisoner here. Send me some help when you can."

"You got it. I'll have units there in under a minute."

"Roger that," Bolan said.

"Oh, I almost forgot. There's a request came through Dispatch, somebody named Jack? Says he needs to talk to you ASAP."

"I copy that. Cooper, out." Bolan clipped the radio to his web belt, then removed his encrypted cell phone and dialed Grimaldi's number. "Eagle, it's Striker. What's up?"

"I need you here and pronto. The Farm called me not ten minutes ago. Apparently the U.S. Marshals Service reported Sergei Cherenko's missing."

"Taken?"

"Hal doesn't think so," Grimaldi replied.

"Any idea where he might have gone?"

"Bear's running down the angles now. But they're asking you to get involved and most pronto."

"Acknowledged. I'll be there within the hour."

Bolan disconnected the call and sighed. He would have preferred a few hours' rest, but it looked like that would have to wait. It didn't make any sense. Why would Cherenko simply split like that? Didn't he know that they had assigned the protection to him and he was no longer in danger? In some ways, Bolan blamed himself for not seeing this coming. He'd felt from the beginning Cherenko was holding back information—especially when he'd asked if either he or Rostov had any ideas where Satyev might be operating from—but Cherenko answered in the negative. Bolan sensed right then Cherenko lied to him, but he didn't want to make the accusation and risk alienating the young man. He couldn't prove it, but Bolan's instincts told him Cherenko knew *exactly* where Satyev was, and he'd decided to go after the guy on his own.

If Bolan had just listened to his instincts, Cherenko

would still be tucked safely away in Seattle. Well, he couldn't do anything about it. Kurtzman had the resources of every advanced piece of tracking technology available to the modern world. He'd find the wayward Russian soon enough. And maybe, just maybe, Cherenko would lead him to Satyev. The tide of gang war had been stemmed and the JI's plot of Western destabilization foiled. All that remained was to hunt down the mastermind behind the terror.

It was a meeting the Executioner looked forward to.

SERGEI CHERENKO HAD NEVER BEEN much of a spontaneous person. Spontaneity was something he'd left to friends like Leonid and Kisa. They were risk-takers, brought up in households where venturing into the unknown and thrill-seeking were encouraged, while Cherenko's upbringing had involved quite a contrary view. His parents had been middle-class working stiffs who didn't believe in "rocking the boat" on any subject, including the merits of socialist living and communism over capitalism and free-rule democracy. Liberalities were simply tools of revolutionaries designed to subvert authority and twist the benefits of government rule.

"Remember, Sergei," his father had once told him. "These people that preach freedom and patriotism under a banner of violent uprising are nothing more than troublemakers and malingerers. They will bring you down one day if you follow in their path. Better to work hard and pay your dues. That is the only way you will get anywhere in life."

That attitude ultimately earned Sergei's father and mother a trip to prison when their boss, to hide his own

dissident activities, framed them as political subver-
sives and resistors to Boris Yeltsin's grab at power. So
at the tender age of eleven, Cherenko was shipped off
to a foster family who ran a State work house in the
south of Moscow. It was there that he met Leonid Rostov, a boy two years younger than he but already full of
life, and spirited beyond words. Through the years their
friendship grew strong, a bond that passed even beyond brotherhood, until at last Rostov convinced Cherenko they could at last *be* part of something by
enlisting with the Sevooborot. At first, the training and
camaraderie had been like something out of a dream—
finally they were together in a place that accepted and
appreciated their individuality—until one day they
graduated to the upper ranks and suddenly the innocence of their youth came crashing down on their heads
in a torrent of reality.

The subsequent years in the Sevooborot were filled
with the bloodshed and violent uprising and the words
of his father echoed in Cherenko's mind day after gruel-
ing day until he considered taking his own life. Once
again, though, Rostov proved his salvation when he
announced his betrothal to Kisa Naryshkin—an intel-
ligent, if outspoken, and impressionable young woman
who'd convinced him to leave behind his revolutionary
ideas for the more peaceable and conventional ones of
love and marriage. But Cherenko had known, like Rostov, they would never be allowed to leave the Sevooborot alive, not after the leaders had revealed their plans
to take arms in exchange for fueling a war among
American gangs to destabilize the West. It was during
the months just prior to this that Rostov had also begun
to show signs of his illness. At first, Cherenko had just

figured this string of colds was a run of bad luck that his friend would eventually overcome. Now he knew of Rostov's illness, knew the probability factor in his speedy recovery, and Cherenko could no more bring himself to stand by and watch all they had run and suffered for come to naught.

Especially not while Colonel Anatoly Satyev lived.

Cherenko wanted to trust Matt Cooper to do as he had promised, oh, how he wanted to, but he could no more put the fate of his friends' lives in the hands of an American than he could cut off his own hand. His friends were a part of him, his flesh and blood, the only family he had really known, and he would not sit idly by while Leo breathed his last because he could no longer endure the pressure of running. As long as Satyev lived, Leo and Kisa had little chance at a normal life. What kind of peace could they know if they were always on the run, always looking over their shoulders and wondering when Satyev or the Sevooborot would rear their ugly heads? No, he would leave the likes of Jurg Kovlun to Cooper, but where it concerned Satyev it was his responsibility to handle it. Personally.

It hadn't proved difficult to get out of his bedroom and climb down the tree.

A few blocks from the safehouse he found a twenty-four-hour pharmacy from which he called a cab to take him to the airport. Obtaining a plane ticket proved even easier. From his intended mission in America, the Sevooborot had provided all the forged identification he required, including a driver's license and social security card, along with a roll of cash. Nobody had bothered to take the items from him, and Cherenko hadn't seen any reason to state he had such things. Now he was glad he'd remained silent.

As soon as Cherenko arrived at the airport, he bought a round-trip ticket from Seattle to Reno, NV. He tried to get a nonstop flight, but the only available flight was by way of San Francisco. It added more than two hours to his trip, but that was the best he could hope for. He wouldn't worry about it; there would be plenty of time to reach Reno and Satyev. Once he arrived at Satyev's house, which he remembered being somewhere in a golf course community nestled in the foothills of the Sierra Vistas, he'd have more than enough time to exact is revenge.

Yes, Cherenko thought as he sat on the plane in San Francisco and waited patiently to continue on to Reno. More than enough time.

"HOW YOU DOING?" Jack Grimaldi said, clapping his friend on the shoulder.

"I've had better days," Bolan replied.

The pilot chuckled at that. "I'm sure."

"We set?"

"Ready and raring. Just as soon as I know where we're going."

Yeah, that had been somewhat of a trick. The Executioner wrapped things up quickly with Tilburg and Brothers. The task force now had a firm handle on the situation. Once they'd taken down the remainder of the Sevooborot strike teams and arrested the small army sent by the Bloods in retaliation for Medford's murder, it wasn't difficult to schedule a meet that would bring both sides to the table so they could hear the explanations and see the proof that the Russian youth gang had duped them all. They had even cooked up a good story to tell the press, although it wouldn't necessarily help the bereaved who had lost a loved one at the club. Bolan knew he couldn't do anything about that—national security had to take precedence. The Portland PD also managed to locate Kovlun's body after spending nearly ten minutes canvassing the grounds surrounding the warehouse. It was then that Bolan realized there had been several calls placed to the same number by the cell phones of both Kovlun and the other leader, a guy Bolan didn't recognize but who several Sevooborot youths identified as Mikhail Pilkin.

On his way to the airport, Bolan had contacted Kurtzman with a request to trace the phone records and get back to him with a probable location. Bolan had also delivered a brief but comprehensive report to Brognola, advising him that the Man and all other concerned parties could rest easy. A gang war had been averted in Portland, and there wouldn't be any escalation to other cities.

"Sounds good," Brognola had said. "What about Satyev and his connection with the JI? They're not likely to give up so easily, Striker."

"Agreed," Bolan told him. "But if I can take at least one of them out of the loop, I think the rest of the plan will fall apart. Considering how much of their operation we've shut down, Satyev won't have bought much goodwill where the JI's concerned. They might even decide it's better to take him out themselves rather than risk further exposure."

Bolan then laid out his theory about Sergei Cherenko.

"You think he might actually go after Satyev himself?"

"It only makes sense," Bolan says. "He really has no

other place to go, and I find it hard to believe he's playing the double agent game here. When I talked to him, I got the impression he'd had about all the fight taken out of him. I think he's tired."

"You know as well as I do that impressions can be wrong," Brognola reminded him.

"I know. But I have to assume he really does want this to end until I can prove otherwise. All the other information I could get from him, and the little I could get from Kisa and Rostov, certainly paid off. If he hadn't spilled about the issue in Portland, we might never have made the connection, Hal."

"All right. You know I trust your judgment implicitly."

"Thanks. Just have Bear get back to me as soon as he has something."

Shortly after Bolan collapsed into a seat aboard the Learjet 36A, the phone aboard the plane rang. Bolan answered, "Striker, here. What do you have, Bear?"

"I'm flattered that you knew it was me."

"You're just that good, Bear."

"Thanks. I tracked that number to phone records belonging to some party in Boston who's so nonexistent he doesn't even have fingerprints or a driver's license."

"Cover for Satyev?"

"I'd say that's a good bet. I eventually traced it back with some effort, and discovered after some intricate switching the number originates in Reno, Nevada." He gave Bolan the address. "I also checked all public transportation logs. A last-minute ticket was purchased for a United flight out of Seattle-Tacoma to Reno-Tahoe not four hours ago with a short layover in San Francisco."

"Cherenko," Bolan said. "Has to be more than coincidence."

"I'd say probably except the ticket was round trip, Striker. Also, all passengers have to show identification. Cherenko wouldn't have had any."

"They were equipping him for a mission here in the States," Bolan reminded his friend. "That would've probably included a whole ID package and plenty of cash."

"You may be right. I hadn't thought of that. I'm trying to get airport camera footage right now just to confirm."

"Keep at it," Bolan said. "In the meantime, we'll get heading that way. Nice job, Bear."

"Thanks. Good luck, Striker."

Bolan hung up the phone and noted Grimaldi's askance expression. "Reno."

Grimaldi rubbed his hands together. "Coming right up."

CHAPTER TWENTY-FIVE

Cherenko shivered against the chill of early morning, thankful that the sun had started to rise and it would soon warm up.

The cabbie had probably thought he was crazy when Cherenko asked the guy to let him out a short distance from the entrance to the gated community, but he didn't want anyone to know where he was going. It hadn't been much trouble getting past the massive, wrought-iron gates—a ridiculous security measure if Cherenko had ever seen one—since the guard shack was apparently operated only during the daylight. Even more pathetic was that the hours of manned security were actually posted, right below the sign that warned the community was private property and no trespassers were permitted. The same sign, sheltered by the elements, also provided a convenient map that listed the location of every house. After Cherenko located Satyev's residence tucked away in a cul-de-sac, he found a place to wait beneath a tree in the woods across from the estate. He could feel the exhaustion to the point where it almost seeped from his pores, but he couldn't sleep. No, he wouldn't sleep soundly until he knew the job had been done.

Now he only faced two more problems. The first was how to get past security; second, he needed some way to kill Satyev. He supposed a gun would do, but it made a lot of noise and could be clumsy in close quarters. Besides, he wanted to make sure Satyev felt pain and experienced misery; he wanted Satyev to know who had beaten him; he wanted Anatoly Satyev to suffer, plain and simple. Once inside the house, Cherenko knew he could find a knife. That left just getting inside the house as his remaining challenge.

He studied the front of the house. The hand-laid drive ran up to a chateau-style house, which included a three-car garage, with a split-timber roof edged with tiles. With the manicured lawn and gardens surrounding it, the house very much took on a rustic appearance. It said something for Satyev: he had excellent taste.

The thing that bothered Cherenko most about the house, though, was the four-man security team walking the perimeter. They didn't carry any visible weapons, but Cherenko had no doubt they were well armed. They would also be well trained, probably former Spetsnaz as Jurg Kovlun had been, and that meant he didn't stand much of a chance against them by himself and unarmed. Stealth would be the key here. The best he could hope for was to get inside the residence by flanking the rear side entry that looked onto Lake Tahoe, and then locate Satyev and finish the business for which he'd come.

Cherenko ducked deeper into the woods and then circled along the wood line until he reached the edge of the lake. The approach wouldn't be easy. He'd checked his watch and timed the sentries, noting they circled the house every thirty seconds. From this vantage point he could see he would have to cross nearly fifty meters of open ground, traverse the house until he reached the back and vault a waist-high flagstone wall that lined the massive back patio. And he would have to do all of that in under thirty seconds. It certainly wouldn't be a task for the faint of heart.

Cherenko put his hand to his chest as he walked to just inside the wood line and crouched. His heart thudded dully, the blood rushing through his ears like a river of whitewater. There wouldn't be any second chances. He'd get just one shot at this and after that, if he failed to gain access, he was finished. Cherenko took a couple of deep breaths and watched the outline of the sentry as he patrolled that side. As soon as he turned the front corner, Cherenko burst from cover and sprinted across the lawn as fast as his cramped legs could carry him. Halfway across he tripped on something and landed hard on his chest, but he immediately regained his feet and kept going. Cherenko reached the edge of the house and edged along the side of the house until he reached the wall. He started to climb over but then spotted the outline of the sentry. With no other choice, Cherenko dropped flat to the ground and laid utterly still, his back pressed to the chill stone of the wall.

The sentry rounded the corner and Cherenko froze, keeping his eyes toward the ground so the whites were not visible. He heard the crunch of shoes on the still-frozen blades of grass as the sentry moved past him. If the sentry decided to look down and to the right, Cherenko knew it was all over. The sentry apparently had his mind on other things, though, because he walked right past Cherenko and didn't notice him. The Russian could hardly believe his good fortune. There he lay in virtually plain view, the shadows cast by the west side of the house his only source of concealment, and yet the guard hadn't seen him. He wondered for a moment if this was by design, if he had walked into a trap, but dismissed the idea. How would Satyev have known he was in the country, let alone coming there to kill him? To men like Anatoly Satyev, Cherenko was nothing more than a chattel to be used or oppressed on a whim.

When the sentry rounded the corner, Cherenko got to his feet and hopped over the wall. He kept his back to the house while he sidestepped to the rear door. He had less than ten seconds before the sentry arrived. Cherenko tried the door handle and, to his complete surprise, it turned smoothly. Obviously, Satyev felt so confident in the sentries that he saw no reason to secure the doors of his house; either that, or a thoughtless servant had forgotten to lock up. Whatever the explanation might be, it had given Cherenko the advantage and he fully intended to exploit it.

The Russian pushed his way through the door and quietly secured it behind him. He let his eyes adjust to the comparative gloom of the interior. Cherenko assumed even the house staff hadn't yet risen, which brought him some measure of relief. He knew there was always a remote possibility he'd have to go up against Satyev's security people, but he saw no reason to harm any of the servants. It wasn't their fault they worked for a murderous thug who didn't even have enough courage to do his own dirty work. Well, Cherenko would settle that account with Satyev that morning.

After his eyes adjusted, Cherenko began to search the house. He had only a single story to contend with, so he knew it wouldn't take him long to find his target. First, he located the kitchen and acquired a filet knife. It would be sharp and perfect for his task. He then began his search for Satyev, who would most likely be in one of the bedrooms. Cherenko soft-stepped along the wall of a long hallway, keeping his back close to it with one hand in front of him as a probe. Eventually, he came to a small side table and stepped around it, but he misjudged and his foot caught on the edge of a leg, causing something to topple off the table and onto the floor. Cherenko froze in place, thankful that whatever had fallen hadn't made too much noise as it landed on the carpet. He remained there for a nearly a minute, listening for the sounds of footsteps or other noises that might signal he had been detected, but only silence greeted his ears. He crouched and patted the plush carpet until his hands wrapped around an object he guessed was a slender, ceramic vase. He put it back on the table and continued down the hall.

The first door he came to was a bathroom. Cherenko proceeded to the next door, this one closed, and reached for the handle. He turned it slowly, agonizingly, intent on maintaining utter silence. The door finally gave inward and Cherenko stepped inside a very dark room. There was a bit of a chill in here, not much, and he could feel the floor had transitioned from carpet to something hard. Wood or tile, maybe? Cherenko waited until his eyes adjusted further before he realized he was in some kind of study.

No, Satyev wouldn't be here. He turned and started to leave when the overhead lights came on and bathed him in a soft-white glow. Cherenko spun on his heel, knife held in the ready position, but there was no one close enough to use it on. Then Cherenko heard the laughter, soft at first but eventually it began to grow in volume until it sounded like it came from speakers throughout the room. Not quite, though. The source sat at a desk near a vast window. It rolled forth from the mouth of Colonel Anatoly Satyev.

"Welcome, Sergei," Satyev finally said after he finished laughing. "I've been expecting you."

"How…" Cherenko finally rasped.

"How is not important," Satyev said. He rose at his desk and nodded toward the knife. "Was that intended for me? How misfortunate for you."

Cherenko's legs felt like rubber and his tongue had gone dry in his mouth. His sixth sense had told him that he might be walking into a trap, and he hadn't bothered to listen. He had come here to assassinate his enemy and instead he found only more deception. Whatever had brought him to this point, Sergei Cherenko knew he'd used up whatever good fortune he might have and had failed. He'd failed his friends and his country. There was no turning back now. If he wished to salvage even an ounce of self-respect, he still needed to try to do what he'd come here to do.

A death's head smile played across Satyev's distinguished features. "You look surprised, Sergei, although I cannot imagine why. Did you really think you could come here and murder me in my sleep? I knew the moment you arrived in this country along with your traitorous friends and that meddlesome American, Cooper. I also knew that Rostov was sick, and that you would eventually come here to settle the score with me. But what I cannot fathom is why you would want to kill me? What have I ever done to you?"

"You stand for everything that is wrong with Mother Russia," Cherenko finally managed to say.

"I *am* Mother Russia, you stupid pig!" Satyev barked. His face flushed with anger. "You were nothing before I came along. *Nothing!* You and your pathetic revolutionary friends made no impact whatsoever, no contribution to the Soviet Union. The Communist party had demonstrated time and again that its way of living could benefit all. But you weren't interested in that. Instead, you wanted to see to the removal of a minority of Arabs from your colleges, to feed your bellies and increase your education while the working class supported you! It's all nonsense. I am trying to restore the former glory of the Soviet Union."

"You are a maniac," Cherenko replied evenly. "And I am here to see you do not go on living."

With that, Sergei Cherenko found the courage to lunge toward Satyev with the knife. He made it only half the distance. Satyev raised a pistol he'd been concealing behind his desk, snap-aimed and squeezed the trigger repeatedly. The first 9 mm round punched through Cherenko's chest. The second hit him in the throat, tearing through the esophagus and windpipe before it blew a chunk of his cervical spine out the back. Satyev's third round entered below Cherenko's left cheek and lodged somewhere in his brain. As the young man went down less than a foot from Satyev's desk, the man pumped three more rounds into the falling body. The door burst open a millisecond later and two of Satyev's bodyguards stared with surprise at the bleeding, broken form lying in front of their master's desk.

The men started to move forward to take the body out but Satyev screamed, "Leave him! Leave his body right here to rot! I don't care. The chopper will be here in a few minutes. We must prepare to depart immediately, so snap to it!"

The men didn't argue, knowing if they opened their mouths to protest they might very well end up like the corpse on the floor. The men turned and left the room. Satyev came around the desk and stared at the motionless form with venom. Then he spit on the body, kicked it once and left his office. As he reached the end of the hall and prepared to descend to the basement, he heard a whomp—an odd noise to hear this early in the morning—followed by an explosion. The concussion blew out a window at the end of the hall and knocked Satyev to the floor, raining glass and bits of wood and stone on him. Satyev shook his head to clear the fog from his head, then looked to see the window had been completely blown out and a heavy cloud of smoke took its place, obscuring his view.

He climbed slowly to his feet and staggered down the hall, intent on getting as far from the carnage as possible.

MACK BOLAN OPENED the hit on Satyev's sprawling estate by firing a 40 mm HE grenade at a massive window on the leeward side of the house. The subsequent blast on impact shattered the glass in the window and sent plumes of dirt and mulch flying in all directions. One of the sentries caught enough of the blast to separate his arms from his upper torso and knock him off his feet. The guy lay on the grass screaming, stringy trails of flesh left in the wake of his separated appendages. As Bolan drew close, he put two mercy rounds from the M-16 A-3 into the man to end his suffering.

Bolan stepped over the base of the shattered window and into a hallway. He swept the muzzle of the assault rifle in either direction, waiting for any sort of a threat to present itself. He was only favored with silence. The Executioner came to a door and kicked it in. A set of steps descended to a basement where he found an array of computers and servers that would've impressed even Kurtzman. So this was where Satyev had been operating. Bolan quickly maneuvered through the room to make sure he hadn't missed an alternate exit, then proceeded up the stairs and on to the next room. He couldn't be sure where Satyev might be hiding so he'd have to conduct a room-by-room search.

Bolan entered through the next doorway and spotted a body lying facedown in a pool of blood. Bolan took a few steps closer, all he needed to identify Sergei Cherenko. He knew there was nothing he could do. Cherenko was clearly dead. The Executioner felt a mixture of anger and regret—he'd arrived just minutes too late.

"Rest in peace, Sergei," Bolan whispered before turning away.

Bolan conducted a search of the remaining rooms in the hallway, then began to sweep the common areas. As he reached the main living area, two more guards with pistols entered the room and tried to bring their weapons into target acquisition. Bolan cut the first one down with a 3-round burst to the gut. The high-velocity slugs punched through his midsection, tearing vital tissue in the stomach and kidneys before ripping out his lower back. The second burst split the remaining man's head open like a mushy cantaloupe and separated it from his neck. The decapitated corpse staggered around a moment, waiting for nerve impulses to receive the signal of death, and finally crumpled to the carpet.

The Executioner heard the steady chopping sound of helicopter rotors beating the air. He burst through the sliding-glass door and onto a patio. He turned in the direction of the sound and jumped a flagstone wall, emerging on the massive expanse of lawn. Nearly fifty yards in the distance he spotted the helicopter with a lone figure climbing aboard with the assistance of two men in suits. Bolan charged the helicopter and triggered his weapon on the run, but the well-dressed pair immediately drew machine pistols and sprayed the area with a horde of 9 mm slugs. The Executioner went prone to avoid the assault and braced his weapon on the ground.

Bolan put his eye close to the rear sight, took half a breath and squeezed the trigger. The man in the suit flipped onto his back, but the soldier was already tracking for his second target. He swept the immediate field of sight but didn't see the man, and then realized he had to have climbed into the chopper. Bolan reacquired by aiming toward the chopper cockpit. The sun was now high enough that it glinted off the glass, and he couldn't make out a viable target. The chopper started to rise and he considered firing, but the earth erupted in front of him as a fresh volley of rounds chewed up grass and dirt. Bolan rolled from the assault and got to one knee, turning in the general direction from which the rounds had come. He spotted the source rushing toward him, another sentry triggering his pistol. Bolan kept the weapon low and tight as he triggered a short burst that caught the guy in the upper torso and knocked him to the ground in midstride.

The roar of chopper blades almost deafened the Executioner as he looked up to see the chopper buzz overhead. He brought his over-and-under assault rifle grenade launcher to bear to target the tail rotor, but the reflection of light on metal flashed on the periphery. Bolan turned to see a late-model Lincoln roar up the drive, windows down and muzzle-flashes winking in steady rhythm from the darkened interior. They could only be JI!

Bolan rolled on his shoulder to the saving cover of a nearby oak tree as he reached into the satchel on his left hip and withdrew another 40 mm grenade. He slammed the cartridge home in the breach of the M-203, aimed through the leaf sight and squeezed the trigger. The weapon bucked against his shoulder with the force of a 12-gauge shotgun as the 40 mm round arced across the lawn and landed just short of the Lincoln. It exploded a moment later, tearing through the gas tank and generating a secondary explosion.

As the Executioner got to his feet slowly, he turned in the direction of the path the chopper had taken and watched helplessly as it became a distant speck against the clear, morning sky. Bolan bet Satyev was aboard that chopper, headed to who knew where. Well, Stony Man satellite contacts would generate intel that would be able to tell him. And with that information, he'd schedule his final appointment with Anatoly Satyev.

CHAPTER TWENTY-SIX

Just as Bolan predicted, Kurtzman had no trouble locating the helicopter using Stony Man's access to satellite technology. He ultimately tracked the helicopter from a refueling stop in Los Angeles and then its subsequent trip to Santa Catalina Island, about twenty-two miles southwest of L.A. Fortunately, the Avalon Airport—aka the "Airport in the Sky"—was large enough to accommodate Stony Man's Learjet, and a quick check with locals there confirmed a taxi had rushed the helicopter occupants away as soon as they landed.

With the address information in hand, Bolan made his way to a secluded area off the southeast coast of Avalon Bay where Satyev had another large estate, this one nestled into one of the many cliff faces among the undulating topography of green and brown brush. It was late afternoon by the time he neared the estate, and a light rain had begun to fall. Bolan had to leave his car off the main road because the dirt trail that led to Satyev's residence had become a thick, slippery trail of red clay.

Bolan reached the crest of the trail and lay in the wet grass at the peak of a cuneiform-shaped ridge that overlooked the grounds. From this vantage point he couldn't make out much more than the roof. The house itself protruded from the cliffs, stabilized with stilts and a line of trees that acted as windbreaks. It looked from that point to be three stories, each with rows of tinted windows that looked onto the ocean, and each sporting a balcony that ran the entire width of the house. The estate around it consisted of a slippery volcanic rock face adorned with patches of slippery moss and the ever-present sheen of moisture. As hideaways went, the design made it seem more like a nearly impregnable fortress than a residence. Such a place would have disheartened lesser men.

For a moment, Bolan wondered if launching an assault via the roof would have been a better option, but he dismissed it as too predictable. Satyev was former Soviet military with a military mind, and he would have accounted for that as the most likely point of entry. Bolan took in the rest of the area before deciding that an attack from the lowest point would prove his best option because it was unconventional and the last thing his enemies would expect.

Bolan had been to Catalina a number of times before, and he knew there was no such thing as flatlands on the island. Armed with that knowledge, he'd elected to bring a pack filled with climbing equipment.

He quickly unslung the pack and rummaged around inside until he retrieved a piton and rubber mallet. He pounded the piton into the ground and then threaded his rope through a climbing pulley system he secured to the trunk of nearby tree. Bolan then checked the edges of his blacksuit to make sure nothing would snag before climbing into the tactical harness, attaching the descender and carabiner. He then shrugged into the pack, which contained his weapons. Bolan positioned his body over the edge until he made forty-five degrees from the cliff face before releasing the rope bag; it bounced and bumped its way down the stones. He then leaned back and when he felt he was out as far as he should be, he kicked away from the cliff. The Executioner went smoothly down the rope, sensing the heat of the friction through his thick gloves. The climbing harness pinched the skin of his inner thighs, but the soldier ignored the pain and continued his descent. He kept one hand at the small of his back as the brake, the other fully extended on the taut rope with just a slight bend at the elbow each time he launched his body off the side of the cliff.

Within a minute Bolan had reached the base of the cliff and disconnected from the rope. The beach could hardly be designed for recreation, as it consisted of very little sand and mostly sharp rock. Bolan stepped carefully along a treacherous path of jagged stones as the turquoise water of the bay slapped violently against them in endless spumes of whitewater. Eventually the rock gave way to a mushy pad of light brown sand no more than two feet wide, and Bolan picked up the pace. He made the cover of several large rocks covered with algae and loam that almost seemed to glow in the twilight of approaching dusk.

Bolan shed his pack once more, but this time he withdrew the pieces of a PSG-90 sniper rifle. Based on the official L96A1 British rifle designed and built by Accuracy International, this variant used by the Swedish army boasted some improvements, including a discarding sabot-ball cartridge. The PSG-90 chambered 7.62 X 51 mm slugs and had a muzzle force of 2500 feet per second.

Bolan attached the scope, put it to his eye and sighted in on the residence. He'd have to take any sentries quickly and quietly, as they had the advantage of high ground. Even that wouldn't give him much time to scramble up the rocks and gain entry to the residence, but he'd made his decision to come this way and saw little point in second-guessing himself. Bolan adjusted the scope for windage when he spotted his first target, estimated the range at ninety meters and then went about locating the second target. As luck would have it, there was only one sentry on each level, and they didn't seem the least bit concerned about anyone below them. Mostly they looked somewhat bored as they paced along the white, metal banisters that ran along the edge of the balconies, automatic rifles cradled in their arms.

Bolan gauged the position where each sentry would be, then made another minor adjustment to the scope before he zeroed in on his first target. He would take them in ascending order. The Executioner took a deep breath, let half out and steadied the folding bipod of the weapon on the rock he used for cover. Bolan became one with the rifle, a technique he'd learned long ago as a U.S. Army sniper, and then squeezed the trigger. The bullet traveled to the target in under one-tenth of a second, caught the man in the left side of the neck and traveled up and out the right, top side of his skull. Bolan confirmed the hit by the red-flower spray of blood before swinging up to the second target. Another half breath, and he squeezed off the second round, this one a kill shot that punched through the sentry's chest. The man dropped from sight as Bolan targeted the last sentry on the topmost floor. The guy had stopped at the sound of the first two rifle shots and now searched the rocks below for the source. That stationary target was no contest for the Executioner's marksmanship. Bolan's last shot caught the sentry in the upper lip and blew off the back of his skull. A crimson geyser filled the scope before the guy's corpse toppled backward and out of view.

Bolan abandoned the rifle, reached into the pack and withdrew four hand grenades, which he clipped to his load-bearing equipment harness. He then procured a pair of MP-5 K machine pistols, which were attached to a sling. He donned the sling, secured it by the chest strap, then charged up the hill toward the house. He'd forgone the Beretta this time, but the .44 Magnum Desert Eagle rode in a military holster on belt webbing against his right thigh. Bolan reached the base of the house in time to come face-to-face with two of Satyev's goons. They burst from a door toting AKSU submachine guns, and they seemed a little surprised at the proximity of their enemy. Bolan seized that opportunity to demonstrate the lethality of hesitation in a combat situation. He leveled the MP-5 K machine pistols and triggered them simultaneously, raking the hardforce with a storm of 9 mm slugs. The pair danced under the assault as the bullets cut through vital organs, then collapsed dead onto the concrete patio.

Bolan jumped over the messy heap and entered through a door that opened onto a massive room. The walls were comprised of flagstones, and at one end of the room was a fireplace with a fake elk head mounted above the mantel. A billiards table took up the center of the room, the balls in random arrangement across the table as if the house guards had been in the middle of a game. So Bolan had the element of surprise after all, as it seemed Satyev's men hadn't expected any sort of offensive. To the right of the recreation room, through a misty glass wall, Bolan made out the shape of a massive pool rimmed by a wooden deck.

The soldier strode through the room, weapons at the ready, until he reached a hallway. He kept his back to the wall as he proceeded until he came on a flight of steps. Ascending quickly, he was aware that he presented as a most viable target while in the stairwells. He arrived at the next floor unchallenged and cleared two more rooms before trouble appeared.

A small force of half a dozen gunners emerged from a room directly across the hallway, bringing weapons to bear on Bolan. The Executioner whirled and threw his body forcefully over the back of a large, overstuffed sofa. He landed gently on the cushions on the other side and continued onto the floor, breaking down the frame of a flimsy coffee table as he landed. The room came alive with the reports of autofire that sounded like it was coming from a hundred guns. Bolan released his hold on the machine pistols even as he heard rounds slap the back of the sofa. It wouldn't hold long under that kind of punishment. Bolan reached to his LBE harness and came away with a pair of grenades. Loaded with PETN explosive, the Diehl DM-51s were a feat of brilliant, German engineering. They were designed as both an offensive and defensive weapon; the grenade body could unleash a blast force adequate enough to destroy equip-

ment and structures, and was equally effective for eliminating personnel when covered by a plastic sleeve containing approximately six thousand 2 mm steel balls.

Bolan removed the sleeve from one, primed it and
let fly with enough force to make sure it adequately
cleared the back of the sofa. He then yanked the pin on
the second, keeping the sleeve in place on this one, and
tossed it after the first. Bolan rolled as close to the base
of the couch as he could manage, opened his mouth and
clapped his palms over his ears. The entire room shook
with the blast a moment later, raining the entire area
with dust, debris and a thick cloud of smoke. Then
came the second blast, this one delivering shrapnel no
longer impeded by furniture or other objects that had
likely been decimated by the first explosion.

As the effects of the after-blast from the second grenade settled, Bolan removed his hands from his ears and
heard the anguished cries of several of his opponents.
He rolled onto his knees and leaned out far enough to
see around the couch. The wood floor had totally
charred in the areas where the two grenades went off,
and small tufts of flames were visible where fabrics and
wallpaper had caught fire. Directly ahead Bolan saw a
blackened and bloody face, eyes open, stare at him with
an expression of shock still evident. Another man near
that one writhed on the floor and his body oozed blood
from wounds in his flesh with charbroiled edges. Bolan
spotted the listless forms of two others along with another live but incapacitated enemy gunner. That brought
the count to five, which left one unaccounted for.

Bolan climbed slowly to his feet and fisted the machine pistols before proceeding carefully in a crouch-
walk so he could see ahead of him. He eventually

spotted the last soldier from the team he'd taken out with grenades, rolling in time to avoid the pair of short bursts the guard directed at him. Bolan came out of the roll on one knee, snap-aimed the MP-5 Ks with fully extended arms and squeezed one trigger then the other. A score of 9 mm Parabellums cut Bolan's opponent across the chest and stomach, tearing holes through his organs and exiting out his back. The man, who'd been on his knees, stiffened and maintained an upright position for several seconds before he toppled forward, dead before his face hit the floor.

The sounds of battled died and Bolan eventually regained his feet. He cleared the last of the rooms before climbing steps to the top and final landing. As with the floors below, the steps opened onto a wide, airy room, this one lined with shelves of books and bric-a-brac from every corner of the globe. The furniture here was mostly for display, and one room was decorated in early Czarist Russia style. Bolan swept each room but found no trace of Satyev, and he began to wonder if this had all been nothing more than a ruse. No, he couldn't buy that. Satyev was clever, but he wasn't stupid—he would never have sacrificed his men only for the purpose of covering his tracks. He was a soldier and he wouldn't run; it was a matter of pride for him and he would stand and fight, defending his stronghold from all enemies until either he had destroyed them or he took his last breath.

The Executioner intended to make sure this matter ended with the latter results.

Bolan double-checked the upper floors, including the garage that opened onto switchbacks up the cliff face to the dirt road, and then descended to the lower floors. He checked every room and closet, certain he would eventually find his prey, but by the time he reached the billiards room on the bottom floor he still hadn't found Satyev. The calm motion of water then caught his eyes and Bolan stepped into the greenhouse-style room that covered the Olympic-size swimming pool. Nothing about the entire place spoke of humility, and this told the Executioner something about his enemy. It wasn't the first time he'd encountered Satyev's kind. They were men who liked to bask in the fineries of life. They enjoyed the money and prestige but none of the hard work required to come by it honestly; they filled their lives with wine, women and song but didn't know happiness; they lived off the hard work and sweat of others but then trod those same benefactors underfoot when it came to giving something in return.

Bolan skirted the pool until he came to a door made of cedar on the far side. He reached for the brass handle and gently depressed the lever with his thumb as he brought one of the MP-5 Ks up to the ready position. The door suddenly snapped outward and with it came a belch of hot air. Steam from the sauna obscured the Executioner's view as a gorilla of a man burst from the swirling mists and drove him backward, knocking the machine pistol out of his grip. Bolan tried to recover his balance but the weight of his attacker proved too much, and a heartbeat later the pair crashed into the deep end of the pool. The weight of his equipment coupled with size of his opponent drove Bolan to the bottom in seconds. The view was still foggy despite the cleanliness of the water, and chlorine burned his eyes. He felt a hand close on his right wrist as he tried to kick toward the surface, dragging him back. Instinctively, Bolan brought his forearm up and felt something bite through his skin. The water around them began to grow dark with blood, but not before the Executioner realized he'd deflected a knife blade meant for his chest.

Bolan wrapped his hand around the knife-wielder's wrist from the inside and twisted outward, simultaneously planting a foot against his enemy's thigh and pushed up. The maneuver spun the man off and away from him, and the boost allowed Bolan to regain the surface long enough to gulp a large breath of air. He immediately ducked beneath the surface, realizing as long as he remained above water he was open to a follow-up attack. He'd maintained his hold on the knife-wielder's wrist, and now the pair grappled under the water like two great sea titans fighting for dominance over the waters of the world. The blood continued to ooze from Bolan's wound, giving the blue water a purplish hue. The man twisted free of the Executioner's grip and lunged for him, wrapping one hand around Bolan's throat while he sought an underhanded opening with the knife. Bolan realized that he could not match his enemy on purely a contest of size or strength.

Only tactics would win this bout.

Bolan reacquired his grip on the wrist of the knife hand while using his free hand to disengage the clip of the weapons sling. He then shot downward and threw both arms overhead to allow the sling to lift from his body. As his feet touched bottom, Bolan grabbed the two machine pistols and pushed off the floor of the pool so his body came up under his enemy's feet. The maneuver worked exactly as planned, the tough leather straps of the sling entangling his opponent's feet and twisting him so his body slipped upside down. Bolan continued toward the surface, pulling the slings until his head broke water. He then placed the soles of his boots against the soles of his enemy's shoes and pulled on the leather sling as he pressed down with all the strength he could muster from his legs.

Bolan froze there, feeling the struggles and panic of his opponent as the man tried to free himself, but to no avail. His feet were too entangled in the strings, and he could not gain enough moment to capsize Bolan and make the surface. Slowly but steadily, the desperate flailing became less pronounced until it was only an occasional reflexive jerk. After five minutes Bolan released his hold and swam to the edge. He paused there a moment to catch his breath, his arms folded atop the deck in front of him. After resting a minute he started to pull himself out of the water.

"Uh-uh!" a voice warned.

Bolan froze and looked up to see Anatoly Satyev approaching him on the deck, a Makarov pistol in his grasp. He stopped in front of Bolan, careful to keep his feet out of reach, and smiled.

"You surprise me, Cooper," Satyev said. "I thought you were going to prove yourself a formidable opponent, and instead I find you falling easily for one of the oldest tricks in the book. Simple misdirection." His eyes flicked to the body in the pool. "I see you've managed to best Ruslan. Too bad, he was a fine soldier. It will be difficult to find a successor."

"What makes you think you'll live that long?"

Satyev produced a sardonic laugh. "Come now, American. You don't actually think I'm afraid to die. Besides, with you out of the way I imagine it will take your countrymen some time to find a suitable replacement to send after me. By that time, I will be long gone. You have put me to a considerable inconvenience, but I do believe I shall recover quite nicely."

Bolan maintained proximity to the wall of the pool as he reached his right hand slowly, steadily, toward one of the Diehl DM-51s on his harness. His hand was concealed beneath his armpit, and Satyev could not tell from where he stood that Bolan was even moving it. All he had to do was keep the guy talking a little while longer.

"If you think the JI will keep you alive after all the trouble you've brought them, you don't know them as well as you think, Satyev."

"Phah!" Satyev countered with a sneer. "They're terrorists. That makes it very simple to manipulate them. They live solely to accomplish their objectives, to destabilize the West…and this country specifically. There are all kinds of ways to do that, and they know I can show them those ways. After all, I have forty some years of experience to draw from, that of the cold war."

Bolan wrapped a hand around the grenade.

"You think so?" Bolan asked.

"I know so."

He snaked his thumb through the pull ring and snapped it clear.

"And what's all in it for you?"

Satyev smiled, this one more genuine as he got a faraway look in his eyes. "To ultimately restore the Communist Party. Don't you get it? You're just like that dolt, Sergei Cherenko and his banal revolutionary friends. You can't see past your own little corner of the world. We were a force at one time, a universal superpower with the resources of an entire continent at our disposal. I want to go back to those times, when the Soviet army was an organization feared and renowned throughout the world."

Bolan slackened his grip and let the spoon come away from the hand bomb.

"And you think an alliance with Islamic terrorists is the path to those ends?"

"I *know* it!" the Russian declared triumphantly.

"You're wrong," Bolan replied as he rolled the grenade onto the deck.

Satyev's eyes widened as he identified the object that rolled to a stop at his feet. The Executioner ducked beneath the water. Scraping his side against the rough granite of the wall proved a small price in contrast to being blown to bits, and Bolan barely managed to get his hands over his ears before the DM-51 went off. The concussion rippled the surface of the water, followed by Satyev's corpse.

Bolan shoved off the wall and crossed to the other end before he surfaced. He dragged his stiff and weary body out of the pool, turned to verify that Satyev—or what was left of him—wasn't moving and then got the hell away from there. He found a sedan in the garage, keys in the ignition and drove from the house. He saw no reason to look back.

EPILOGUE

Mack Bolan stood alongside Kisa Naryshkin, arms folded, as she kept vigil next to the bed of Leonid Rostov. The doctors had just come to discuss his condition, advising Rostov had a long road to recovery in front of him, but promising he could look forward to a long life with the proper treatment and therapy. It was Naryshkin who had promised to keep an eye out for him. Bolan shook hands with Rostov, left him with a brief repose to the couple and then departed from the room.

The Executioner was halfway down the hall when the young woman called for him and ran to catch up.

"What is it?" he asked

"You, um—" she lowered her eyes "—we owe you our lives. I forgot to thank you for that."

Bolan smiled. "The fact you came through it in one piece is thanks enough, Kisa."

She nodded, letting the uncomfortable moment pass, and then said, "I spoke with my father this morning. He was very happy to hear I was alive. And he asked me to thank you for keeping your word."

"Yeah, well, you tell him it was my pleasure."

"Leo and I have decided to return to St. Petersburg. It is where we belong. He will probably face some charges for his part in the Sevooborot, but my father believes they will show him leniency. With a good word from the American government, of course."

"Of course."

"I don't suppose we'll see you again?"

"It's not likely," Bolan said. "Then again, I suppose anything's possible."

"I understand," Naryshkin replied in almost a whisper, and Bolan could see she tried to hide her disappointment. "But you *do* know you will always be welcome in my home, and that we shall always consider you a friend."

"I'd like that."

"Okay," she finally said a little hesitantly.

Before Bolan could react, she threw her arms around his midsection and hugged him tightly before turning and marching the way she'd come without a backward glance. The memories of the mission and the days they had spent together flooded his memory. The Executioner wanted to say something, some words that might make Kisa feel better, but he couldn't think of a thing. So he turned and headed for the exit, silently wishing her and Rostov a long and happy life. Then it dawned on him that they *would* have a long and happy life because of the sacrifice of others—the selflessness of friends like Sergei Cherenko.

And the dedication to duty by a new friend.

The Don Pendleton's® Executioner
COLLISION COURSE

The global trade in prohibited weapons has reached terrifying proportions, and as Mack Bolan digs deeper, he realizes the outcome could be war. Racing against the clock to infiltrate terrorist cells, he realizes the entire situation was engineered by a traitor—an *American* traitor. Now the U.S. is on the brink of disaster...and the Executioner is running out of time.

GOLD EAGLE ®

Available April 2009 wherever books are sold.

Don Pendleton
HOSTILE DAWN

Rogue organizations within anti-Western nations are banding together to attack their common enemy on a new front. New Dawn Rising is the bad boys club of the Middle East, Africa and Asia, using money, influence and politics to access global seats of corporate power and cripple the free world from the boardroom. The target: Los Angeles. The goal: to wreak mass terror.

STONY MAN® 100

Look for the 100th StonyMan book, available April 2009 wherever books are sold.

JAMES AXLER

DEATH LANDS®

Eden's Twilight

Rumors of an untouched predark ville in the mountains of West Virginia lure traders in search of unimaginable wealth. Ryan and his warrior group join in, although it means an uneasy truce with an old enemy. But as their journey reveals more of Deathlands' darkest secrets, it remains to be seen if this place will become their salvation...or their final resting place.

Available June 2009 wherever books are sold.

AleX Archer
SACRIFICE

On assignment in the Philippines, archaeologist
Annja Creed meets with a contact to verify
some information. But when the man doesn't
turn out to be who he said he was, Annja
finds herself a prisoner of a
notorious terrorist group.
Though she manages to
escape, Annja is soon
struggling to stay alive
amidst terrorists and not-
so-dead jungle spirits with
a taste for human flesh.

**Available May 2009
wherever books are sold.**